TOUCH HER
AND DIE

McRae Bodyguards - #1

Jolie Vines

Cover design - Natasha Snow https://natashasnow.com/

Formatting - Cleo Moran / Devoted Pages Designs

Cover photography - Wander Aguiar

https://www.wanderbookclub.com/

Cover model - Zac Van Alphen

To all you lasses who love the brooding, instinctively protective hero. This is for you.

BLURB

A grumpy Scottish bodyguard with an iced-over heart, and the sunshine woman who might just melt it.

Daisy

Phoneless, carless, and trapped by my relatives, I make a daring escape in just my fancy underwear. Right as a grouchy but gorgeous bodyguard arrives to rescue me.

Enemies pursue us on our West Coast road trip, so Ben whisks me away to a snowed-in cabin in Scotland. I start falling until I'm ready to let him guard my body in every way possible.

But breaking his rules could cost me everything—including him.

Ben

As a bodyguard, I have one rule: don't get attached. Yet Daisy's got me hooked. When I'm asked to protect her, I can't resist. She's warmth and kindness wrapped up in a curvy package, and I'm willing to cross any line to keep her safe.

Almost.

No matter how torn I am between duty and desire, there's only one chance I can't take.

For her, I'll risk anything—except for my heart.

--

Touch Her and Die is the first in a brand new bodyguard series that brings steam, mystery, and adventure, plus a little revenge plot for our heroines. This is standalone romantic suspense with only-one-bed (twice) and a forbidden element.

READER NOTE

Dear reader,

Thank you for picking up *Touch Her and Die,* the first in my series about the McRae Bodyguard team.

In case you didn't know, this series comes directly after the *Wild Mountain Scots* books, which contain the romances of the Mountain Rescue team who are based on the same Scottish estate.

All the stories are standalone and each has its own happily ever after.

The audiobooks are delicious.

In fact, there are five series in total. If you like my style, find the list at the end. I've been told devouring them all provides weeks of swoony, Scottish distraction.

Love, Jolie x

1

The quiet rush of my office door opening broke my sleep, and I monitored the padding of footsteps across the room, keeping my eyes closed.

"Found him," followed a little whisper. "He's asleep. Like a bear in a cave."

I placed the voice—Jamie-Beth, one of the kids from the Scottish estate where I'd lived and worked for the past five years.

I relaxed my muscles, aching from being on-shift the previous twenty-four hours straight, and played dead. It wasn't a challenge. A few hours of rest on the hard-edged couch hadn't done much for me, but there'd been no point going home when I'd needed to return for an early meeting.

Such was the life of a bodyguard. Always available, especially when you led the service.

"Should we wake him?" Jamie-Beth asked. "His face is all crumpled."

Another voice answered her. "He obviously needs his beauty sleep, but I have to talk to him."

That was Ariel. I joined the dots.

Ariel taught snowboarding on the mountain and often took out groups of youngsters. Several years ago, she and her two older brothers had fled here and gone into hiding, and I'd helped them stay out of danger. I considered them to be friends. The younger of her brothers was gunning to join my crew. The elder, Gabe, used to work for me before he'd taken a job elsewhere.

For a while, Ariel had a crush on me. Back then, she'd been fourteen to my twenty-eight, and I'd happily played the responsible adult she could practice flirting on, never seeing her as anything other than a younger sister. Now she was nineteen, her affections had leapt elsewhere, and I'd settled into the role of a trusted family friend.

Call it strong protective instincts, but her needing to talk to me set me on high alert.

Jamie-Beth giggled. "I'm going to tickle his feet."

With the stealth of a drunk in a china shop, the little girl crept closer.

I bided my time, keeping my breathing regular.

3...2...1...

Something touched my foot.

I burst from the couch with a roar.

Jamie-Beth squealed, scrambling back and stumbling over her snow boots. Ariel yelped in shock and whipped her polar-patterned beanie hat at me.

Then she tripped over the girl.

Both lasses landed their arses on the floor.

I roared again for effect and stomped closer. "A bear, am

I? Is it any wonder I woke up with a sore head with ye two messing with me?"

Ariel scowled and climbed up to poke me in the arm. "That was mean. We weren't expecting you to be out cold. Since when do you sleep here?"

I scooped up Jamie-Beth and planted her back on her feet, hiding a smile at the girl's indignant look. Identical to Isobel, her ma who ran a garage on the estate. "I got back at four this morning from working security in Edinburgh. To what do I owe the pleasure of the rude awakening?"

The amusement fled Ariel's expression. She turned to the six-year-old. "JB, can you give us a minute? I need to ask the grumpy bear for a favour."

Once the child had skipped out into the corridor, Ariel came back to me. "I heard from Daisy."

The last vestiges of drowsiness left me. A few days ago, during a snowy Christmas party, Ariel had come to me with a problem. Her best friend from childhood had gone silent, prompting Ariel to panic. Daisy was in California where Ariel and her brothers used to live. Their families had links with organised crime, so any problems came with a list of dangerous add-ons, particularly for women.

"What did she say?" I pointed Ariel to the visitor's chair at my desk then opened the blinds to the fucking gorgeous Scottish Highlands view I could never get enough of.

"It's a voice message. Listen for yourself." She pulled out her phone, poked at the screen, then a message played.

"I have to be quick," Daisy said, hushed and fast. "So sorry for the radio silence, but things are a little freaky right now. I'm staying with my aunt and uncle, and my aunt has this no-phones deal going on. She took me away for a week on a detox cleanse, you know, with the usual commentary about how one day she'll make me a skinny Minnie, then we had a tech-free Christmas." Her voice tightened. "Mom never showed, and my uncle took my car for repair so I can't just up and leave. They keep telling me I need to stay. I just have this feeling that something's about to happen—"

A click sounded in the background of the call. Daisy came back. "Shit, someone's coming. Gotta go. Love you."

Ariel set the phone down on my desk and eyed me. "Daisy's a grown woman, but her family are assholes. What reason could they have to confiscate her phone, take her car, and keep her under lock and key? I've got a really bad feeling about this."

I did, too.

I knew better than to completely trust my gut instincts, but they were usually right, and my adrenaline was rising. A young woman being isolated by her family was exactly what had happened to Ariel. They'd intended to use her as a pawn, and I'd bet any money that Daisy was about to suffer the same fate.

"Ye think she's in danger," I said slowly.

"I really do. She's kind. Sweet. Easy for someone to use. Plus her family have always treated her like a maid rather than an equal member. If they need something and she's a solution to getting it, I don't doubt that they'd take the opportunity. I'm scared for her."

A tap came at the door.

My boss poked his head in. "Ben, got a minute?"

I lifted my chin to him. Gordain McRae owned the aircraft hangar where my office was based, along with the land for miles around it in our isolated stretch of the Cairngorm mountains. From the hangar, a helicopter school operated, and the mountain rescue team was based here, too.

I used it as the centre for the bodyguard operations,

though mostly we were out in the world, carrying out our protective service. In recent months, the people on my crew had dwindled, and we needed to recruit fresh blood, hence this morning's interview.

Which would be starting in a few minutes. Fuck.

Gordain sighted Ariel and gave her a grin. If I was the trusted friend, he was the father figure to Ariel and her brothers. "Sorry to interrupt," he said to her.

Ariel slumped, not returning the boss's smile. "It's fine. Rein me in. I'm trying to steal your employee's time. I can go if you're busy?"

"Nah. This won't take a sec," he replied.

"Has our candidate arrived?" I asked, though my mind was still stuck on the Daisy situation.

"Cancelled. He wasnae suitable."

I frowned and jiggled my laptop to wake it. The guy's application was open onscreen from where I'd refreshed my memory ahead of my snatched sleep. In his photo, he stared straight at the camera, a thick neck denoting a muscular frame.

"He passed all the background checks and came with recommendations," I recalled.

"Aye, on paper. I did a little digging. Two years ago, he was let go from a close protection position. On his application to us, he put that the contract ended, but there was more to the story, as I found out when the company owner rang me back an hour ago. He took advantage of the woman he was supposed to be guarding. Slept with her while promising her the world."

Ariel wrinkled her nose. "Let me guess, his wedding ring slipped off and he forgot he was married?"

"Got it in one," Gordain agreed. "He was with the client

when his wife rang, a picture of her and their baby on the screen. Of course the client then refused to have him work with her, leaving them short-staffed and unable to deliver the service. A right royal fuck-up."

I glowered in annoyance then closed and deleted the application. "What a jackass. I had high hopes for him. Back to the drawing board."

My boss raised a shoulder. "It's a good time to rethink what we're looking for. We don't have any work lined up for a week or two, so there's time to play with." He cocked his head at me. "Didn't ye say your brother is just out of the military? There's no one I trust more than family."

I had mentioned that. My mother had asked me to consider offering him a job.

Whether the brother in question would even talk to me was another matter.

A yawn threatened to overtake me, and I stifled it, taking a second before I replied. "I do, and he'd be an asset. But he's in the US and could be hard to get hold of. I'd need to see him face to face."

"No pressure, but if he's interested, it'd help us. In fact, isn't your ma after ye for a visit? Maybe take some time off and go see your family?" Gordain made a pointed gesture at my unshaven face. "When was the last time ye took a break? It looks bad for my HR report if my people aren't using their full entitlement. Float the idea to your brother and take a few days to wind down while you're at it."

He tapped the doorframe and walked away.

My thoughts turned inward. Gordain was right. My mother had been asking to see me for a long while now, but I kept finding reasons not to. I didn't like taking time off work. It had never suited me to be idle.

Let alone the fact that the last time I spent any significant time with my family, I'd caused more problems than I could ever hope to fix.

Ariel hummed, bringing my attention back to her. "Don't your folks live on the West Coast?"

"They're in Washington. Olympic National Park."

"Near to Daisy."

I drew my eyebrows in. "Isn't she in LA?"

That's where Ariel's family had lived, pretty much the entirety of the western coastline south from mine.

"It's a short plane hop away. Or a slightly longer drive."

"Two fucking days behind the wheel," I groused back, but my mind was already sprinting ahead.

Ariel needed someone to check in on her friend. For all I knew, Daisy was in real trouble. It would give me another purpose for returning to the States.

As if knowing my internal balancing act, Ariel leaned in, fixing me with her serious gaze. "Daisy is the one person I care most about in the world who isn't here in Scotland. If I could, I'd go there myself to see her. Get her out if her family are planning something."

"Don't talk crazy," I muttered. Without conscious decision, I tapped my keyboard and searched on flights from the UK to Los Angeles.

Data scrolled before my eyes, a pathway forming.

If I could drive to Inverness airport in the next hour, I could catch a connecting flight and arrive in LA tonight.

Get a rental car.

Check in on Daisy to be sure the lass was okay.

I didn't let my brain advance beyond that part of the trip. Instead, I grumbled to let Ariel know her request was a chore but then got on with booking a ticket.

2

Daisy

An envelope waited on the floor of my bedroom, crumpled under the door.

I stooped and collected it, slicing it open with a finger to reveal a single piece of yellow paper inside.

You need to leave, it read.

Where the mother-loving heck had this come from? I mean, I agreed with the statement—I'd been stuck here forever, but no one else in the house had made any noises about me going.

I flipped the sheet over. Examined the envelope. But there was nothing else. No name or explanation.

I stuffed it into my pocket and peered back into the hall.

Empty, save for the morning sunlight that pierced the all-glass frontage of the modern Los Angeles mansion. The light stretched past the empty, unused bedrooms of my cousins, falling short of reaching my door.

Curious, and a little unnerved, I tiptoed along the polished floor, peeking into doorways and listening for the sound of any other person. But as usual, the vast space was mostly vacant. The polar opposite of a cosy family home.

I'd grown up here, on and off, as my mother had moved us in with my aunt and uncle each time she lost a job and subsequently our apartment.

Family is everything, she'd say, and Aunt Sigrid and Uncle Paul had agreed, readily taking us in with them and their much older daughters.

I loved my mother, but she was the definition of a hot mess. The stress of holding down a job and raising me had been too much for her. She'd disappear for months on end, leaving me with her brother and sister-in-law. There had always been a warning with it—never to upset them because we owed them big time.

The admonition had never come the other way. Not verbally, at least. Paul and Sigrid had tolerated my existence in their home, their driver taking me to school, an allowance gifted when they went on vacation and I was left with a sitter and a list of chores.

It wasn't a home spilling over with love, and I was under no illusion about how they got their money—by means of the organised-crime-adjacent business they ran—but it was a roof over my head, food in my belly. I'd always be grateful.

I'd earned my keep by cleaning and polishing, becoming part of their maid service, though they'd never asked.

I reached the doorway of their oldest daughter. She had ten years on me and had long moved away. Her room was kept clean and neat, though I couldn't remember the last time she'd stayed in it.

Nothing looked out of place.

Moving past, I came to the second daughter's room. Luna was a year younger than her sister and had fled for college the minute she could, then disappeared overseas.

We might be related, but I barely knew either. Between them, they'd returned for a matter of hours in recent times, one for Thanksgiving, one for Christmas.

Voices came from the lobby down the steel-and-glass staircase at the end of the hall. I padded over and peeked down. Uncle Paul stood in the doorway with Camila, his office manager. He continued giving some instruction to her, but Camila's focus landed on me.

Her eyes narrowed.

I swallowed down a spike of unhappiness.

At eighteen, I'd left for college on a scholarship with the intention of working my butt off and never looking back. But the minute I'd graduated last year, Uncle Paul begged for my help at their LA office. I'd worked there for months, resisting the pleas to move back in with them.

I had an apartment share with friends. My own business I'd wanted to get off the ground.

But *family came first,* even if I hadn't enjoyed the work. Or been paid much for it.

Camila was there every day in the office and had made it clear she disliked the nepotism that landed me the job I didn't want.

Then somehow, I found myself back here in the mansion and unable to go.

I was torn up over what to do.

Simply upping and leaving would feel like the worst kind of bad manners, and I was controlled by a sense of obligation to the people who'd given me everything.

"Daisy," Aunt Sigrid's voice found me as my uncle and

Camila exited the mansion. "Just who I was trying to find. I have some people coming for lunch. Be my companion?"

I faked a smile and trotted down to my aunt at the bottom of the stairs. I'd hoped to hide in my room, but it seemed my luck was out.

"A lunch? Who are you expecting?"

"A business contact. She's bringing her son and daughter-in-law who are newlyweds. An arranged marriage, like myself and your uncle. The picture of a couple in love, so I'm told. Your romantic heart will get a kick out of seeing them, I know it."

I hid a sigh.

My romantic heart had other ideas.

For weeks, my aunt had kept me close. First by way of her Christmas gift to me, a week at a health resort, and then for Christmas and New Year's celebrations. Every day, we did yoga, meditation, juice cleanses, lunch dates which were mostly business-focused, and I was grateful to be included, but we were into January now. I had a life to get back to.

I pulled up my big girl panties. "Actually, I really need to think about going home."

Aunt Sigrid's face fell. "Oh, sweet girl, no. Don't say that. I enjoy your company so much, and you know your mother is due for a visit. It's not like you have anywhere urgent to go until we see her. Please stay. Just another day will do it. Learn more about the business. Besides, we have a party tonight, and you wouldn't want to miss that."

That was the first I'd heard of it. "A party, too?"

Aunt Sigrid beamed. "Just a small gathering. Willow's going to come over and give you a makeover. Hair, make-up, an outfit fit for royalty." My aunt curled her yoga-toned arm through mine. "You'll need to appear the part. It would be a shame to let all the work we've done on your health go to waste."

I gave a quick nod, gritting my teeth. As a chubby kid, I'd usually been sequestered in my room during parties. To be included was new. Butterflies made of mixed emotions flitted around my belly.

I was made for hard work, not socialising, but it was nice to be asked.

Also my aunt's friend, Willow, was stepmother to my bestie, Ariel, who I missed beyond belief. Maybe she'd have some news of my friend.

"Act the part, too," my aunt continued. "No going on about school or those books you read. You're representing our family. Think poise and elegance. Smile and say yes."

No chat about my favourite smutty romance novels with her fancy guests, or discussion on how I wanted to set up my own cleaning business now I'd finished my degree.

"Got it," I breathed. "Could I please have my phone back so I can take pictures?"

Sigrid's mouth worked then resolved into a smile. "Cluttering our brains with mindless notifications stands in the way of all the great things the world has to offer. Wouldn't you rather be looking up and ahead for opportunities, or have your nose buried in your screen?"

"I... I guess you're right."

This earned me a warm smile, then I spent the world's dullest lunch imagining how I'd be transformed from Cinders to Cinderella.

*S*everal hours later, I inched out of the entertaining area, a cool wine glass clutched in my hand and my oppressively tight body contour underwear making it almost impossible to eat any of the fancy canapés being circulated by wait staff.

What I really needed was my phone.

If what Sigrid had said about phone addictions was true, I didn't care. Being cut off was a punishment.

Ariel would get such a kick out of helping me decide who could've left the note. I'd been eyeing the staff, as surely it couldn't have been my uncle or aunt, the only two other people who lived here.

Ariel would also love seeing how Willow had made me up. Even by my own pretty low standards, I was killing it, with my brown hair swept into a single coil over one shoulder. I'd always been larger chested, and the soft, velvet bustier under my midnight-blue evening dress contained and boosted my ladies to perfection.

I was rocking a Big Boob Bonanza and needed to preserve the fact with a photo.

More, I just missed talking to my friend. Her daily updates on living in the Scottish Highlands gave me life. She was so happy and free in the wide-open landscape, with green rolling hills, snow-topped mountain peaks, and heather-strewn glens.

The occasional pictures of the men she was crushing on didn't hurt either.

Light music and a smattering of conversation echoed through the hall from the two dozen or so people in glittering gowns and evening wear. My uncle had introduced me around, but only out of politeness. Whatever business deal he and my aunt were concocting clearly had him on edge because the thin, nervous man had been even more tense than usual.

I inched away from the party and towards the office.

My best guess for the location of my phone was my aunt's bedroom, but she'd been in there all afternoon, so I'd been unable to search it. My next bet was the office she and my uncle shared, down the hall and around the corner from the party. I'd try there first then slip upstairs.

Out of sight, I prowled the corridor.

The office door was open, and I stole closer, pausing by a window that overlooked the parking area beside the house. The glass was opaque but had been left ajar, and male tones came through the gap, two voices speaking low.

"No, I have to wait around to handle the niece," one said. My uncle's driver, I was sure.

I froze. Did he say niece? Meaning me?

Ahead, the office door closed, someone unseen within the room.

Shit. I would've had some explaining to do if I'd strolled right in. What was I thinking?

I really should return to the party, but the voices outside continued. With the obscured glass, the people outside couldn't see me, but I clung to the wall so I didn't cast a shadow.

"What does she think of it? Doesn't seem the type, looking at her."

He said something else too low for me to hear, ending with a laugh.

The first man was all too clear. "Does it matter? They've already sealed the deal."

Several thoughts struck me at once.

There was a deal being made with my name included when no one had said a word to me. Instantly, that notion was chased by the fact that never once in my family's history had I ever been consulted on a decision that impacted me. The elementary school I attended, where Mom and I lived, even what I did with my free time.

But to be dealt with as some part of an offer beat out any previous implications.

What was it, free labour? Cleaning, housesitting, babysitting?

Upset curdled my blood, and I stared at the window, willing myself to storm around the house and demand to be told everything. Except I wasn't moving. Not through fear, but because I didn't want to know.

You need to leave.

Yeah, note writer. Gotcha loud and clear.

Then the first man said something else, ending with, "... taking her with me this evening."

Taking me?

I recoiled.

Memories hit me from my lunch with Sigrid this afternoon. She and her friend had talked about the benefits of an arranged marriage while the young couple made eyes at each other across the table.

My aunt had talked about opportunities.

Surely not.

There was no way she could've been trying to prepare me, was there?

I goggled at the picture I'd conjured. It couldn't be. I was only thinking like this because Ariel had been on my mind.

Her dad had tried to sell her off, literally giving her away as a child bride to some old man he'd had business dealings with. Ariel had been a target for men's attention since she'd been ten years old. She was stunning. An easy target for men to want to misuse as currency. I was a potato in comparison, even made over like I had been tonight. I was letting my imagination run away.

Footsteps at the other end of the corridor jerked me out of my stupor. My pulse sped, and I swung my gaze around to the looming figure.

Just a waiter carrying a tray.

He cast a curious look at me then continued on, but the interruption was enough. Whatever the deal, I wasn't down for it. I kicked my stiletto heels into an alcove, hiked up my gown, and sprinted for the stairs.

In my room, I stuffed my possessions into my bag. I hadn't brought much, not expecting to stay this long, and half my things were already in it, so packing was easy. Then I slipped across the hall to my aunt's room, really needing my phone if I was going to make a break for it and avoid whatever was meant to happen tonight.

I crept through the darkened space, senses alert for any sound.

Inside her all-white walk-in wardrobe, I eased open the top drawer of a dresser, wincing as it squeaked.

No phone lurked among the neat piles of clothes.

Rapid-fire, I continued down the drawers, then over to her jewellery display. Panic hastened my search. Like a thief, I pawed through the plush boxes that I'd always treated so respectfully when I dusted around them.

Urgency rose in me, screaming that I needed to get out of here before the man outside came for me. But getting away was going to be a problem.

I had no car. Armed security manned the gate as well as the end of the road. Cameras guarded the exterior of the house, but that didn't worry me so much. Once I was gone, I was gone. They couldn't force me to come back.

I absolutely needed my damn phone, though. Hard to call an Uber out to the middle-of-nowhere suburban hills without one.

My hunt through the jewellery display came up empty, and I turned, scanning the small space and the room beyond. This was taking too long. I was wasting time. Perhaps I could escape to a neighbour's house and ask for help.

I took a step towards the exit.

The bedroom door swung open. I sucked in a breath and dove into an open wardrobe, silently concealing myself behind a wealth of beautiful dresses.

The light sprang on.

My aunt chattered away to someone. I closed my eyes and pressed back against the wall, my heartbeat loud in my ears.

Laughter rang out, closer still.

Heels clicked on the polished floor then became muted, telling me that my aunt stood on the fluffy white rug directly outside my hiding place. I held deathly still, not even breathing.

"See, this is it," she said to whoever she was with.

"It's darling," cooed her friend. "Such a pretty piece of jewellery. She's going to adore it."

I itched to peek, my mind supplying wedding jewellery. An engagement ring. Holy shit.

In my crouched position, I shifted my fingertips, touching something beside me. A white box, concealed in the depths of the wardrobe.

Outside, the women's voices returned to the bedroom then out to the hall.

I stared at the box, then infinitely slowly, lifted the lid.

My phone sat on top of a pile of papers.

I gaped at it then snatched it up. But I knew better than to activate it right now, and instead checked the ringer was off.

I counted my heartbeats to be sure the voices had gone, and waited a minute more. On my bare feet, I crept back into the bedroom and peeked out into the hall.

Empty now.

From my own room, I grasped my overnight bag and the ballet flats I'd set on top of it and stole to the stairs.

Below, a group of people stood chatting in the foyer.

Marching down there barefoot and with a bag on my back was out of the question. They'd stop me for sure.

I needed another way out.

At a guest room down the hall, I closed myself in. Locked the door. The window opened onto a low roof. If I got out there, I could jump down to the path below.

I peered out into the dark night, no sign of anyone. The two men who'd talked about me had been over at the far side of the house.

The coast was clear, but I had to be quick.

Was I really going to do this? Make a moonlit escape with no explanation to the people who'd supported me for much of my life?

I couldn't ignore what I'd heard, the note, or my gut instinct.

Then I glanced down at myself and the beautiful dress I'd been loaned. Climbing out in it would ruin it and probably restrict my movements, too. Plus I didn't want there to be a single thing I owed my family after tonight. No cause of recrimination beyond bad manners in not saying goodbye.

In a flash, I unzipped and stripped the evening gown, draping it over a chair. I just needed something from my bag to cover my half-naked body.

"Daisy? Are you up here?" my aunt hollered. "I have someone I want you to meet."

My panic overspilled. It was now or never.

I eased open the window and let the night air rush in.

3

Ben

Under the cover of the shadowy hedgerow, I prowled down the side of the brightly lit Los Angeles mansion.

I'd got here in good time.

From LAX, I'd jumped in a car and hit the road, a message from Ariel spurring me on. She'd seen her stepmother's Instagram pictures of a party happening this evening and recognised the house as Daisy's.

Call me suspicious, but if I was planning to do something nefarious with a family member, having the cover of an event would prove useful.

It was a fancy-as-fuck residence, too.

Not only was the street gated, but the house had its own security. Two guards at the entrance. Except they weren't doing a great job. I'd bypassed them easily and found my way through the perimeter and right up to the building itself.

The next part would be harder—locating and securing my target.

Striding into the party was out of the question.

I needed a distraction.

Above me, on the upper floor of the wide house, a window opened, then a pair of feet swung out followed by the bare legs of a woman. Before my very eyes, a curvy lass dressed in tight, brain-cell-destroying lingerie eased out of the window and dropped down onto the low roof beneath her.

For a good few seconds, I was entirely stuck on the spectacular sight. Grabbable hips, gleaming skin. The most incredible tits, presented in some sort of corset like the world's most delicious offering.

Deep and unexpected lust slammed into me.

I swallowed, but it didn't ease. Dirty images that centred on the bouncy frame of this stranger flew before my eyes. So hot and fast it stopped every other brain process.

Being ridden so I could tear open that corset and get to the goods.

Going balls-deep until we both yelled in pleasure.

I was a professional, a grown man able to check himself. But it had been a long time since I'd got laid. In fact, I'd promised myself that during this trip, I'd find an energetic hook-up or three to take the edge off. Indulge myself like I didn't have the time to in Scotland.

Maybe it was because of the fact I didn't want any local woman to get the wrong idea about me that I didn't screw around on home territory. I was nobody's boyfriend-in-waiting.

But that didn't stop me being hot-blooded.

Finally, my haze of horniness relaxed its grip, and the

face and body I'd been staring at morphed into recognition.

Fuck. Holy fucking fuck.

The sexiest woman I'd ever seen was Daisy Devereux, Ariel's friend. And she was staring right back at me.

"Please," she whispered from her rooftop perch, her eyes rounded in panic. "Please don't call out. I know what this looks like. I just need to get away."

I unhinged my jaw and forced out a sentence. "I'm here to help."

"Appreciated, but I don't need it." She released a bag I hadn't even noticed to the ground with a dull thud then dangled off the roof.

Before I could question my motives, I darted over to catch her fall. "C'mere, shortie."

Those perfectly padded hips were in my hands for a second that was too brief as I released her and stepped back.

"Are you kidding? I said I don't need help. Back away, buddy," she hissed. But then her face fell. "By which I mean please don't tell anyone I'm out here. Just give me a head start."

She was scared.

And escaping.

My brain rebooted, and the inappropriate lust evaporated entirely. Ariel was nineteen, which meant Daisy was way too young for the likes of me to be ogling.

"No, I really am here to help. Ariel sent me. You've saved me a job in getting ye out of the house."

Her mouth opened in a perfect O. Then she cast her gaze over my features, and her eyes widened all the more. "Oh my God. Are you Ben?"

"Ben Graham, at your service."

Daisy made a sound that was a cross between a muted squeak of outrage and one of happiness. She flung out her arms and launched at me in a tight, half-naked hug.

Smashing those insanely hot tits against me.

I couldn't remember the last time I'd been hugged, but that wasn't the main issue on my mind. An inch closer between our lower bodies and she'd feel exactly how hard up I was. I had no intention of scaring the lass I'd come here to save.

I broke away and hid my embarrassment by collecting her overnight bag from the path and scanning the grounds to be sure the guards hadn't heard us. "I'll explain everything once we're in the car."

"You have a car?" she gasped. "Of course you do. What are we waiting for? Lead the way. People will be looking for me, including two men the other side of the building."

"No problem. Let's move."

She curled an arm through my free one, awarding me the status of trust I barely deserved. But at least now I could use up my energies on action.

Keeping vigilant for all sounds and movement, I retraced my steps to where I'd entered the property, guiding Daisy with me. The boundary was marked by rising, dusty ground and thick shrubs, the next house only metres away. Daisy pushed through, scrambling over the crumbling earth and through the greenery at the top. I kept my focus resolutely off her peach of an arse and followed her.

We emerged on a driveway, the house beyond smaller than Daisy's relatives' but thankfully dark. I opened my mouth to whisper a question on our next move, but a rapid, staccato barking commenced, cutting me off. From the steps leading up to the entrance, a miniature dog burst out, baring its tiny white teeth at us.

It stopped at the gate but continued its tirade.

Fuck. It was going to blow our cover.

Daisy took two steps towards it and hissed like a cat, her arms out to make herself big. The little dog yelped and scampered back up the steps.

Silence fell once more.

"For an animal lover, I'm not sweet on that pampered pet," the woman commented. "Barks all night."

A light blinked on above us.

I grasped Daisy by the hand and took off at a jog.

Though the street was one long loop around a hillside with the security gate at the single-road exit, a five-minute scan of an overhead map had given me a way in. The houses here were built on top of each other, no space wasted except where essential. Further down, the exclusive road curved back on itself, separated from the street below by a run-off gully and a five-foot concrete wall. That street was a thoroughfare, and I'd parked within a nice striking distance of the house.

Far easier and quicker than obtaining the code for the gate, but tricky for a half-naked woman to navigate.

Dutifully, Daisy followed me down the side of another property and under the shelter of trees. From here, the city lights of Los Angeles spread out far and wide.

It was pretty, if you liked that kind of thing. I preferred cold, steep mountains at first light.

I stooped low to put my lips next to Daisy's ear, ignoring her little rushed intake of breath that sounded far more erotic than it should've.

"Two choices. We can run down the street and exit out of the walking gate, assuming ye know the code. Or, just beyond these trees, there's a gully and a five-foot wall, which is the route I used to get in."

"I can handle a climb. I just need to get far away from here." She cast a look behind.

A shout came from up the street, and Daisy stiffened, her fingers seeking mine once more.

"I think that was my aunt. Go!" she urged.

I directed our steps to the edge of the rough gully, dropping down first so I could take Daisy's hands. She didn't hesitate and landed lightly beside me on the branch-strewn concrete then stared up at our next challenge.

From the depth of the channel we were in, it appeared intimidatingly high, the moonlight casting hard shadows around it.

"Put on something from your bag," I suggested. Straddling the rough wall would scratch her skin.

I fought the image of red lines marring her perfect thighs, though it was a battle.

Another shout came, followed by voices closer still.

Daisy jumped. "No time. Your car's nearby, right?"

At my nod, she sucked in a breath then scrambled out of the shadowed gully. I followed and made a foothold for her at the base of the wall. With no hesitation, she planted her foot in my palms and let me boost her upwards. But adrenaline fuelled my move.

She sailed over and crashed down the other side.

Shite. Grasping the ridge, I hauled myself up, pausing for a second at the top to check where she'd fallen.

Daisy sat in the earth, her hand over her mouth and her shoulders shaking.

I dropped beside her at a crouch, urgently scanning her for injuries. "Fuck, I'm sorry. I put more power into that than I needed."

She pulled her hand away, revealing silent laughter. Not tears.

"I'm fine. I get it, I'm a big girl so you overestimated. Congrats on the muscles."

The muted laughter continued, and I scrubbed a hand over my face, confused.

What the fuck did that mean? She was curvy as hell, but I got the impression I'd somehow offended her.

But now wasn't the time for questions.

The shouts from above continued. In tandem, we upped and moved through the bushes to the road. My hired car was exactly where I'd left it, and I unlocked it on our approach, jogging ahead to open the door for Daisy.

She settled inside without a word, and I rounded to the driver's seat, tossing her bag in the back.

Then I got us the hell out of there, for once lost for words despite everything that had just gone down.

4

Daisy

Of all the guys Ariel had ever liked, none had ever captured my interest. Aside from the man adjacent to me in the car, one hand on the wheel, his finger tapping like he was deep in thought.

Ben Graham. A strong, confident name. I'd been sixteen when I'd first seen a picture of him and I'd thought him the hottest man alive. That hastily taken shot did nothing for him, not compared with reality.

He was tall, much bigger than me, and built, his shoulders bulky under his close-fitting long-sleeved shirt. I'd hugged him and felt exactly how hard those muscles were.

Though it was dark, I knew his hair to be a dirty blond, cut short but not enough to hide how it curled.

But I hadn't counted on how confidence-inspiring his presence was. A single word from him and I was ready to sit up and obey. He could tell me the world was flat and I'd one hundred percent believe him, having faith that the land-scapes had changed and he'd noticed before me.

A few minutes in his company had rewritten five years of being distantly aware of him, and I was happy keeping up.

But then I'd set my fingertips to his shoulder, and he'd power slammed me over the wall. The memory brought a shuddering halt to my musings. Everything about this evening was embarrassing. The fact I'd needed rescuing from my own family, that I'd pranced around in my underwear, nice as it was, or that I'd got a fit of giggles at the humiliation of him needing to put extra strength into getting me airborne.

"Talk me through what happened tonight." His deep voice with a Scottish brogue cut through the silence.

It set me in motion, and I stretched to grab my bag, unable to avoid grazing his arm with my boob.

I righted myself, sneaking a glance at my rescuer, and a tiny bit caught on the flush of pink on his cheeks.

"Is it okay if I do that at the same time as telling Ariel?"

Ben jerked his head in agreement. "She's been blowing up my phone all evening, so you'd better. But first, go into your location settings and turn them off."

"You think someone will try to track me?"

"Wouldn't rule it out."

My cell phone didn't power on, so I plugged the charging cable into the car.

"It'll take a second to start up. Old phone. Poor battery life," I explained then fished in my bag for something to wear.

In the close confines of the car, getting dressed became an immediate necessity. By LA nightlife standards, I wasn't that underdressed, but I felt practically naked beside the big man. I shrugged on a light-grey hoodie that was long enough to cover my ass, wriggling it under my seat belt and down my body. Next, I found underwear, but changing into that meant first peeling off the ultra-tight shapewear.

The escapade had left me hot and a little sweaty. If anything, the giant panties felt tighter, and ridding myself of the instrument of torture would be impossible at this angle.

I could barely get my thumb under the waistband.

"Damn," I mumbled.

"What?" Ben shot his gaze to me.

I considered making something up, but he'd already seen what I'd been wearing. "The shapewear I've got on is slowly killing me. I'm not sure how I'm going to get it off."

He swallowed and returned his attention to the freeway. "Cut it?"

"Got a knife on you over there, Boy Scout?"

He reached into his pocket and pulled out a pocketknife, thumbing the silver blade free. Then he held it out to me, handle first.

I stared for a second then took it. "You're one of those always-prepared people, then."

"In my job, I have to be."

I sensed rather than saw his smile, concentrating instead on not nicking myself as I hiked up my hoodie and guided the blade under the edge of my underwear at my hip.

On the side by the door, obviously.

It split, shredding halfway down with a silent tear. I moaned in relief at my body taking its natural shape, then angled the knife for the final hem.

The panties split completely.

But I put too much effort into it. My hand kept going, and

the knife flicked out, missing cutting my thigh by millimetres.

"Shit!" I squeaked.

Ben's gaze instantly came my way. "Are ye hurt?"

My cheeks flamed. I had everything on display.

I yanked down my hem to hide my coochie, then whipped the underwear completely off, tugging on my comfy boy shorts.

"No, just me and this knife are not friends."

I didn't dare look at Ben.

He had gentlemanly manners, but I didn't know him. I already felt a mixture of embarrassment and gratitude I couldn't quite reconcile.

Let alone the tendrils of a powerful insta-crush.

"All better?" he asked, amusement as well as something a little gravelly in his voice. "I'll dispose of the knife before I travel home and I'll make sure to treat it badly for not being nice to ye."

I was saved from answering by my phone springing to life. I swiped to call back one of the hundreds of missed calls from Ariel.

"Daisy," my best friend yelped. "Tell me that's you."

"Alive and free," I replied. "Coming at you from a car with Ben. He can hear you, too. Boss bitch move in sending in the big gun."

I hadn't actually thanked Ben himself yet, but I would. Who knows how far I would have got without him.

"Tell me everything," she demanded.

I filled both of them in on the back story of the past few weeks, struggling to make sense of the events of the evening.

"Wait up. You had a cosy lunch where the virtues of arranged marriage were paraded, got a makeover, then were introduced around at a party?" Ariel summarised. "I don't think there's any doubt over what you overheard from those men. They were going to marry you off. Ben, back me up here."

My rescuer palmed his jaw. "A fair assessment. My question would always be: what's the motive? Something they'd stand to gain. If we understand that, it gives us a better defence."

"There was something else," I added. "A note appeared in my bedroom this afternoon. It warned me to leave."

Ben's eyebrows dove together. "Did ye keep it?"

"In my bag," I said.

"Good. Don't throw it away. It tells us this situation was not only premeditated but not everyone agreed."

I gulped, the events seeming far worse from the other side. It had all happened so fast, my head was spinning.

Ariel made a sound of agreement. "Where will you go now?"

Ben slid a look my way, waiting on my word.

"Probably not home," I said slowly.

"Where do ye live?" he asked.

"I don't have a place of my own. After college, I moved in with friends in downtown LA, close to my aunt and uncle's office."

He shook his head in a firm no. "First place they'll try. Ye need somewhere else for the night. Does anywhere spring to mind that they don't know about?"

For all my thoughts of escape, I hadn't progressed beyond the desire to get away. The fact was, I didn't have many choices.

"Can you call your mom?" Ariel asked.

I hid a sigh. "I'll try. If not, I'll think of something. I don't want you worrying. For all I know, I could've got it wrong. Maybe they'll be glad to see the back of me." I gave a shaky laugh, not liking the feeling that had descended over me.

"Oh no," Ariel said. "Don't do that thing where you think you're a burden. Ben, promise me you'll take care of her and get her somewhere safe."

The big man curled his fingers around the steering wheel. "That's my job."

"Good. Daisy, call your mom then text me so I know how it all goes down. I don't care how late it is, I've missed you so much and I need you back in circulation. Ben, don't drive all night. You were already on limited sleep, and I bet you couldn't rest on the plane. I don't want to find out that you've crashed on a freeway somewhere."

Belatedly, I realised what time it was for my friend. Nine p.m. in LA was the early hours of the morning in Scotland.

I held in my instant apology, thanked her again, and hung up, taking a second to summon my strength for the next conversation.

"Where's your mother?" Ben asked.

I scrolled through my contacts. "Last time we spoke, San Diego. The time before that, San Francisco. So your guess is as good as mine. But honestly, I don't need you to play cab driver, especially since Ariel implied you've had a stressful couple of days. You helped me, and I'm so grateful, but I can take care of myself from here."

He huffed, the corner of his mouth curving like I was funny. "Make your call, Daisy."

Daisy. The way he said my name gave me shivers.

I dragged my gaze off him and pressed Mom's number.

The dial tone filled the car, and I realised my error. Whereas I'd been happy for Ben to hear anything Ariel said, my mother was another matter. She had the habit of being casually outrageous, and I cringed when she picked up, music in the background of the call.

"Baby?"

"Hey, Mom."

Last time we'd spoken, I'd been sitting with Aunt Sigrid in her office. Mom had been cagey and got off the call in a hurry.

"What's going on? Who's with you?" she asked.

"Just a friend."

"Not my brother or Sigrid? Can they hear me?"

"No. You're on loudspeaker in my friend's car."

"Ooh," my mother cooed, her tone changing from defensive to higher pitched. "A guy? Is he pretty?"

"What, um, yes?" I answered, flustered.

Mom didn't miss a beat. "Hey, hot guy. I'm Betty, Daisy's mom, but people usually mistake us for sisters. I had her when I was very young."

"Pleasure to meet ye," Ben replied, his tone dry.

"Oh my God, that accent. Are you Scottish?"

I palmed my face. "Mom, where are you?"

She paused. "Why are you asking?"

"I'm..." I pulled up short on explaining what had happened. Mom either had big opinions or could be totally dismissive, and I wanted to talk to her face to face. I started again. "I've left Paul and Sigrid's house and I need somewhere to stay."

She took a rapid inhale. "You left? Holy shit. Is that a good idea? Tell me everything."

I wrinkled my nose. "I will when I see you."

"Seriously, you can't just up and leave. Sigrid really wanted you to stay. I know how important that was to her."

"I didn't exactly ask."

"You just walked out? Baby!" Mom sputtered.

I expected this. She was allowed to flit away. I had to stay put and make nice. But I couldn't do that anymore.

"It's for the best," I cut in. "We can talk it over better in person."

She paused for a moment, and I had no idea which way this would go. Then she took a breath, and her voice returned brighter. "Yeah, okay, then bring it on in. Come straight to me. I mean that. Don't go anywhere else. I just started a new job. Oh my God, you can work with me, too!"

"What kind of work?"

"Cleaning, kinda. Inspired by you. It pays well." She hastened on, the music getting louder. "Call me when you get to Seattle, and I'll give you my address. Got to go. Bye to you too, mister Scottish guy."

She hung up.

I stared at my phone.

"Cleaning, kinda," Ben repeated.

I'd skipped over that detail for another more pressing matter. I couldn't afford a flight to Seattle, even if I could stomach getting on a plane without a full-body meltdown, which meant I needed to work out how I'd make the trip.

I tapped my browser and searched on the bus options.

"Am I heading to the airport?" Ben asked.

I grimaced, remembering to flip my phone to airplane mode to take it offline, like he'd asked. "I have a morbid fear of flying, so no. There's a bus that leaves tomorrow morning. It calls at Sacramento, Portland, then Seattle." And took over twenty-seven hours, but I left that information out. "I just need somewhere to sleep tonight then I'll make my way to Union Station in the morning."

Ben went quiet. Throughout our drive, he'd kept to the bigger, faster roads, his focus occasionally flicking to the lanes behind us as if checking whether we were being followed. Something Ariel told me about him registered in my mind.

He was a bodyguard. Or some kind of security personnel. It made sense of how he behaved and the quiet professionalism that came off him in waves. What didn't track was how he flicked tiny glances at me. Just a couple of times, I'd noticed, but it happened. And each time, he tightened his muscles and aggressively faced forward.

One of my wildest dreams was to visit Ariel in Scotland. I desperately wanted to see the place she'd run to, and where she'd built a happy life. Chill out with her in the mountains and breathe in the clean air. But now, a new element joined that mix. I liked the company she kept, too. I didn't want Ben to drop me off and drive away. Just a little longer with him would be nice, not only because I felt safer with this stranger than I had in weeks with my own family, but because he reminded me of all things good.

I adjusted my position, easing one bare knee over the other.

Ben's gaze darted to my movement, lingering on my legs, then sharply away as he did the same grip-the-steering-wheel, eyes-on-the-road action.

I liked that, too.

Then he opened his mouth and said words that sent my pulse racing.

"I'm driving north to see my folks. Fuck getting the bus.

I'll take ye to Seattle."

All I could do was agree.

5

Ben

*O*n paper, my offer was a logical one.

Daisy was going in the same direction as me—Seattle wasn't far from my family in relative terms. It was late at night, and her other options were sketchy at best. We were connected by our mutual friend, Ariel, who'd tear me a new one if she knew I'd had the chance to help further but blanked on it.

Alongside that was my personal discipline to see a job through. Though Daisy had downplayed the events of the evening, my senses were wired for danger. Her relatives wouldn't so easily let her go if they'd been willing to force her into a marriage. They'd already broken the boundaries of reasonable behaviour which meant there was more to this picture than I knew.

She wasn't safe yet.

On the other hand, neither was I.

I could blame the adrenaline of the night or my dry spell

but I couldn't ignore the soaring attraction I felt for this woman. I'd control it, sure, but it wouldn't quit.

Every little thing about her put my senses on high alert.

Her scent. Her pretty voice. Her stripping in the car next to me which had me picturing her in all kinds of fun ways. It sank my mood to fucking miserable.

We sailed northwards on I-5, leaving Los Angeles behind.

Just one night and one day, I coached myself. See her to her mother's place, head straight into the city, find a bar, and take out my horniness on a willing body.

"So you're a bodyguard," Daisy said, blithely unaware of my turmoil. "What kind of bodies do you guard?"

"I go wherever I'm sent," I forced my reply.

"Ever protected anyone famous?"

"Now and then."

Daisy twisted in her seat to face me, apparently not put off by my non-answers. "It's so interesting to me that you'd put yourself on the line for someone else. Using your body to defend theirs."

She was killing me.

I managed a grunt to acknowledge her.

Around us, traffic flowed, the roads still busy despite the late hour. As always, I'd picked a fast car so I had the muscle if I needed it. I'd have killed for a car chase right now just to take the pressure off so I could focus on anything other than Daisy.

But it seemed we'd got away without being followed.

The fact made me even grumpier.

"I remember Ariel telling me what you did for her and her brothers. They were on the run, but you helped make them safe. Didn't you negotiate with their dad as well?"

This question was wide open, and I was being an arse-hole in not giving her the conversation she wanted, but my ability to speak had got lost in my mood.

"Something like that," I forced out. "Can we not talk? I need to concentrate."

For a long moment, Daisy stared at me, her eyes wide in surprise. Then she turned to face the window, thankfully falling into silence.

Guilt stabbed at me for how I was treating her. It was better like this, even if I couldn't tell her why.

A few hours on, Daisy had made another couple of attempts at conversation but then got lost in her phone. Though I was playing ignorant, I still noticed every move she made, including her hand resting on her belly.

The last time I'd eaten had been food served on the plane God knows how many hours ago. I was burning up fuel I didn't have from lack of sleep.

Continuing without a break would be dangerous. I knew my limits.

"Have ye eaten?" I asked.

Daisy lifted her head. "Actually, I haven't had anything since lunch."

She shut her mouth with an audible snap like she was cutting off all the other words she wanted to say.

Another guilty pang hit me, but I buried it in finding an off-ramp and services.

I cruised through rows of parked cars and slid ours into a single space between two RVs, providing a little bit of cover. Then I killed the engine and turned to Daisy.

"It'll be better if ye stay in the car—"

She yanked on the handle and leapt out.

I scrambled after her.

But she took off at a fast clip. "See you back here in ten," she tossed over her shoulder then disappeared into the nearest building.

I had that coming.

More slowly, I trudged after her, entering a burger bar. Daisy was nowhere to be seen, so I checked out the menu and ordered the protein feast my body was crying out for. I tacked on a cheeseburger and fries, in case the woman came back from the ladies' room with hunger equalling mine, but by the time the food appeared, she hadn't emerged. I ate slowly, relishing the oversized meal and drink.

Daisy still hadn't shown when I'd finished, asked the waiter to bag up the remaining food, and hit the men's bathroom. I was starting to get worried.

Also even more tired.

Exhaustion had caught up with me, and the food I'd intended as fuel had put me into hibernation mode. I trudged back to the car, relief flooring me at the sight of Daisy leaning on the doorframe.

She'd tugged on a pair of cropped leggings under the oversized hoodie and brushed her hair out of the fancy style and into a high ponytail. She'd swiped off most of her make-up, too, and the change took me by surprise.

From starlet to girl next door.

And I was still staring.

"Where did ye go?" I barked to hide my confusion.

Daisy cocked her head at me. "Didn't we say ten minutes? You're the one who's late."

I went to answer, but a yawn took me over before I could stifle it.

When I opened my eyes, her gaze had softened. I'd pissed her off, but she'd half forgiven me in a heartbeat.

"You're exhausted. I heard what Ariel said about you not sleeping. Tell you what," she said. "I'll take the next driving shift. Do we have a stopping place in mind or are we just going to go all night?"

I hid yet another groan at the unintended innuendo. Then I gave up a confession. "In any other circumstance, I'd want to get ye as far away as possible, but we have a long journey ahead, and I want to do it quickly and safely. Maybe another hour or so and we find a motel. That way, I'll be well rested and able to drive the full day tomorrow."

I didn't like to sleep in a vehicle, unless I had no choice. It left me feeling vulnerable, and the rest was for shite. Getting some sleep tonight and being back on the road early would bring us into Seattle by late evening, assuming the traffic played ball.

Daisy held my gaze for a moment then nodded. She extended her hand. "Keys," she demanded. Before I could protest, she gave me a look that took no prisoners. "I'll drive, and you find us a motel for the night. Don't worry, I'll be out of your hair before you know it."

An image hit me of curling that ponytail of dark hair around my fist. Using it to bring her soft mouth to mine.

For fuck's sake.

I handed over the keys and held up the burger bag.

"Hungry?"

"Not for food," she answered smartly and bypassed me to get into the car.

What the hell did that mean?

Better I didn't ask.

In our reversed positions, I polished off the second burger and stared at my phone while Daisy took the wheel. Motels were plentiful, and I booked one online, an hour ahead of us on the road.

"I've got us rooms but given our details as a married couple," I informed her.

"Sure."

"Just to conceal your identity."

"Uh-huh."

"You have nothing to fear from me. I'm a professional on the job."

"Right," Daisy gave the same sort of monosyllabic response I'd been giving her.

God-fucking-dammit.

Mixed in with my unending lust was that nagging edge of guilt. I'd hurt her feelings twice this evening, the first time inadvertently, the second one more purposefully. I didn't like it, and I didn't like that I didn't like it.

Normally, in my line of work, it was my way or the highway. People obeyed me because it kept them safe. They didn't usually want to chat or get to know me.

"Tell me more about your relatives," I blurted for the sake of saying something.

"Don't really want to talk about it."

I glowered at her.

"It'll help me understand how to protect ye."

Daisy raised a shoulder, giving me nothing.

"All right. What did your ma mean when she said you'd inspired her job?" I tried.

"Beats me."

My frustration swirled.

But it was fine. Hadn't I already decided it was better if she didn't try to be my friend?

We sped on into the night, neither of us trying to make small talk.

At the motel, the disinterested guy behind the counter handed over a key. I passed it to Daisy, following her to the door.

Outside, she took a deep breath of night air then turned back to me. "I'm just going to say this. Thank you for coming so far to help me tonight. I'm aware of how huge that is and I won't forget it. I'm also sorry you've been dragged into this. I get that you don't like me or the fact you're forced to babysit me for this trip. It's a burden you weren't banking on. For the record? You're not on the job. If you want to quit, that's fine with me. I won't even tell Ariel if you prefer. Goodnight, Ben."

She said it all without making eye contact then fled down the path. I watched her disappear inside a room, my heart sinking.

At the reception desk, the attendant raised his tired gaze to me once more. "Do you need something else?"

"The other room key?"

"You need two keys for one room?"

I summoned my patience. "No, I need one for my room."

He blinked. "Come again?"

A deep breath did nothing for my frustration. "I have two rooms booked. Ye gave me the key for one, now I need the key for the other."

The guy wrinkled his pierced nose. "Sorry, mister. There was only one room booked, and we're full. Yours has two beds, so you can sleep apart if you're arguing or whatever."

Fuck no.

I whipped out my phone and showed him the booking, but got only a shrug in response. The guy explained it was provisional only until people showed up, because often they didn't. There was no way around it.

We only had one room, and Daisy was in it.

I trudged from the office and down the path where she'd disappeared. I needed to explain that I'd be sleeping in the car, but also I owed her an apology. Outside her door, I paused for a second with my hand to the wooden frame, pulling the right words into order in my mind.

Then I picked up voices. She was on the phone. I sank my arse on the ground to wait her out.

A breathy moan came from inside the room.

I stilled and listened harder. The murmur of a voice continued, as if someone was reading a story. I picked up a few words.

"...he grasped her by the hips and pulled her down astride him on the bed."

Holy shite. Was that an audiobook?

A soft moan came again, and instantly, my blood rushed to my dick. She was nineteen, I reminded myself. Not for me.

But as I scrambled up, aiming to give Daisy her privacy, my elbow hit the door in a solid knock.

I was two steps away when it swung open.

6

Daisy

An orgasm, a shower, then sleep. All very much needed. The bathroom beckoned, and I had my audiobook playing, ready to help me get Ben out of my head.

The moment he'd turned surly, my hormones shot up to record levels.

I liked the grump. It made me want to pet him until he growled.

A flush of heat hit me, and I stripped my leggings.

A knock came at the motel room door.

Flustered, I padded over and opened it. My hot body-guard was walking away.

"Shite, I didn't mean—" he started.

At my back, the audiobook kept playing.

"*Don't make me beg,*" the heroine pleaded. "*Hard and fast. Now.*"

My cheeks burned, and I whipped around to snatch my phone from the bed, jabbing at the screen to stop the story.

Slowly, I turned back to Ben.

His vision looked a little hazy.

"You were saying?" I asked.

He scrubbed his face with his hands before answering. "Just needed to let ye know there's been a misunderstanding and we only have one room. I'll be sleeping in the car."

His gaze jumped from me to the comfortable space at my back.

I had no explanation, absolutely zero, for the words that came out of my mouth. "Don't be silly. There's two beds, we can share."

Ben stood like a statue, his focus returning to me and his cheeks distinctly flushed. I didn't get this man at all, and I was crazy to consider sleeping in the same room with him, but his remark about being no danger to me had stuck.

Despite the hot looks, he wasn't interested.

I'd be the one lusting over him from a whole bed away.

Cursing inwardly, I opened the door wider and gestured. "I mean it, come on in. You said yourself that you need the rest. Sleeping in the car won't give you that."

With cautious, hesitant steps, the big man entered the room, suddenly making it feel a lot smaller. He placed down his bag then sat on the bed I hadn't spread my possessions across and fixed me with his gaze. "I'm still going to sleep in the car, but a shower would be good, plus I have something to say. I apologise for my attitude on the drive."

"Doesn't matter," I said, aiming for breezy.

"It does. I've given ye the wrong idea about me."

"No, I worked it out. You were already coming here to

see your folks, right? That's where you're driving now. Ariel sidetracked your plans and tacked me on. It's reasonable to be pissed off in that scenario."

Ben pinched the bridge of his nose. "Apart from the fact about my folks, you're dead wrong."

I folded my arms, not believing him. "So set me right."

My pose boosted my boobs, and Ben's attention landed squarely on my chest. He closed his eyes and spoke through gritted teeth. "Somehow I've given ye the wrong impression of how I see ye. For example, I didn't put extra effort into boosting ye over the wall on purpose. I was just fuelled by adrenaline and facing off with a short, half-naked woman whose curves were driving me insane."

"My curves?"

"Just needed to be said."

"Why?"

"To explain why I cannae sleep here."

I floundered, completely lost. "Of course you can. It's not a big deal."

"It is, Daisy."

God. How could one person saying my name so differently affect me so much?

"There's two beds," I continued, fast. "It's late, we're just going to crash. Jeez, you look like you're a minute from passing out anyway. Give me a good reason."

"For Christ's sake. My problem is that I'm attracted to ye."

His words fell like a grenade.

My mouth dropped open. I snapped it closed, stunned.

Attracted to me.

Holy hell. I hadn't imagined it.

"You're nineteen and under my charge," he continued, his tone harsh. "Everything about that is wrong, so forgive my rudeness, and the fact I never should have said a fucking word. I just needed to explain. I'll be sleeping in the back of the car. Now ye know why."

He kept his gaze down and waited on my response.

My breathing came faster, my heart hammering. I was no virgin but I had zero experience with a man like him. My nerves wanted me to run a mile, but other parts of me had a better idea. Starting with correcting his wayward assumptions.

Almost silently, I crept to stand in front of him. Then I placed my fingertip under his chin to tip his face up, the instant eye contact staggering.

"I'm twenty-one, not the same age as Ariel, and I already told you you're not on the job. No one's paying you here."

"Twenty-one...? Fuck. You're still under my protection."

"Great. But no more so than you are under mine."

His brown-eyed gaze held mine, a dangerous kind of urgency lurking behind his neutral expression.

Slowly, and with confidence I didn't know myself to have, I collected his work-roughened hands and set them on my hips.

His fingers indented my skin through my clothes.

"Don't tease me," he growled.

"I'm not. I'm attracted to you as well. Hence needing the smutty audiobook. I wasn't going to be able to sleep without it. After tomorrow, I'll more than likely never see you again..." My words came out with a tremble.

I had no idea where my boldness was coming from, only that I was sick of the way my relatives and their associates had treated me. Like a commodity, like someone who'd roll over and agree to their plans. I had my own life to live. My own wants and needs. And right now, I wanted and needed the grumpy bodyguard's control to break.

"I'm no blushing virgin," I added. "I like sex."

I mean, I probably would with him.

Dangerous electricity licked me, the anticipation alone enough to set my whole body on fire.

For a long moment, he just stared at me. "Just one night."

"Just one night," I repeated.

Abruptly, Ben pulled me down to straddle his lap, simultaneously sinking his mouth onto mine.

I gasped against his lips, steadying myself on his broad shoulders. God, one slide, a single taste, and I was a goner.

In the past, my experiences of intimacy had been limited to two college boyfriends and one in high school. None had really rocked my world, usually meaning I had to resort to the battery-operated toy thankfully still concealed in my bag. I had the feeling Ben was about to overturn my experience completely.

His lips worked mine, the kiss fierce and promising a whole lot more. He wrapped my ponytail in his fist.

Emboldened, I grazed my nails through his chest hair, scratching lightly.

Ben gave a groan that hit me straight between the legs. Then he stood, turning to drop me on the mattress with a bounce. He stared down at me and stripped his long-sleeved top, barely breaking eye contact.

A lean, muscular frame filled my view, tattoos down one of Ben's arms and reaching across his chest. My mouth watered.

I was so out of my depth, the hot bodyguard was about

to drown me.

"Take off the hoodie," he ordered.

I reached for the hem and dragged it up, loving how fast things had changed, willing for nothing to stop this. The man was fighting exhaustion, that was plain, but his need was greater. He wanted me. I was a little bit in lust with that.

I threw the hoodie to the bed, revealing my corset which I hadn't dared try to remove yet, and my mismatched comfy shorts. Ben breathed out and dropped to kneel in front of me. With his big hands, he grasped my knees and pushed them apart, inserting himself in the gap.

He kissed me again.

Held me to him.

Then he spoke against my lips, that gorgeous accent making me crazy. "All evening, I've been dreaming of getting this off ye."

He grazed up the sides of the corset, sending spirals of pleasure through my body. Instantly, I moved to the first fastening, poised to start undoing it. But he caught my hands. Drew both behind me.

"Keep them there," he ordered.

In this position, perched on the edge of the bed with my knees wide and my hands behind me, I was his to play with, my boobs high and forward, constrained like they were about to burst out.

Shades of embarrassment battled my need. He might be looking at me with deep hunger, but I didn't have a tight body like he did. He was all hard ridges, the opposite to my softness. But I kept my mouth shut and my insecurities locked down.

Ben dropped a kiss on my mouth then another to my throat. He moved to my chest and pressed his lips to the upper curve of my breasts.

I loved having my boobs played with. Hopefully he'd share the idea.

"So perfect," he muttered.

He framed my sides again then cupped my boobs, continuing to the top fastening. Delight rippled through me, but if he went hook by hook, we'd be here forever.

"I'm not all that attached to the corset," I confided.

"Dinna tell me that," he said. "Because I really want to tear it off ye like ye did with the underwear. Which, by the way, nearly gave me a heart attack."

My thrill ramped up a notch. "Do it."

Ben gave a devilish smirk, grasped the two sides, and wrenched. The corset fastenings shredded, spilling my boobs free. He groaned and tore through the remaining hooks, completely freeing my breasts. Then his hands were all over them, cupping them, his thumbs driving over my pebbled nipples.

I made some ungodly sound and tipped my head back, gasping again as he buried his face then took his hot mouth to my nipple. He sucked me, plumping my bare flesh with his hand, simultaneously working the other side to a peak.

Lust and shock zinged through my nerves.

Nothing had ever felt this good, and we'd barely started. Maybe the evening had been a kind of foreplay, attraction prepping me. Either way, Ben was giving me a masterclass in playing my body.

He worked me till I was rigid, pulling back to admire his efforts. Then he raised his gaze to my face. "You're so fucking beautiful."

I gave a startled laugh. "Tell that to my boobs. They like hearing it."

He gave me an amused smile then eased back, bringing his hands over my not-so-flat belly and to the waistband of my shorts.

"I'd really like to repeat it to your pussy. May I?"

Dimly, I was aware that I should be doing more than just sitting here like a pillow princess. I'd barely touched him, and I really wanted to. But all I could do was nod and lift my backside so he could ease the boy shorts off me.

We were going straight into the danger zone, and I didn't care.

He tossed the underwear behind him and palmed my thighs. I had the urge to close my legs from his avid gaze, but he wouldn't let me.

"I would've waxed," I started, but his bark of a laugh shut me up.

"No complaints here. Not a fucking single one."

He kissed my thigh, dragging his thumbs up my flesh in electric lines. Then he was at the core of me, his knuckle sliding through my wet centre. I moaned and closed my eyes, the sight of him far too much, far too huge a boost of hormones and lust.

He trailed kisses until he was right at my centre, and as with everything else I'd seen him do tonight, Ben didn't wait around. He licked me, drawing one leg up and over his shoulder for better access. I dropped onto the mattress, the ruined corset half down my arms now and trapped behind my back. It didn't matter. All I could feel was what he was doing to me.

Ben French kissed my pussy, gliding his tongue inside me before focusing on my clit. He sucked on me, and I bucked on the bed, amazed, and jerking my hips to get closer to his mouth. He gave a dark laugh and slid a long finger straight inside me, instantly finding my G-spot.

His other hand gripped my hip, holding me exactly where he wanted me.

I couldn't have moved anyway. It was so obvious how experienced he was. Later, I'd probably be too aware of the difference between us, but in this moment, all I could do was feel.

A second finger stretched me.

He coupled the action with his mouth and tongue getting to work, and the first spasms of a fast orgasm hit.

"You're going to make me come," I spluttered.

He didn't answer, instead, keeping the exact pressure up with the suction at my clit and his fingers moving in and out of me.

I'd never known such a fast rush or the whole-body takeover. The motel could burn down around us and I wouldn't care.

Then I tightened around his hand. Ben gave a groan of desire, and my orgasm smashed into me, out of control and so hard. My brain flipped, the pleasure almost knocking me out, and I melted into the bed, sure I'd momentarily levitated.

Sheer joy filled me. Every nerve lit up in the relief of a stunning climax. I could've sobbed, except this had been one-sided. I needed to take care of him in the same way he'd done to me.

But as I pushed up on my elbows, ridding myself of the corset, Ben was taking matters into his own hands. He yanked the button of his jeans, quickly freeing one massive erection.

"Push your tits together," he demanded, gripping his dick.

I obliged, earning a flush of lust across his features. He flicked his avid gaze between my pussy, my face, and my tits, working his length. I wanted to offer my assistance. I really wanted to explore his body. Take him in my hands and mouth. But the urgency between us hadn't quit. Ben jacked himself fast and hard.

"Going to come on ye," he forced out.

I tipped my head back and pushed my chest forward more.

With a pained growl, he came, spurting hot cum onto my breasts and belly. His groan of pleasure had me gasping, wildly crazy about our spectacular and entirely unexpected clash.

Then he was done. Spent.

And he collapsed down next to me like the act of finishing on me had broken him.

7

Daisy

Ben shoved his dick back into his boxer shorts and curled on the bed, eyes closed. His arm across my waist grew even heavier, and as my breathing slowed, and my heart rate got somewhere back to normal, he fell into a heavy sleep.

My heart panged.

He really had been exhausted.

Easing out from under him, I scampered to the bathroom and turned the shower on, closing the door so I didn't disturb him. I washed him from my skin, parts of me deliciously tender from the fast and frantic use. Once cleaned up, I slipped into fresh underwear and a T-shirt, then came back to the bedroom.

Ben hadn't moved.

I considered waking him, but he looked comfortable enough, facedown now with his arm extended. I tucked the blanket over him, turned off the light, peeked outside in case a convoy of angry relatives had found us, then when nothing stirred beyond waving palm trees, I got into the other bed.

Sleep took me under almost as quickly as it had him.

I woke to the sound of running water and a slice of light under the bathroom door. It was still dark outside, so I snuggled down, idly wondering how on earth I'd got to this blissfully relaxed and content state when I should've been panicked and sad. He really was a great bodyguard with all the services he'd offered me. A giggle hit me, and I smothered it.

The shower stopped, and Ben emerged, killing the light first. He crossed to his bag, rummaged quietly inside, then tugged on a fresh pair of black boxer shorts.

For a heady moment, I indulged in a fantasy that this was real and not a blip in time. But surely that kind of passion only existed in small doses.

He moved to the window and watched the parking lot. His car was tucked out of sight of the road, rather than directly outside our room, so we had a clear view of the quiet motel space.

"I checked earlier and saw nothing," I spoke quietly.

Ben jerked his gaze to me. "You're awake."

"True. Anything out there?"

"No. Though no thanks to me," he muttered. "I should've stayed outside and provided a night watch, instead of...other things."

Instead of sexy times with me?

"Ouch," I countered.

Ben stole another look outside then returned to the bed and sat, giving me a once-over from the mattress opposite.

"Listen, about earlier," he said.

Oh God, no. I didn't want to hear it. I flopped back, embarrassment rising. "Please don't. I had the worst evening and I'd really rather not know your regrets on the one good thing."

His eyebrows drew in as two dark slashes. "Regrets?"

"Yes!"

I dropped my arm over my eyes with a groan.

Ben shifted, and the bed dipped beside me.

He traced a line up my arm until he circled my wrist, unaware that he was making me crazy. Then he drew my arm away so he could see my eyes.

The orgasm he'd given me had knocked every other climax I'd ever had on the head. Except now, my body was alert again and anticipating more, a pulse beating at the apex of my thighs.

His voice returned, low and rough. "I won't sleep again tonight. I've rested enough and will keep watch until dawn so I'm sure you're safe. Then we'll leave. At no point during that am I going to regret what we did together, only my lack of professionalism and my falling asleep without cleaning ye up. Our hook-up blew my mind. I'll be dreaming about that for months."

"Didn't we agree we'd have the whole night?" I asked.

Where the heck had Ms Confidence come from and where had she been my whole life?

Ben stilled, and his grip on me tightened. "Want to know how much I'd give to roll ye over and fuck ye right now?"

My breath caught. "Okay."

He let out a groan. "Don't. Unless there happens to be a box of condoms in your bag, that's a no-go. I just beat myself off in the shower when I realised my stupidity."

I exhaled in disappointment.

Ben ducked and sank his mouth down on mine. God, his kiss did things to me. I threw aside the blanket and pulled him down on my body.

We were magnets, pushing apart or clamping together. I'd never known anything like it.

His hand went straight between my legs. Under my shorts. Feeling me up while he groaned against my lips. Then he found my clit, dipping down to gather my wetness first. He drove fast but steady circles into my flesh. The whole time, he kept up his devastating kiss. The pressure just right. Each slide of his tongue driving me higher.

In minutes, I was gasping then I shattered, another soul-stealing climax eclipsing my senses.

Ben worked me through it then removed his hand from my underwear and brought it to his lips.

Holding my gaze, he licked his fingers clean.

I had the momentary wish that he'd shove his fingers into my mouth. A thought I'd never once had before.

Ben kissed me again, frowning as he did it. Then he rolled me away from him and cuddled my back.

"Go to sleep," he ordered.

With the big, protective bodyguard spooning me, and his hard dick poking my butt, I drifted off again, unexpectedly satisfied for a second time tonight.

*T*he next time I woke, it was to a lighter room and an empty bed. I stretched, deliciously well used and content, and propped myself up on my elbows. Across the room, Ben packed his rucksack.

He glanced at me, his gaze dipping to my T-shirt-clad boobs like he couldn't avoid a cheeky peek.

He seemed...different. No lust in his eyes. Only cool professionalism, despite the glance.

"Morning," I said.

Ben turned back to his packing. "It's early, but we need to make a dent in the trip. I'll clear the room so ye can get ready."

"Sure we can't delay a little?" I asked.

What I wanted was for him to crawl back into bed. Another hour or two wouldn't make a difference, and the full-body contact would set me up for months.

He ducked his head, and a muscle ticked at his jaw. Clearly, he was trying to frame what he had to say next.

The long pause spoke volumes.

My heart sank. *Right. He really had meant* one night only, and now he was trying to find a way to let me down gently. Wasn't that a kick in the lady balls?

It shouldn't have been. I didn't know him. I didn't need anything more from him. But I couldn't ignore the stab of hurt.

Then I pulled up my proverbial big girl panties and gave myself a mental shake. I needed to be the sort of woman who could make this no big deal. My emotional armour was weak, and I let too much hurt me when it had no right to, like my relatives, like Mom.

Straightening my shoulders, I took back control. "Look, it's fine. I was only trying to use you for your body again. I'll just name my vibrator after you instead."

His pained gaze shot back to mine.

Heh. *Yep, I have a vibrator, and nope, you don't get to use it on me.*

"Go on outside. I won't be long," I promised.

Ben left the room, and I got my stuff together, washed up, brushed up, took a little more care with my make-up—physical armour to go with the emotional—straightened up the room, then joined him at the car.

Inside, he handed me a wrapped breakfast roll and pointed to the second of two coffee cups in the drinks holder. "Didnae ken how ye took it, so it's a latte. There are sugar packets in the bag."

He'd bought me breakfast.

Damn. A girl could get used to that.

"Thank you," I replied brightly then tucked into the food. "Does 'didnae ken' mean you didn't know?"

"Exactly that."

I grinned. "Great sex and learning a new language. Go me."

Ben drove, visibly pulling himself back into the professional role I'd seen during my rescue. While I ate, he kept his focus on the road.

"I just want to clear the air about last night," he announced abruptly. "We did what we did, and it was fucking amazing, but now I'm back on the clock. It can't happen again."

I uttered a laugh that was only fifty percent fake. "It's fine, really. I'm not expecting a proposal because we fooled around. I'll be your dirty secret."

He exhaled through his nose. "No, ye won't. I'm not asking for secrecy. I just don't make promises I can't keep."

"One and done. Got it."

"Exactly that. It's a rule I don't break."

I was glad he didn't need secrecy because I needed to talk it out. Just not with him. I'd call Ariel when I was next alone. I drank my latte and allowed myself to idly wonder why he never broke his rule.

Further on down the road, the uncomfortable air in the car lifted, and we lapsed into conversation.

"Help me understand why your relatives treated ye like they did," Ben asked.

I took a steady breath and considered his question. "I don't know. I'm still not entirely sure they were going to marry me off. Maybe they knew nothing about it."

"At their own party? Usually the most obvious answer is the correct one."

I pondered that. "It's a little extreme, though, isn't it? They'd need a very good reason."

"Money?"

"They're not exactly hard up."

"No signs of stress in their business or tense meetings?"

I gave a shrug. "They provide services to the Mafia, so every meeting is tense, but I know their business is doing well as I worked in their office. Their motivation is a mystery to me."

Even though it bothered me that I'd gone from valued houseguest to sellable, I didn't want to delve too deeply into the mindset of my aunt and uncle. It touched on a lifetime of needing to make nice with them because of my lowly status. I didn't want to feel like that anymore. I also slightly feared my mother's reaction when she found out the full details of what had happened. If she'd blame me for a family row in some way.

I heaved a sigh and found my phone. "It doesn't matter anyway. I'm going where they can't find me, considering that even I don't know where that is yet. Please don't worry about it. I'll be fine. I'm going to ring Mom. That's okay, right?"

I waggled my phone to demonstrate it, then at Ben's nod, flipped it off airplane mode.

A string of text messages came in, plus missed calls from my aunt and uncle and voicemails I'd never listened to.

I skimmed the previews, my heart sinking. Interspersed were ones from Damon, the boyfriend who'd broken up with me in the spring.

Discomfort curled in my gut.

Damon: Am I not owed a reply?

Damon: You're being cruel, do you know that? It isn't like you.

Damon: Tell me where you are.

For a while now, whenever I'd spotted his name on my screen, I dismissed the messages without opening any, and I did the same now with my teeth clenched.

"Problem?" Ben asked.

"Just an ex trying to find me," I grumbled back, not looking his way.

"What does he want?"

"Not planning on reading his complaints to find out. My guess is my aunt contacted him to help in the hunt, but who knows."

I dialled Mom's number. It rang but with no answer.

I tried a second time then hung up. "I guess she's working."

Ben grumbled. "And she hasn't sent ye her address yet? Not liking this option."

I checked her social media. Mom hadn't posted in a while, but a friend of hers had commented on her last photo. It was a woman I'd known growing up, and who I used to call auntie, though we weren't related in any way. She was my mom's bestie, and I even had her phone number.

SandieD: Can't wait to see you on Friday.

The comment had been posted within the past week, and I considered it. "I'm going to try one of her friends."

I dialled Sandie. She answered right away, chirpy as ever. "Daisy, my sweet little flower girl! Long time, no hear. Your mom said we'd be seeing you soon."

"Hey, yes, that's the plan. Except I'm not sure where I'm going." I dug my fingers into my thigh. "Any idea where Mom's at? She isn't answering her phone."

"She was working all night. Probably sleeping now."

"Cleaning late at night?"

Sandie giggled. "Topless cleaning, sweet thing. It's not always daytime hours, but it pays good, and what with her brother breathing down her neck, you bet she's piling on the hours. She's fit to burst that you're joining her crew. Her schedule is full tonight, but if you get here tomorrow, she has a day off."

I closed my eyes. Topless? Damn.

"I'm on my way now," I said weakly. "Can I have an address?"

"Uh, not sure I can give that. She's moving from one place to another. Call her later and speak to her yourself." Sandie gave a cheery goodbye and hung up.

I dropped the phone to my lap and twisted it in my fingers.

Ben cleared his throat. "Just so ye know, I could hear most of that phone call."

I rubbed my forehead with the heel of my hand. The very last thing I wanted was for him to think I was any more pathetic.

"Topless cleaning. First I've heard of that," he added.

There was a hint of amusement in his usually growly tones, and amusement bubbled up my throat, mixing with my embarrassment.

"And I'm joining the team. Not exactly the job I had in mind," I spluttered. "At least I'd be putting my main assets to work."

The bodyguard's grip on the steering wheel tightened, his knuckles standing proud. Like yesterday, his gaze jumped over to me, but not to my boobs, instead lingering on my face.

"Sure ye want to go there tonight?" he asked.

"I don't really have a choice."

"I'm not happy with dropping ye off in Seattle with no address."

"Yeah, not ideal. I'll find somewhere to stay."

He chewed on that for a moment, his focus back on the road ahead. "The woman on the phone said something about your uncle breathing down your mother's neck. Does she owe him money?"

She had said that. I'd blipped over it, instead assaulted by the image of my bare-chested mom mopping floors while dirty old homeowners watched on.

"Mom owing money to her brother," I summarised. "First

I've heard of it, though I wouldn't be surprised. It explains why she's avoiding them."

"Considering what your aunt and uncle intended to do, I wonder if there's a connection."

"There's no way my mother knew what they were planning," I retorted.

"I didnae say that. Only that it could be part of a bigger picture. The motivation we're looking for."

I twisted in my seat to watch the world fly by outside. The next city we'd come to would be Sacramento, and spanning our route was wide-open dusty land.

Mom loved me. She would've warned me if she heard anything about me being used and a potential marriage being set up. There's no way she would have kept quiet, not for all the debt in the world. It was gossip, exciting and shocking. She'd revel in the telling as much as want to protect me.

Still, the doubt was there. I cringed in on myself.

"Come back with me to Falls Ridge," Ben said suddenly.

"What?"

"It's the town where my folks live. It's quiet and friendly. I'll feel better if I know you're in a safe place for the night, then I'll drive ye over in the morning."

After last night, and the emotions of the morning, I kinda wanted to get away from him completely. Cut off the series of embarrassing incidents. But on the other hand, going to work with my boobs out every day wasn't all that appealing either.

A sudden laugh bubbled up in me. Mom had claimed I'd inspired her work. I'd had no idea she meant this.

"It's fine. You don't need to feel responsible for me anymore," I said.

But Ben played his ace card. He set his phone on the dash and dialled a number, loudspeaker on.

"Hello? Ben? Talk to me," Ariel answered.

In a minute, he had her begging me to agree.

"I'll think about it," I conceded. There was a long road ahead, and Mom could call back at any time.

One thing was certain. If I went home with Ben, this time, I definitely would not be falling into bed with him.

Both of us had agreed on that.

8

Daisy

We made good time through Sacramento and hit the stretch to Portland with an estimated arrival time of nine p.m. After that, I needed to make a decision. It was a little over three hours either to Seattle or to Olympic National Forest where Ben's family lived.

As we drove, we talked. Ben asked what I'd studied at college, and I told him about my business economics degree at UCLA. I hadn't meant to go into any depth, but I found myself confiding my plan. He was an easy listener.

"I'm going to set up a cleaning company. With a specialty in deep cleans as well as maintenance ones."

"Like crime scenes?"

Before we'd left the motel, I'd straightened up our room. A force of habit, but also a minor need I had to create order.

But my greatest love was facing off with something others would run from.

I kept my gaze on the flat vista outside the window. "No, not that. It's something I discovered I really enjoyed in college. I had to work to pay my way, and by far, the better money was in taking on a big project. There are people who really struggle to look after themselves, let alone their homes. They're alone, they get sick, maybe emotionally, maybe physically, and they barely make it through each day. Keeping the place clean and tidy is beyond them. So you have these situations where an unbearable, unfixable mess accumulates. I'm talking piled-up trash in the kitchen, floors covered with boxes stacked up to above head height, bathrooms so awful they can barely stand to go in them. It's a vicious circle because the worse their home becomes, the less able they are to cope."

I took a deep inhale, my fingers itching to get stuck into the picture I'd painted.

"I advertised that specific service along with pictures of the worst cases I've seen. It was heartbreaking to hear the hope in people's voices when they contacted me. They felt so ashamed of how bad things had gotten. Some were hoarders with a real condition, others had gone through some awful experiences like surviving cancer or a family breakdown. The common factor being there was no way in the world they could fix it on their own. Cue me. I breeze in with all the kit and zero judgement. I'd pop in my headphones, stick on an audiobook, and get to work. Typically, I'd be there for a few days, and you want to know the best part?"

Ben inclined his head, his brow furrowed. Maybe he knew someone who struggled like this. Many people did.

"Oftentimes, they didn't even have to pay," I confided in a flurry of pure happiness. "I set up social media pages and showed what I was doing. Strangers sponsored the cleans."

"Wait. Random people from the Internet would stump up to pay for someone else's mess to be fixed?"

I raised my eyebrows. "That sounded awfully judge-mental there."

He lifted a hand, shaking his head lightly. "It's not. I'm just surprised. How long did this continue for?"

"Over a year, then I graduated and ended up working for my aunt and uncle because they were in a bind. Now I'm here. Unemployed and homeless."

"But with big plans. I admire that," he said simply.

My little burst of happiness set itself free in my chest. Most people thought my business ideas were weird. Who'd want to clean someone else's filth? But they didn't get the satisfaction. The worthiness of helping someone reset their life. It meant a lot to me that Ben recognised that.

With my cheeks warm, I revised my plans in my mind. I was free to pursue them now.

For the ten-hour stretch to Portland, I told stories of my jobs, spurred on by Ben's interest. Then I dozed.

Messages landing on Ben's phone woke me. He frowned at his screen.

"We're going to need to make a stop. Someone needs to talk to me."

"Is there a problem?"

"I offered to help out another bodyguard service over on the East Coast. They need me to talk them through an active plan now. It's urgent and could take a while. Not great timing."

I stretched out my arms and yawned. We'd already made a food stop, so were good for a while. "Quick bathroom break, then I'll take over the driving?"

He scanned the road. "I'm pretty sure we haven't been tracked."

I'd kept my phone in airplane mode since that one call after we'd left the motel, so I knew I wasn't sending a signal. "If we had, they'd have found us during the night, right? Do your thing and let me drive you. I'll just check my cell first."

He relented with a curt nod and pulled over at the next rest stop.

When I returned from the bathroom, Ben was glowering at his screen again.

We were late into the afternoon now, a cold wind promising a bracing evening, that much cooler the farther north we'd come. The point in which I'd have to make a decision was fast approaching. Amid the further missed calls and messages from my aunt, Mom hadn't rung back. I could either take a second to find accommodation on my phone in Seattle, or in Falls Ridge.

"I'm going to book us a room," I told Ben across the hood of the car.

He lifted his gaze to me but at the same second his cell phone rang. "Ben Graham," he answered his caller.

Though he was listening to them, his focus remained on me. He gave me goosebumps. A shiver down my spine.

That was the only explanation I had for what I did next.

On my phone, I searched for his hometown then called the first inn that came up.

"You're speaking to Kelly at Bhaltair's," a pleasant voice answered me. "How can I help you today?"

"Hi, I know it's late notice, but I need a room for this evening."

"Sure thing! We have one left. If you tell me your name, I'll book you in."

"Mr and Mrs Ben Graham."

The hotel receptionist went quiet. "Mrs Ben Graham?" she repeated, a weird tone in her voice.

I was still enjoying looking at Ben, though he was talking to his contact. "That's right. It'll be late when we get in. Probably after midnight. Will that be okay?"

Kelly stuttered agreement, taking a few details before she hurried off the call.

I put it out of my mind, reeling a little from my decision.

We weren't going to sleep together. That wasn't why I'd booked a single room. I merely used the cover he'd given me last night while knowing he'd no doubt stay with his parents. Still, a woman could dream.

Then once again, we were driving. This time into the dark, frigid evening.

The further north we went, the more the surroundings changed. Scrubby trees gave way to evergreens until night hid it all from my view. Ben's call didn't end. He was talking a crew through a live event and managing them from what I could understand.

I didn't mind. It was fun to hear his world unfold through the long and otherwise eventless drive. He pulled a tablet from his bag, loading floor plans and even a camera feed. His management skills and confidence in bossing the team around with easy commands added to how I saw him.

I'd never met anyone so competent. Hella sexy.

Then again, if I was on his crew, I'd follow him without hesitation. I'd fixate on his fine ass and trail around after him like a puppy. I stifled a grin that he caught, sliding me an intrigued look before returning his focus to the job.

With only an hour left of the trip, he leaned to the car's navigation screen, and as he talked to the other bodyguards, programmed in the address in Falls Ridge.

He'd obviously heard me reserve the room at Bhaltair's as that was the location he chose.

I drove on until snow lined the road in thick drifts.

Signs for Falls Ridge eventually appeared in the middle of a thick, frosted forest. The roads were clear enough to drive without worry, but it was a different world from where we'd come.

At the inn, Ben was still talking, though trying to get off the call. I gave his shoulder a squeeze and hopped out of the car, grabbing my bag. I'd check in so the receptionist could go to bed then come back out to say goodnight.

The building was a cute two-storey with wooden clapboards and a homey feel. I practically skipped inside to the small desk and smiled at the woman behind the counter. She was probably a little older than me and...frazzled. Her fair hair escaped her ponytail in right angle wisps around her head, and her gaze darted up and down me.

"Mrs Ben Graham?" she asked, her voice bearing that same odd tension I'd picked up on before.

"Yes, Daisy," I chirped.

"You're not what I expected."

"Um, okay? Thanks for staying up to check us in. This place is so sweet. It must be lovely working here."

It was also going to be even better spending the night. I pictured a soft bed. No, a warm shower first. Get rid of the road dust.

But to my surprise, the receptionist, who I assumed to be Kelly from the earlier call, took a step back, knocking into a stand of postcards and leaflets. They fell, scattering to the floor.

"Oh shoot." I stooped to help pick up the mess.

But instead of joining me, the woman let out a sob and fled from the room.

I stared after her.

"What happened there?" another voice came.

A huge man with dark hair and a black beard emerged from the back.

At the same moment, Ben entered from the front. "Who was that who just ran across the street?" Then his gaze fixed on the other man. "Da?"

The bearded man gave a gasp and bypassed me to wrap Ben in a hard hug.

My mouth dropped open. I stood, setting handfuls of leaflets down on the counter.

"That was Kelly," Ben's father told him. "She wanted to wait around to see ye both. Valentine's back in town but leaving early in the morning, if he hasn't already gone, so she's been a wee bit upset."

He held his son at arm's length then gestured pointedly at me. "Why the ever-loving fuck didn't ye tell us ye were married?"

God.

Uh no.

I'd messed up. Somehow, but badly, and involving Ben's family.

Ben stared at his dad then turned to me. "Valentine's my brother. I really need to... I'll be back." He turned and left, the door swinging behind him.

Leaving me to explain myself to the man why I was faking being his daughter-in-law.

For a long moment, I closed my eyes, opening them to find Ben's father watching me. But as I went to speak, another woman slipped into the reception, a baby in her arms.

Ben's dad extended an arm, and she tucked under it. He spoke to me. "I'm Bull, and this is Autumn. Ben's our boy." To his lady, he said, "This is Ben's wife."

The woman gave me a wide-eyed but pleasant smile. "You're a surprise, sweetheart. But not an unwelcome one. Please, come and join us. Our grandson has kept us up anyway, so don't worry about the time."

She was English, and the father Scottish. They seemed lovely, but I was dying, and I wanted to curl up in a ball and hide. Instead, I took a shaky breath and confessed my sin.

"I'm so sorry. There's been a mistake. Ben and I are just friends. I had no idea this was his place. I mean yours. I think I've made a terrible mess for him."

Both regarded me with curious expressions, no harsh words forthcoming as I'd expected.

"You're naw married?" his dad confirmed.

"No! We're not. I only said it to your receptionist for the sake of booking a room. I'm sorry," I babbled. "God, I upset her, didn't I?"

Kelly had looked me over, confirmed my lie, then ran. That spoke volumes.

Ben's mom passed the baby off to her husband. "Don't fret. You haven't done anything wrong. Or at least it isn't your fault. This was coming anyway, what with all the history between Valentine, Kelly, and Ben. Would you like to come sit with us and have some hot tea? I'll explain it all."

In equal measures, I did and I didn't. The embarrassment wouldn't stop hitting me in waves, and I shook my head, entirely miserable. "Is it okay if I just go to bed? It's been a long day, and I'm suddenly really tired."

Ben's mother gave me an understanding smile and took

a key from the reception counter, pointing me to the stairs. Along a corridor, she opened a door for me to a lovely room I didn't deserve. "This is you. I'll send Ben up when he gets back. We'll talk over breakfast. Please don't worry."

As if I could do anything but. Ben wouldn't come to my room. He probably wouldn't speak to me again after I'd caused trouble in whatever way I had.

I took the key, thanked his mom, and locked myself in.

Then I curled up on the mattress and hid my face in my hands.

During the night, I couldn't stop my thoughts colliding. Kelly must have been a girlfriend. Maybe an estranged one because Ben lived so far away in Scotland, but her reaction made sense. She cared about him.

The thing that carved a hole in my chest? He'd run straight after her.

He cared about her, too.

She was the reason he didn't sleep with the same person more than once. Perhaps they planned to get back together one day and that was their deal. Perhaps she was the one who got away and he'd intended to return to reclaim her.

All I was certain of was how I was in the way.

When dawn came, I got up, stripped the bed and cleaned the bathroom, then got the hell out of the Graham family's inn.

A local driver took me to Olympia, the next biggest town. From there, with practically the last of my money, I booked a ticket for a bus to take me to Seattle.

It didn't leave until after lunch, so I killed time by taking a walk.

As I did, I took out my phone. First I needed to talk to Mom to get that address, but also I had to get hold of Ariel.

There was so much to tell her. Not only to dissect what had happened with my family, but also about Ben.

It was worth the risk.

I was far enough away from home and about to leave this town. Taking my phone off airplane mode wouldn't make a lot of difference now, and after all, no one had come after me.

But before I deactivated it, I noticed the location services tick in the corner of my screen. Still running, even with my phone offline.

"Shit," I muttered.

Surely that couldn't have been running in the background the whole time. What had Ben said? I'd been so flustered after leaving my aunt and uncle's house that I hadn't listened properly.

My stomach sank. Something about settings. Not the method I'd used.

A little spooked, I made my call.

"Hello?" my best friend answered.

I didn't spot the truck pulling up alongside me until it was too late.

Nor could I tell the identity of the person in a mask and hood who snatched at my arms to wrench me into the back.

9

Ben

I trudged to the inn, my mission to find my brother partially successful. Chances with him were always slim, which was why I'd had to grab it. Da had told me he was here until morning, and I knew my brother to be an early starter.

If I'd waited, he would've been gone.

I hadn't counted on him being out most of the night, leaving me trying to stay awake in the cabin he always used.

In the cosy reception, Ma was behind the counter.

Her eyes lit, and she bustled out to take me into her arms in a hug. It didn't matter that I was a man of thirty-three. A hug from Autumn always took me back to that place of feeling like a kid.

Even if she wasn't technically my mother, I'd only ever considered her to be so, particularly as the alternative wasn't interested.

A fact which Autumn and Bull could never find out.

She pulled back and palmed my face. "There you are. I was beginning to worry you'd gone before I got a chance to see you."

"No, I just needed to find Valentine before he left. I didn't mean to be out all night."

"You're looking so well. I'd say that married life agrees with you, but it sounds like something got confused there."

I'd worked out during my cold vigil that Daisy must've booked us in as a married couple, and my da hadn't been messing with me. It explained why Kelly made a run for it, sobbing, no doubt. For her, I should've felt pity, but instead, only annoyance rose.

Da came out, his gaze taking me in once more.

"The confusion was mine," I told them. "In the last place we stayed, I booked us in as a couple. Daisy is a...friend."

My father's shrewd gaze bored into me. "Funny that. Whenever I book accommodation for my friends, I automatically make them family members. Many a time I've been married to the boys on fishing trips."

I dead-eyed him, earning a smirk.

Bull didn't seem like the type to enjoy a joke, but he saved all his teasing for me and my siblings.

Ma guided me through the reception and into the living quarters at the back. Our family home was on the outskirts of town, but they often stayed here when working. Thirty years ago, Autumn had fled Scotland and relocated to this little snowy backwater with me. She'd met Bull and fallen in love. At the time, he was running a bar and had my brother, Archie, then together, they had another two kids. My next brother, Valentine, and our younger sister, Merci, who was away at college.

Archie now ran the bar. My parents had opened the inn.

Somehow, Daisy had picked this as the perfect place for us to spend the night.

Beyond the comfortable living room, the door to my parents' bedroom lay open, and Ma gestured for me to go in to take a peek at the crib. Inside, a chubby blond baby slept.

Meeting my first nephew was a trip. I leaned over the crib and pressed his pudgy hand in mine.

"Meet AJ," Ma whispered. "Awake half the night and now happily sleeping the morning away. Your brother owes me big time."

"Same for me," Da grumped. "The lad has a set of lungs on him."

I gazed at the bairn. "He's cute. How come he's here?"

"Archie and Lily are away for the night. They'll be back later this afternoon, so you can catch up then."

Ma peered from the baby to me, then seemed to make a decision. She stooped, and infinitely carefully, picked up the lad, blankets and all, and placed him in my arms. Automatically, I cradled him. My eyes wide. A little terrified.

Kids like Jamie-Beth with a fun and sassy personality were okay, but babies scared the life out of me. They were too fragile for a big lump like me. I never imagined having my own.

Ma snickered to herself and took a picture, then carefully returned the baby to his cot, all without waking him.

I didn't breathe until she ushered me out of the room and pulled the door mostly closed.

Ma took up her favourite spot on the comfortable sofa, my father settling into his usual position at her side. They always cuddled up together.

Memories of the closeness of my family were the reason I'd wanted to rest holding Daisy last night. I loved my life in

Scotland and didn't want to leave it, but I'd been away from my family for a long time.

"So, ye found Valentine?" Da asked.

"Eventually. He's turned wild man of the woods."

Valentine had grown his black hair long and shaggy in the year since he'd left the military. He had our father's build—topping six-five or six—and a thick frame. If I didn't know him to be sporting a broken heart, I'd think him dangerous.

Both my parents chuckled but let me continue. They knew I'd wanted to find him to make a job offer because I'd messaged them so. They also knew why my brother would hate the sight of me, even after all this time.

"He spoke to ye then?" Da asked.

"Just about. He heard out my offer. He's taken a contract with a logging company based outside of Olympia for three months, but he said he'd consider coming to work with me after."

Da rumbled approval. "It'll do him good to have steady work with people to talk to instead of keeping away from all human life."

It would, though I had the opposite feeling. I'd set out to make Valentine an offer yet had been strangely disappointed when he hadn't given an outright no.

Ma settled her gaze on me, speculation in her eyes.

I stiffened, knowing what was coming.

This was the other reason for avoiding home. The evasion I had to deploy when I despised lying above all things.

"Is your mother okay?" Ma asked.

Cold slid through my veins. "You're my mother."

She smiled softly. "You know I mean Tabby."

I tried and failed to hide a recoil. "She's fine."

"And still putting in the effort to see you?"

"Everything's the same." I hated the words.

Every memory.

Yesterday, Daisy had told me about her stranger-sponsored cleaning efforts. As much as I thought her pretty fucking amazing for what she did, I fundamentally didn't agree that all people deserved help.

Some were better left to the mess they'd made.

Under my mother's scrutiny, I changed the subject.

"Has Daisy come downstairs yet? After breakfast, I'll take her over to see the bar and give her a tour of the town. I'm driving her to Seattle later, and I may or may not spend the night there."

Ma squinted at me. "Daisy? Then you don't know. She already left."

I stilled. "What?"

"Really early, before we'd even started breakfast. She found the time to clean the room, though. I like her. If you plan to make the fake marriage real, you have my approval."

My heart sank. I couldn't even smile at Ma's joke.

Gone.

Without even saying goodbye. Guilt burned a hole in my chest. I probably deserved that. I'd treated her as disposable then wasted my evening on a work call, leaving her with no one to talk to. Then I'd run after my brother, assuming she'd just go to bed and be waiting for me come morning.

Fuck.

I found my phone. No messages. Daisy didn't have my number, so even if she'd wanted to leave me a message, she couldn't.

"Did anyone see her go?" I asked.

Da scratched his thick beard. "Naw, but there's only one cab driver in town, so if ye want to find her, ask old Buck."

I did want to. I still felt responsible for her. What if she never got an address to go to? Where would she stay?

I leapt up and crossed the room to kiss Ma's cheek and hug my father. "I'm going to track her down. Sorry for rushing off."

"If you don't make it back here, we'll come and see you soon," Ma promised.

A threat, too, though she didn't know it.

With a final goodbye, I jogged out to my car.

But as I crunched through the snow, my phone rang.

Ariel, the screen read.

I thumbed to answer it. Ahead of my greeting, she was yelling.

"Daisy's in trouble."

My heart froze. "What?"

"Someone found her in Olympia. They tried to grab her, and she's running scared. Ben, she needs your help!"

10

Daisy

Concealed behind a dense shrub in a stranger's yard, I clutched my phone with trembling fingers.

"Ben's on his way," Ariel breathed down the line. "I gave him the description you told me. I'm going to hang up, and he'll call you immediately. Stay hidden. I love you."

I pressed my lips together and gave her a tiny nod, even though she couldn't see, and she hung up.

In seconds, another call came in.

I answered it, keeping absolutely silent, though I wanted to sob.

"Daisy? It's Ben. Ariel told me what happened. I'm on my way, but it'll take me an hour to reach ye." He swore and blared his horn at someone, sounding as frantic as I felt. "I have someone closer by so I'll get help to ye faster. I've called the cops, too, and we'll liaise with them, but listen, I need ye to do something for me. Give me a minute to call my brother, then call the number I send, if it's safe to. It'll connect ye to a video call. Keep us on mute. Ariel said ye didn't know the name of the street, but don't worry. I will find ye."

Swift relief jostled my panic.

Ben disconnected, and I peered out from the thick evergreen bush, a cap of snow giving it just enough height to hide me.

At the end of the drive, the black truck cruised past.

Him. I shrank back, my heart pounding. Cold and fear gripped me.

After I'd bought my ticket at the bus station, I'd wandered down a busy road alongside a wide river, aiming to keep to a route I could easily follow back.

A truck screeched up beside me, and someone leapt out. A man, I'd assumed, from his size. He'd grabbed at me, snatching a handful of my hoodie, but then he'd slipped. It had given me a precious second to wrench away.

Without hesitation, I'd run.

Flat out across the road and dodging cars, scrambling up a grassy, icy hill to where apartment blocks overlooked the water. I'd lost my footing twice, sensing the man right behind me, but then I reached the buildings, rushed between, and fled across a quieter street.

The man had disappeared, so I'd hidden in a front yard, not trusting that he'd gone.

And he hadn't. He'd merely retrieved his truck.

I cursed myself for not running farther.

But I didn't know this town at all. For all I knew, I'd be shot on sight by the homeowner if they discovered me. And now, my would-be kidnapper was twenty yards away.

Which meant I was trapped.

I had to hope Ben could get someone here soon.

I waited out his minute, happy to keep statue still while being hunted. I didn't dare peek again but used the time to correct my mistake with location services and turn them off in the settings.

A message came in from Ben. A link. I clicked it.

The video call connected. Three boxes appeared, mine, Ben's, and a stranger in the third. I hit mute, staring at Ben in his car. He stole glances at his screen then said something. It appeared as text onscreen.

Ben: Is the man who tried to grab you near?

I nodded, unable to stop shaking.

Creeping up the drive, for all I knew.

Ben: Pan the camera. Valentine's in Olympia and can get to you faster than me.

Valentine, who I gathered to be his brother, leaned in. He had thick dark hair tied back and was driving, same as Ben. I flipped my camera to show my surroundings. The clapperboard house with its neat brickwork wall lining the drive. The house number—854—which I zoomed in on. Then risking a view down the street to where the winter sun reflected off the cold river in a slice of shining white.

When I came back, there was a message from the brother.

Valentine: I know that street. Be there in ten.

Ben: Put your fucking foot down.

The wind whistled through the trees that lined the road. It bit into me, and I shivered harder. I didn't have a thick coat. In LA, I'd got by with hoodies and sweaters, but that didn't cut it here, despite me pulling on all the layers I had at the bus station. The cold sapped my strength. If the man was searching the street for me, I didn't have it in me to run again.

I shuddered, my breathing shallow.

My hand holding the phone dropped to my side, my fright taking over. I'd been such an idiot. I'd underestimated the trouble I was in, thinking that all I needed was to leave my relatives' home and strike out on my own. I'd not paid enough attention to what Ben had asked of me.

Or perhaps this was nothing to do with that? Could a random person have seen me and decided to stop and make a kidnapping attempt?

Either way, I'd wandered straight into the path of someone dangerous.

When I glanced back at the screen, there was a flurry of messages from Ben.

Ben: Just breathe, sweetheart. He won't take you.

Ben: I promise we'll get to you in time.

Ben: Daisy, eyes on me.

He sent the last as if I could hear him, but it worked. I let the sight of the huge, competent bodyguard rushing to my side calm me a small degree. He had his phone right in front of him on the dash so I could see his face.

He said something else, and it converted to text.

Ben: Need you to hear me. Do you have your earbuds?

How did he...? Oh—I'd told him I cleaned using headphones to listen to audiobooks. Damn! Why hadn't I thought of that? Moving slow, I rummaged in my bag until I found the case. Then I popped one in and took the video call off mute.

"Can ye hear me?" Ben asked.

I nodded, flushing warmer at his familiar tones.

"Thank fuck. Everything's going to be fine. Valentine, how far away are ye?"

Another voice joined in, similar to Ben's but even gruffer. "At the end of your lass's road. Lucky I was getting supplies in the centre of town."

"Can ye see the truck?" Ben asked.

"Not yet."

I gripped my arm, so cold I couldn't feel my fingertips.

"Okay, Daisy, sit tight," Ben coached. "You're a minute away from being safe. You've done so well."

But I hadn't. I should've run further. I should've taken his professional advice in the first place.

"First stretch of road, clear," Valentine reported.

"No sign of the black truck?"

"None. No pedestrians in sight either. Proceeding up-hill."

Ben acknowledged him, then his voice gentled again. "Hear that? My brother's closing in. Raise your phone so we can see the path to the road."

In my misery, I'd dropped the camera view to the gravel bed beneath me. I raised it again.

I couldn't look in case someone was there. Ben became my eyes.

"There's no one in the front yard. He doesn't know where ye are. Great job in hiding. I'm so proud of ye."

Startled, I brought the phone back to my face and mouthed *thank you,* my lip trembling.

I'd done nothing to be proud of except run and follow orders, but I liked his praise. Wanted more of it.

God help me, instead of watching Valentine's progress, I stared at Ben instead.

His gaze fierce. Jaw locked. Frequent glances back at me. Or more likely at his brother. But when he spoke, it was for my ears.

"I'm over halfway there. Pushing the car as fast as it'll go. I'll be with ye soon, and it'll all be over."

If it had just been me and him, I would probably still have felt safe, but having his brother prowl the streets worked doubly well. As he walked, Valentine took a call from the local police, filling them in on the incident then reporting back to us that a car would be dispatched soon.

Footsteps crunched the gravel path beyond where I hid.

Onscreen, Valentine was striding up the long road. It wasn't him.

I held my breath, curling in on myself so I was as small as possible.

It was the man who'd attacked me. Had to be.

The footsteps moved in, so close he had to be the other side of the thick bush. A figure cast a shadow. Two yards away. All he had to do was poke around and he'd find me.

My heart beat so loud it was going to give me away. Panic electrified me, readying me to run again. Even if it meant being caught straightaway.

I clamped my lips closed so I didn't scream.

"Daisy, what's happening?" Ben asked with urgency.

I gestured with my eyes to indicate the man.

"Someone's close?" he guessed.

I couldn't nod so I blinked twice, my face on the screen ghost-pale white. He'd done so much, but it was going to be too late. If the man had a gun, or a knife…

"Miss?" a quavering voice came.

In shock, I snapped my gaze up. An elderly woman watched me, both hands resting on a cane. It was her shadow I'd seen. Oh hell.

"What are you doing in my yard? Give me one good reason not to call the cops," she added.

"Fuck, is that the homeowner?" Ben asked.

Had to be. Behind her, the front door was ajar. I nodded, still barely moving.

She was about to give me away.

"Get inside the house," Ben said in my ear.

"What?" I mouthed.

"If Val's driving the man your way, he'll see the lady talking to someone hidden. We don't know what he's prepared to do. Ye need to move."

He was right. God. But I wasn't about to rush a kindly senior. I twisted to face her, showing every ounce of my fear.

"Someone's chasing me. He tried to grab me off the street. Please don't give me away."

Her eyes widened, and she peered from me to the road. "And he's still out there now?"

"Yes, ma'am."

"You been taking drugs, honey?"

"No," I gasped.

I expected her to tell me to go. Not to bring trouble to her door. Instead, she set her expression to stubborn and gestured with her hand.

"Lord! Get your butt inside. I'll see him off."

On frozen limbs, I half stood, keeping as low as I could.

The woman straightened. "There's no one in sight, get

going," she said without looking at me and her jaw set. Just a lady taking in the cold winter air.

God, I loved the resilience of older folks.

I darted for the house, flinging myself in the front door and hiding behind it. The woman surveyed her property then slowly ambled after me, closing us in.

Sagging to the floor, I spoke to Ben. "I'm safe. The homeowner let me inside."

"Roger that. Stay out of sight of the windows. Val, anything?"

"Negative. I'm passing the house your lass entered. All clear," his brother replied.

"Who are you talking to?" the lady asked.

"My...my bodyguard," I managed.

Then a flood of emotion hit me, and I could do nothing but drop my head to my hands and shake.

11

Ben

Breaking every speed limit, I pushed the rental car hard, fighting to reach Daisy. Finally, I was powering through Olympia and up the hill to the address Valentine had given me.

I screeched to a halt and leapt from the car, spotting my brother leaning against the house.

With his arms folded and his hair tied up in a bun, he scowled, the same expression he'd worn when he'd found me at his cabin last night.

"Update," I demanded, striding to him.

He pushed off the wall. "No sign of the man or his truck."

"And the police?"

He shrugged, infuriating me with his indifference. "Not here."

For fuck's sake.

I opened my mouth to say exactly what I thought of their response time, when the door burst open, and a blur that was Daisy flew at me.

I caught her, a good chunk of my worry easing at the sight of her intact. At the feel of her still alive and breathing.

It was just a hug. The same as Ariel would've given her. I was only a proxy, barely a friend. Though none of that explained the clamp that tightened around my chest.

The lass released me and stepped back, her hands flying to her mouth. "Sorry. I didn't mean to plaster myself to you. I was just so scared."

"You're safe now," I promised.

And I meant it. I'd get her to a safe place if it was the last thing I did.

"This the wife?" Valentine asked.

Daisy's cheeks flushed pink, and she slowly turned to him, taking in his glower. "Oh no, we're not... I mean..."

All I'd mentioned to him about Daisy was that we'd come into town together. Valentine must've heard the gossip from our parents or one of our siblings and not yet been corrected. On my frantic call earlier, I'd simply said Daisy was in urgent need.

Considering our history, it was a miracle he'd shown up at all.

"Which one is the bodyguard? Is the other your boyfriend?" a grey-haired lady called from the house. "Hey, boys. Did you catch the attacker?"

Daisy spun around then took me by the sleeve and led me to the homeowner. "Mrs Jessie, this is Ben Graham, a friend but also a bodyguard."

Mrs Jessie squinted at me, giving me a thorough once-over before huffing. "Well, you'd better come in. Daisy here was helping me run up a new set of drapes while your man stood guard against the kidnapper. No good you all standing out in the cold."

She turned and trod inside, using a cane to stab at the snowy ground.

"Ye were doing what with drapes?" I asked for Daisy's ears only.

She wrinkled her nose. "I had a lot of nervous energy when I was hiding and noticed her lounge room curtains were hanging unevenly. Mrs Jessie said she'd bought a new set but hadn't put them up, so I offered to do it while we waited. She fed me cake. It was a nice gesture."

I snorted a laugh and glanced back for my brother. But the street was empty. Valentine was nowhere to be seen.

Like a ghost, he'd vanished, but it didn't matter. He'd done everything I'd needed him to do, and I'd be forever grateful.

Half an hour later, Daisy was finishing up a conversation with the cops. With her safe and little evidence to go on, the two officers had exchanged a glance and queried whether she could have imagined the attempt. Maybe someone had stopped to ask directions and she'd taken fright.

Fucking idiots.

I'd given her a minute shake of my head so she didn't bother arguing. Before Mrs Jessie had let them in the house, Daisy had asked me if it was better not to involve them, but I saw no need for that. Whoever was chasing her knew she was here, and it was better to have the law on our side.

The homeowner escorted the cops out again, demanding patrols of the neighbourhood, and Daisy raised her big brown eyes to me.

"I didn't imagine it."

"I know."

Her hand went to her biceps, just above her elbow, then

she pulled up her sleeve. Red and purple marks bloomed on her arm. Bruising from the attack. She stared, her shock cutting into me.

My blood boiled.

I reached to trace a finger over them, circling the marks like I could somehow erase them by will alone.

Daisy shivered and whipped her sleeve down again. Her phone buzzed, and she picked it up. "It's Ariel."

She accepted the video call, and Ariel appeared on her screen.

"Are you done with the cops yet?"

"They've just left. They weren't really interested."

Daisy's friend tutted, the wind whistling her end of the line, snowy trees behind her. She was outdoors somewhere on the Scottish estate.

A pang of homesickness struck me.

Her gaze darted to me. "Ben, how do you think the attacker found Daisy?"

Daisy winced and spoke before I could. "I think I have that answer. When I rang you, I realised I still had location services on. Easy to track, I guess."

Holy shite.

I stared at her, and her cheeks pinkened again.

"Ben!" Ariel exclaimed. "Why didn't you tell her to switch it off?"

Daisy's blush darkened. "Oh, he did. I got it wrong and used airplane mode."

I grimaced, annoyed at myself, not her. "That doesn't stop tracking. Even turning location services off doesn't stop it for all things, only for apps. We should've ditched your phone from the start."

Daisy wilted. "I went to a lot of effort to get it back from my aunt, so I would've fought you on it. I've never been on the run before. And honestly, I didn't think anyone would be interested in me the moment I left Paul and Sigrid's."

"It was my fault. I knew better," I said. Most people underestimated the extent to which their phone tracked them and how easy it was for another person to access that. I'd done everything wrong in protecting this lass.

"No," Daisy protested. "It was all me."

"Well, one thing for certain is that you can't stay there," Ariel decided.

I nodded. "Agreed. It's a second incident in two days which tells us someone is in active pursuit. They followed ye here. The next thing they'll look for is known associates in the vicinity."

Daisy dropped her gaze. "Meaning I can't stay with Mom."

I resisted the urge to take hold of her hand and press her fingers in mine. While fucking handcuffing her to my arm. "Sorry, but that would be a bad idea. You'll also need to toss your phone."

She gave a fast nod, still not making eye contact with me. "Yeah, I figured. God. What a mess. Now I need to work out a new plan, but..."

She trailed off, but it was easy to fill in the gap. She had nowhere else to go. And she didn't want to say—Ariel had clued me in to the fact that Daisy never wanted to be seen as a burden.

It only increased my need to take care of her.

I could drive her back with me to Falls Ridge, but that would only be temporary. I had to return to Scotland in a few days at the latest.

"Got your passport on you?" Ariel asked.

Daisy reached into her bag and produced the document, showing it to Ariel with a small frown.

"Come to Scotland," her friend suggested.

Daisy opened and closed her mouth. "I'd love to. I'd even suffer through a transatlantic flight just to see you and the place you've told me so much about, but I can't. I don't have the money for a ticket."

I sat taller. I had money. Not a huge amount, but I'd been saving. Running the bodyguard service gave me a decent income, and I had little to spend it on, so it was just sitting there in the bank.

"Is that your only concern?" Ariel said.

At Daisy's minute nod, she continued.

"I have an open ticket my dad sent me. Never used, because fuck visiting him. It was paid for in cash so I can transfer it to your name and he'll never know." She stopped walking, the scenery behind her revealing Castle McRae, where Ariel shared a tower apartment with her brother.

A fortified castle was a damn sight safer than here.

"Please, Daisy. There's nothing keeping you there and every reason to come to Scotland. Ben, back me up. Oh! You two can take the same flight. Ben can help you with your fear of flying and make sure you get here safe."

Those big brown eyes returned to me.

Uncertainty filled her gaze.

My reaction, on the other hand, was immediate and absolute.

I produced my phone and searched for the next flight out of Seattle. "There's a flight to Manchester that leaves in a few hours. From there, we can pick up a connecting flight to Inverness, though there's risk attached to your passport being logged in Scotland. A problem that's hard to avoid, but I'll think on that. The first leg of the journey is set, but we'll need to move fast if we're to catch it." I lifted my gaze to Daisy. "Are ye sure ye want to do this?"

Inside, I urged her to accept.

It was the best thing for her safety. It would give her a chance to reset and me space to help her uncover who was trying to hurt her.

Still, she had to choose to come.

Watching me, she slowly inclined her head, so fucking pretty with a flush of pink across her cheeks. "All I really want is to be with friends. You, Ariel, and your brothers. Others. I can't think of anything I'd like better." She gave a short laugh. "And I guess it beats becoming a topless cleaner with my mother."

Onscreen, Ariel's eyebrows rose. "Well, that needs unpacking."

"I'll explain when I see you."

It was a moment of levity in the middle of a dangerous situation, but I couldn't laugh.

I was occupied trying not to examine the reason behind my relief that she'd accepted.

Or the burst of desperate energy I had to drag her to my cave and fuck her seven ways from Sunday, and the thousand and one reasons why I couldn't.

12

Ben

We left Olympia for SeaTac, Mrs Jessie the proud new owner of Daisy's phone, stripped of data by me. For the rest of the day, she'd stay home with the phone off, then tomorrow, her son was driving her over the border to Canada where she'd visit with her grandchildren. Daisy's phone would make the trip with her. On the way there, Mrs Jessie would turn it on, make a call to a local store then toss it into a lake, effectively ending the trail of anyone following the trace.

Depending on the skill of whoever was chasing Daisy, it possibly wouldn't be enough. But it was the most we could do right now.

In the passenger seat of my car, Daisy nibbled at a bag of peppermint bark the old lady had gifted her. I'd been on call after call, dealing with handing in the hire car then calling my folks to say I wouldn't be back.

They let me off with a little protesting, but Daisy cringed, clearly feeling it was her fault. I'd correct that when we had a minute.

At the airport, we set our tracks directly for check-in. But as we passed a flower shop, she stalled.

I instantly stopped with her. "Problem?"

"Can we stop here a minute?"

I glanced around, jumping my gaze from face to face. Scanning every man for any unnatural interest in Daisy.

I needed to get her through security. Out of the public area. It still wouldn't be safe, but it would be a damn sight better than here.

"No," I barked.

Her shoulders came up around her ears, and her cheeks reddened. "Yikes. Sorry."

I gritted my teeth and clamped down on my urge to throw her over my shoulder and stalk away. While we were still in the States, I needed to retreat to professionalism. Fully back in bodyguard mode. Yet she still wasn't a client.

I inhaled frustration and exhaled calm. "What did ye want to do?"

"Order a bunch of flowers to be sent to Mrs Jessie and another for your mom. I've got just enough cash left for it."

She was too sweet, and I hated myself for her crestfallen look.

"Kind gesture. We'll do it on my phone from the UK. Mrs J won't be home for a week, and Ma can wait."

Daisy gave a soft smile and nodded, easily accepting my decision. That ready obedience went straight to my dick.

Through security, we settled into the departures lounge, and I made another call, strolling away to talk to my boss.

Never for a second did I let Daisy out of my sight.

Even in this slightly safer environment, I wouldn't take

my eyes off her.

Without a phone to lose herself in like all the other passengers around her, she watched the planes outside and twisted her fingers together. She was scared of flying. The reminder lodged in my mind.

"I'll work out a solution," Gordain said to my question over where Daisy could stay. For a day or two, she couldn't be under Ariel's roof. We couldn't hide her passport being registered in England at the other end of the flight, and though I needed a solution for the same happening in Inverness, we had to have plausible deniability if her family came looking. Ariel had an idea for that. Her brothers were getting involved, too.

Daisy would be far safer in Scotland than here, but there were still hurdles to get over.

While Gordain talked in my ear, I stared at her. She tucked her feet under her legs and wrapped her arms around her knees, as if trying to make herself small. Not a target.

I wanted to make her smile again.

Next to me was a bookshop, a table of novels displayed right next to the entrance.

Front and centre was a romance novel with a half-naked guy on the cover, all abs and moody glower. *Start a War,* it was titled, the packaging promising steam with a reverse harem, whatever the hell that was. Without thinking too much on it, I entered the shop, bought the book, then strolled back to Daisy.

She looked up on my approach and I handed over the gift, muting my side of the call.

"Here ye go, shortie."

Daisy took it, then her jaw dropped. She clutched it to

her chest and...smirked at me. Curved lips, an amused glint in her pretty eyes.

"You called me that at my aunt's house. I'll ignore the nickname because you, Mr Guard of my Body, are a beautiful man."

Damn it. I might've provided a distraction but as a result made myself hornier than ever. And where the fuck did shortie come from? I'd never in my life given a nickname to anyone. I turned my back and stalked away to make another call.

A short while later, boarding was announced. We joined the queue, Daisy still clutching her book.

"I haven't thanked you properly."

I raised a shoulder. "No need."

"Yes, there is. For coming to California, for taking me with you on that long drive north, and then arranging my rescue after I upped and left." She swallowed and forced out the words. "You must hate me. I messed things up for you, including with your ex-girlfriend."

"My who?"

"Kelly at the inn."

"She isn't an ex."

We shuffled forward as the line of people moved, but Daisy was obviously puzzling over my words as much as she was cringing the closer we got to boarding. I wasn't in the habit of sharing my life story, but I wanted her to know she hadn't done any wrong.

Depending on how much I told her, the distraction might work for her, too.

"When we're seated, I'll tell ye the basics."

Briefly, I curled my fingers around her arm in a comforting gesture, but she was rapidly slipping into flight or fight mode. We crossed to the plane, and at every step closer, she trembled all the more.

Inside the craft, Daisy could barely greet the flight attendant, relying on my gentle guidance to get her to our seats. I stowed our possessions in the lockers then sat beside her. She'd taken the window seat, which was either a good decision or very bad. I got the impression she was barely thinking at all.

Around us, the plane filled, people chattering and finding their places.

The attendants helped with suitcases and answered questions, all while Daisy curled up in a ball and closed her eyes. Every little thing seemed to add to her panic. The air came on and made her jump. The engine changed tone, and she recoiled and softly moaned.

"I'm too warm," she mumbled then stripped her hoodie, clutching it in her lap over her seat belt.

The reveal of her strappy shirt had me likewise hot under the collar.

Those incredible, bouncy tits stretching the material.

In our bubble of space on the plane, no one taking the seat the other side of me, I could picture all kinds of shenanigans that might stop her spiralling.

Once had been nowhere near enough.

But I'd promised her a story, so I opened my mouth and got to telling it.

"Kelly, the receptionist at my parents' inn, used to date Valentine, not me. I fucked things up for him, though I never intended to. Considering the fact I didn't even live with my family in the States past being a young teenager, it was all a fucking nightmare."

She lifted her head, listening. "How come you didn't live with them? I liked your family, from the time I spent with them."

"For ye to understand, that means I need to delve into ancient family history."

"I'm listening. You already know some of mine, so it's only fair."

My nerves grated. I'd barely told anyone this, but Daisy needed my help, and in focusing on me, she'd become distracted. I dug deep.

"Our family is a hybrid of three different nationalities. Autumn's English, Bull, Valentine, and I were born in Scotland, and Archie and my younger sister were born in America. It might also interest ye to know that Autumn and Bull are not my biological parents. Autumn's my aunt. Bull stepped up to the role of father as I didn't have another. My birth mother got knocked up by a squaddie in the RAF and basically handed me over to her sister for care, not all that interested in her baby, then got imprisoned in a military jail after embezzling a fuck load of money. There were people after her, and they broke into the house where we lived. Autumn took me and ran, ending up in Falls Ridge where she met and fell in love with Bull. He already had Archie, and they got pregnant pretty quick with Valentine."

"Didn't you say Valentine was born in Scotland?"

"I'm getting to that part," I grumped. "Up until that point, my birth mother had expressed zero interest in me, but out of the blue she demanded Ma take me back to Scotland to see her in jail. Ma was five months pregnant, but she went, then ended up getting sick, and we were there several more months until she'd given birth, hence how Valentine was born there. In that time, she took me to see my birth mother often so I could form a relationship."

Daisy twisted in her seat, fully engaged, though every clank or rumble of the plane had her flinching. "That can't have been easy."

I gave a hard laugh. "Even though I was tiny, I remember that time. Certainly the lack of parental concern from Tabby. That's bio mother's name. Turns out Tabby only wanted me there so she could apply for a sentence reduction and have the sympathy of the military court. Her appeal failed, and she lost interest in me instantly. We all came back to the US and for the next decade got on with life. When I turned thirteen, Tabby got moved to a minimum-security jail and again asked to see me. She gave Ma a hard time, pleading with her that she'd changed, so my whole family travelled back to Scotland for a long summer. In itself, that was no hardship. We loved it there, and our parents showed us the places they'd lived and where Bull had grown up. Autumn and Tabby's father had been a wing commander in the air force, so we got to see the base that he'd run, though we never met the man because he died years before. Now we come back to Tabby. After the first visit, she insisted on seeing me alone. I agreed, so Ma allowed it."

I hesitated. Gordain had heard a very brief version of this when he'd interviewed me, as I needed to be upfront. A no-lies-detected response to a job that demanded trust. But Daisy curled her fingers into mine, and somehow the words flowed.

"Those sessions were strange. She talked a lot about herself, about conspiracies in the prison, about how hard done by she was. She never asked me anything about myself, not a single question on my life, what it was like where I lived, anything about my personality at all. I didn't like her, even you'd find it hard to see good in her, but for Autumn's sake, I went. Ma thought it would help me. Then Tabby betrayed us all. She flexed her rights to have access to me, forcing me to remain there. She had two years left on her sentence after which she'd claim benefits and get a sweet two-bedroomed flat, using me as part of her plan. It meant my family had to hustle to find someone to run the bar and change their entire world for my sake. Our lives were completely upturned by the forced relocation. Never once did anyone blame me, not for changing schools, not for the hassle of finding somewhere to live, but it was a trap all the same. When I reached fifteen, Tabby was freed and her penance to society paid. She got that new apartment, and I told my family to go back to the US."

Daisy's fingers tightened around mine, and her soft voice soothed the roughened edges of telling the full version of this. "I can't imagine how hard it was for teenage-you to make a decision like that."

"The bar needed attention, and the bed-and-breakfast place Ma had been eyeing for years finally became available. She badly wanted to open an inn, and the timing was perfect. I was closing in on six feet tall and knew my mind. I wanted my family to be happy and I didn't need coddling. Home for them was back in the US, and I'd been offered a place at a small Scottish boarding school with a focus on sports. I didn't want to live with Tabby but that way I could honour the obligation and she'd get to keep her flat. What I didn't anticipate was Valentine. He was twelve and had fallen in love with Scotland. He wanted to stay with me. After a lot of pleading, heartache, and stress, our parents agreed to a trial. They enrolled him in the same school, and we gave it a term. I loved having him there. Archie and I are closer in age, but Val and I have similar personalities. He's shrewd, smart, and he has a wicked sense of humour, at least he used to. We got up to all kinds of pranks in our dorms. I hated the summers where he'd spend the whole time in Falls Ridge while I only got a couple of weeks before

Tabby'd demand I return."

Daisy frowned, her dark eyebrows pulling in, and I guessed she'd seen how distant Valentine and I had been outside Mrs Jessie's.

"You and your brother were close," she said.

At the front of the plane, a flight attendant closed the doors. We were getting ready to fly just as I was getting into the meat of the story. Reliving all the old times was like poking burning-hot knives into my iced-over heart, but it was working. Daisy didn't blink as the world was shut out.

"Very close. After school, I went into the army then ended up in this industry, and he joined the military, too. On a trip back to Falls Ridge, he started seeing Kelly, a local girl we'd known on and off while growing up, and he fell hard for her despite the long-distance relationship. But the feeling wasn't mutual, even though she said it was. Several years ago, at Archie and Lily's wedding, Kelly made a pass at me. It was out of the blue, and I'd never seen her as anything apart from my brother's girlfriend. No different to Lily. On my visits, I'd happily talked to Kelly, not noticing how she hung on my every word. Later, Lily told me she'd suspected something, but Kelly denied it, and both Valentine and I were blind to it. But at that wedding reception, Kelly got drunk, broke things off with Val, and kissed me in front of everyone."

Daisy parted her lips in shock, presumably picturing the drama.

I rubbed my mouth with our joined hands like I could erase that awful kiss.

"She claimed I was the one she'd always wanted and that we were meant to be together. I was the strong brother Valentine had learned everything from, and every story about me only proved how I was perfect for her. It was me she wanted, not him. She gave all of this in an emotional speech in front of the wedding guests like it was a big romantic moment in a movie. Valentine walked out before I'd even had a chance to react. Last night was the first time I've seen him since. He served another four-year term and at best gave me one-word answers to my messages. Obviously, I stopped Kelly's advances and went after my brother, but he was long gone. The next day, Kelly came to find me, devastated but still hopeful. I pitied her but I was also cut up for my brother, and pretty angry about how she'd gone about things. It had all been a fantasy on her part, and somehow I felt like the bad guy for telling her no. She went away for a couple of years but is back in Falls Ridge now and made good with my family, even taking a job with them. Valentine claims to have forgiven and forgotten her, but I'm guessing from her reaction after hearing I was married, she still has feelings on the subject."

Maybe Val still did, too, despite his claims. I wasn't sure.

For a minute, I got lost in the uncomfortable feeling the telling had given me. It felt good to get it off my chest. Cleansing, in a way. Maybe the visit back with my fake wife had drawn a line under it all.

Daisy's grip on me tightened. I tuned back in to the sounds of the aircraft, picking up on the lass's panic.

The plane was readying to go.

It jerked, then began taxiing.

"Daisy," I said. "Keep looking at me."

She snapped her gaze to the porthole window, the airport falling away behind us, a tall mountain towering in the landscape.

"Oh God," she mumbled.

Fuck. Her fright had returned. I needed to do something

else to help her.

The plane reached the end of the runway.

Daisy squeaked in fear.

The sound zapped through me.

"Please, Ben," she uttered, desperate. *Terrified.*

But my story was told. I had nothing else to say.

I palmed her cheek, brought her focus back to me, then swept in with a hard and heavy kiss.

13

Daisy

Ben's lips moved on mine, the unexpected kiss blocking out almost everything else. My panic turned into instant heat.

Around us, the plane shuddered.

I did, too.

Ben upped the pressure in a bossy, insistent move. Lust bloomed through me, carried on the waves of adrenaline from my fear of flying. He angled his head and licked the seam of my lips to gain entry, then slicked his tongue over mine in a scorching-hot action.

It promised so much more than we'd already done together. Dirtier, darker activities. Him laying me out and taking ownership of my body. Teasing me, winding me up.

It promised him fucking me.

God, I wanted that. The brief glimpse I'd had of his dick had fascinated me. He was big. Thick. I bet he knew—

Something clanked in the engine.

I broke away, eyes wide.

"Ignore that. Just normal takeoff procedures," Ben promised, setting his lips to my cheek, his palm still cradling my face.

"Why did you kiss me?" I spluttered.

"Shouldnae I have?"

Another press just below my ear, the sensitive spot giving me the good kind of shivers.

"Not according to your rules. Was it to distract me or because you wanted to?"

"Both, adding how I'm liking the distraction myself. Want me to stop?"

In his story, he'd revealed a lot. Exposing a wound from not only being the unwilling reason for the breakup of his brother's relationship, but also another from the rejection from his birth mother.

I wondered how deep that second part went.

I lost every thought when he nudged my face up and our lips met again.

Kissing Ben for the first time had been a desperate clash, coupled with the urgency of needing relief. Here on the plane, we couldn't do anything other than enjoy the slow winding up of passion. Teasing each other. He was in charge, wanting to dominate me. Then when I pushed back, he groaned, and the sound hit me straight between my legs.

I wanted so much more of this. He gave me confidence I'd never felt in the past. He made me feel so sexy. Even freaked out by the plane, I hadn't missed how his gaze clung to my boobs when I'd stripped my hoodie.

His confession that he needed this gave me such a boost.

Hadn't he told me he never fooled around twice? Why did that make me want him so badly? So much so that if he touched me, I'd probably orgasm in ten seconds flat.

That was impossible, though. There were people all around.

The plane's engines whined, powering up.

I broke away once more, taking a rapid, scared little inhale as the world started moving outside the window.

Holy hell. This was it. We'd speed up, the plane would lift, anything could happen.

Ben put his lips next to my ear. "We're going to take off now. Tell me, how far did ye get in the book I bought ye?"

"Th...three chapters."

"Anyone fucking yet?"

God, him saying *fucking* broke my brain. I shook my head, dragging my gaze off the fast-moving surroundings. The dark, compelling, and serious expression in Ben's eyes claimed my full attention.

He reached over me, taking the Elle Thorpe novel from where I'd stashed it in the seat pocket. He flicked through it and handed it to me, open on a page which he tapped with his finger. Then he positioned himself to appear like he was looking out of the window while neatly blocking the view of me from anyone in nearby seats.

"Read."

I stared at him. Ben lifted my hoodie and draped it across my lap. He held my gaze then purposefully glanced his knuckles down the side of my breast.

"I said read to me."

"Out loud?" I squeaked.

The scene he'd found was a smutty one. My favourite

kind.

His lips curved, but it was his hands that were up to no good. He lifted my top, slid his fingers beneath my leggings, and grazed the line of my underwear. "Aye, sweetheart. So I get to enjoy it, too."

"War's hands slid up the backs of my thighs, spreading them as wide as I could go," I read, my words spilling over each other, *"before coming to rest on my ass. He spread me there, too, and I gasped."*

"You heard the man. Spread those thighs," Ben ordered.

Entirely overwhelmed, I obeyed him and adjusted my position, widening my knees in the plane seat to give him space to touch me.

Across the aisle, the passengers peered out their window, not looking our way.

"Keep reading," Ben said, caressing me over my underwear.

I took a series of short breaths, barely able to force my concentration back on the page and definitely missing a few lines. *"...then his mouth was covering my pussy. He kissed me there like he kissed my mouth."*

But Ben eased his hand into my underwear, cutting me off mid-scene. His fingers slid over my clit then further down. I was soaked from just his kiss, and embarrassment had me slamming my eyes closed.

He gave up a sound of pained need and kissed my cheek, gliding a thick finger directly inside me. "You're so fucking wet for me. I want to tear your clothes off and tongue fuck ye like your man in the story. The whole plane would hear ye scream and see ye come so hard from everything I did. But I'm pretty sure we'd end up being arrested by the airline police, so you'll have to pretend this is my mouth and try to stay quiet."

He added another finger, tight against the seat and stretching me around his hand with the heel pressing down on my clit. Then he eased them in and out, hitting my G-spot, and I gripped the seat arm and his thigh, desperately trying to keep from crying out.

He finger-fucked me.

The angle intensifying his moves, how horny he made me amplifying it.

Thank God for loose clothes and a semi-private place. I wouldn't have him stop for all the money in the world. It felt too good. My body winding tighter, every slide building me up towards a crash.

"Next line," Ben commanded, his torture unending. "Daisy, read the next fucking line."

I fluttered my eyes open and tried to focus. "*...slow and intruding strokes of his tongue. It flickered over my clit, sending the little bud wild.*"

He rumbled approval and added a third finger. I whimpered, so close already. Then his thumb landed on my clit and flicked.

Two times, three, then harder.

The book fell.

I detonated.

A cry flew from my lips, and Ben's mouth landed on mine to smother the sound. His hand moved slower, and I tightened around him in hot spasms, wetter again and brainless from the wave after wave of knockout pleasure. My chest heaved as I tried to take in air, and dimly, I picked up Ben's groan then smiled when he briefly buried his face in my cleavage with a hard kiss.

He righted himself quickly, keeping up his role of blocking anyone from seeing me, letting me slowly come back to earth. Then he brought his fingers to his mouth. Licked them clean like he'd done in the motel.

I could only stare at him, still trying to catch my breath.

Why was that so hot?

Why was everything he did so devastatingly sexy?

His ardent and desperate expression showed me exactly how into this he had got. He'd so easily taken me over the edge. I wanted to do the same to him.

From my huddle, I couldn't see anyone behind his bulky frame. He protected me from view, but maybe that would work in reverse as well.

In the past, I'd never really understood how women enjoyed blow jobs, but now, I got the bigger picture. With the right guy, it wouldn't be awful. In fact, I was convinced of the opposite. I wanted him in my mouth. I wanted to lick and suck him and drive him insane like he'd just done to me. Desperately, I wanted to make him lose control. To grab me, take over, and fuck my face. God.

"Keep your back to the aisle," I ordered. "I'm going to unbuckle your jeans."

His fevered gaze darkened.

Ping.

An announcement came over the plane's intercom, and people around us started moving.

I glanced around. The seat belt sign had gone off. We'd reached cruising altitude, and I hadn't even noticed us leave the ground.

My jaw dropped, and Ben reached out a fingertip to my chin and closed it.

"Another time," he said in a deliciously gruff tone, then

gave me a final, sweet kiss.

Then there was nothing else to do but settle in, relaxed and sated, and maybe even enjoy the rest of the flight.

14

Ariel

Stomping the snow from my boots, I entered the tower of Castle McRae where I shared an apartment with my brother, Raphael.

"Anyone home?" I hollered, my voice echoing.

No answer came from the darkened space, so I shed my outerwear and sprinted up the ancient stone spiral staircase, a lot to do this evening.

It had been a long day at work, with endless snowboarding sessions, and even though the slopes closed at dusk, two hours ago, it had taken a while to return my students to their parents, chat, and slalom back down the mountain to home.

Pounding up the stairs, I untwisted the braid from my hair and shook it out, almost groaning with relief at how good it felt.

Not that I had time to hang around. I needed to shower, change, speed eat if I was lucky, then get stuck into the preparation for Daisy's arrival tomorrow. It was a dream come true that my best friend who I hadn't seen in five years was coming to stay. We spoke daily, but visiting had been out of the question. My father had once upon a time tried to sell me off. He pretended now to be friendly, but going anywhere near Los Angeles felt risky in case he forgot his promises and I found myself at the wrong end of a priest and a wedding dress once again.

Grumbling, I pulled off my thermal top and then my sweaty sports bra. In the octagonal hallway outside my bedroom, I paused to strip my leggings, balancing with a hand to the stonework, then I tossed the bundle of clothing into my room.

My brother would be at work still as he had training, so the place was all mine.

The tower was arranged with a kitchen and lounge room on the top floor, with slit windows that a thousand years ago had been used to shoot arrows at marauders, and two bedrooms with one bathroom on the floor below. At the ground-floor level, there was a narrow hall where we kept our winter boots and coats, and a locked door with a passageway that led into the great hall of Castle McRae.

It was safe in the fortified structure, with several people living in apartments throughout the castle, and many more in the wide and secluded estate.

I felt protected. Even prancing around buck-ass naked apart from my panties and alpine socks.

I hoped eventually Daisy could stay here with me, though definitely not at the start.

It was too dangerous. She'd be at too much risk of discovery.

We had to keep Daisy—

A man in a black beanie stepped from my brother's bedroom doorway.

An outraged shriek ripped from me.

I twisted on the spot, kicking out as hard as I could. It connected, driving my socked foot into his gut.

My assailant dropped, clutching his belly.

I'd had enough self-defence instincts to know that the element of surprise could mean the difference between life and death. With the man giving nothing other than a pained groan, I needed to run.

Spinning on the spot, I staggered away.

"Ariel, wait," the stranger gritted out.

I froze at the top of the steps.

Oh shit. I knew that voice.

Slowly, I turned, my eyes wide in shock. In Raphael's doorway, Jackson, his best friend, slumped.

I covered my mouth with a hand, the other across my boobs. "Oh my God, oh my God!"

He wasn't supposed to be here. Over Christmas, Raphael had invited him to stay for a couple of days, but he'd *left*. He'd been gone over a week.

Him sleeping on our sofa had been a special kind of torture, because the most unfortunate thing had happened. I'd developed feelings for the man who had only ever been polite to me, and they wouldn't quit.

Throughout his stay, I'd managed to almost completely avoid him.

All those efforts had been upturned by my unexpected beatdown.

Jackson drew himself up to his full height of a good foot taller than me and dragged back his hoodie from his dark hair. A frown pinched his eyebrows in, and he reached into the bathroom to toss a towel at me. "My fault for startling ye."

Did I mention his voice? Deep and ridiculously sexy. His face was all cut angles. He was a god on earth, sent to torture me.

I bundled myself up, wanting the floor to swallow me whole.

"I didn't expect—" I started.

"Your brother invited me—" Jackson said at the same time.

We both stopped.

I could cry. I'd never been that body conscious, but everyone who'd ever seen me naked in the past, I'd been prepared for. But him? I'd *fantasised* about this. In the depths of my bed, my subconscious had concocted all kinds of dirty and delicious scenes involving Jackson.

And what was infinitely worse? He didn't look. That sober gaze trained on my face only.

Who wouldn't steal a peek? I would if the situation had been reversed, though I'd deny it until the end of my days.

Filled with brimming devastation, I wheeled away and pointed at my bedroom. Then I stepped inside, closed the door, and sank down against it.

Ten minutes on, my heart had slowed a fraction, and I strip washed using wet wipes then dressed again, not daring to poke my head outside.

My phone buzzed. I collected it from my leggings' zip pocket. A message landed from Gabriel, my oldest brother. Not the one I planned to murder for his lack of visitor notification.

Gabriel: On my way with Gordain. We'll come straight up.

Ariel: Roger that.

When we'd relocated to Scotland, Gabe had this tower apartment, but he'd moved out to a cottage with Effie, his wife. She was also my boss and had taught me all kinds of extreme sports which had become my career.

It had given me killer thigh muscles and great balance, all the better for taking down intruders who weren't really intruders.

I groaned and smacked my head with my palm.

Footsteps outside coupled with voices told me Gabe had let himself in. Jackson answered his shouted greeting.

Huh, look at that. He *was* able to speak up and identify his presence. Then I picked up Gordain's and finally Raphael's tones.

Raph was a dead man. I was going to kill my brother. He should have warned me that Jackson would be here, but he hadn't, and for that his life would be forfeit.

In the meantime, I stood in front of my mirror, quickly assessed my subtle pretend-it's-not-there make-up and my cute skater dress and winter tights, and put on my game face.

Jackson would get a private but swift apology, and if he never mentioned it again, I wouldn't either. I needed to focus on my best friend. That was all.

Thirty minutes on, our task force had organised pickup for her and Ben, a place for her to stay, and actions that I'd take to go on the offensive and throw my father, and therefore her relatives, off the scent.

At no point did I look at my brother's best friend.

Not even when he muttered something to Raphael about me putting myself in danger.

Too late for that.

Trouble had walked in the door when he'd shown up. Maybe Daisy wouldn't be the only one on the run. For the sake of my sanity, I'd probably join her.

15

Daisy

Cold, grey morning met us in Manchester, the plane piercing thick clouds to land. I'd slept a good amount of the flight, then traded places with Ben so he could rest, too. He'd protested, but I had the inkling he couldn't relax so easily, and I'd been right. In the window seat, he'd closed his eyes and sunk into an instant and deep sleep.

When he'd woken, it was into his cool professional attitude once more, with a cursory glance at me and our surroundings before he got lost in thought, probably picturing all the things that needed to happen next. We were nearing landing, but I kept in the centre seat, and this time, closed my eyes, knowing I wouldn't get a repeat of Ben's takeoff procedure. Still, he let me clutch his hand in a death grip until we taxied to a stop.

Gone was the gruff smile and sexy, heated eye contact, though.

I understood. And I was grateful for it. Even if I missed it.

We exited the aircraft, and an icy wind tore across the blacktop.

Ben bounded down the steps and led me into the arrivals hall. We queued with everyone else at immigration, and a spark of panic passed through me at my passport being scanned. A digital footprint left. Wasn't much I could do about that now.

Inside the terminal, Ben continued his silent direction, his muscles tensed as if he was on high alert, and he led me in the opposite direction to the rest of the passengers. I didn't ask questions, trusting him entirely. Besides, I was distracted by being in another country.

This was England, though obviously Manchester airport looked like any airport anywhere. But the accents were different. Signage and words used distinct. Maybe it was my romantic, fanciful heart, but my excitement grew and my fear turned into a sense of adventure. We were now only a short plane hop from my best friend. I fully intended to make the most of the trip.

Our journey through the airport took us not out of the main exit, but through a long corridor and then to a waiting airport vehicle. It sped us out to an airfield, far away from where we landed, and populated with small planes plus a few helicopters.

I'd been expecting a smaller passenger plane. Resigned myself to it. "What are we doing here?"

At the same moment, my name was carried on the wind, called by someone I hadn't seen in years.

I snapped my head around. Sighted two men approaching. Raphael and Gabe, Ariel's brothers.

"Oh my God," I uttered.

"I wasn't sure if they'd be able to get here until we landed. Thought you'd like the surprise and familiar faces," Ben returned. "Go greet them."

I took off, jogging to Raphael's open arms and banding him in a hug. He was a year younger than me but now a head taller. So different from the boy I'd last seen in California. I often chatted with him over Ariel's video calls, where she'd teased him about having a crush on me, but seeing his friendly face caught me square in the emotions.

"What are you doing here?" I sobbed.

Raphael held me at arm's length and took me in. "Aw hell, don't cry. We're providing the world's most expensive taxi service and keeping ye off the radar. I copiloted for Gabe." He tipped his head at a helicopter waiting in the middle of the concourse.

I gaped at it. I'd been mentally prepared for another flight, not wanting to embarrass myself like earlier, even though it had turned into a spectacular win, but a helicopter?

I swallowed and remembered my manners, giving a small wave to the oldest of the siblings. I'd never really known Gabriel, except as Ariel's decade-older brother, but I knew he'd turned his world upside down to protect his family from their awful father, and for that, he had my friendship.

"Thank you both. But seriously," I came back to Raphael. "You flew down here for me?"

"We did. Ariel's running interference with our father, so it was too risky for her to come along. I'll tell ye more about that on the way back, but she's dying to see ye."

It was a trip seeing him, too. Gabriel had always sounded Scottish, as they'd originally relocated from here, and now Raphael did, too. It was only Ariel who'd retained a mostly American accent. My stubborn bestie through and through.

A presence loomed behind me, and I didn't even need to look to know Ben had my back.

"Gabe, Raphael," he said. "Are we ready to go?"

Gabe gave a curt nod and turned, gesturing for us to follow. "All fuelled up. The weather's been tricky, but we'll get ye home, Daisy."

Home. For a short time, it would be.

I badly liked the sound of that.

In the helicopter, Raphael helped me strap in and put on headphones then took the copilot seat alongside Gabriel. Ben sat rigid beside me. I tried to get him to look at me and cursed my soft heart for the sense of loss when he refused.

Then we were underway. I turned to the window with my eyes closed and counted my breaths.

Lift off. Except I didn't get the waves of panic plane flight gave me. This felt more like the sickening feeling of being on a roller coaster. Tense, alarming, but not wildly out of control.

"Daisy, how are ye doing back there?" Raphael asked after a few minutes of presumably flying on.

"Still conscious," I managed.

Through the headphones, he explained about Ariel's plan. She was going to make a call to Willow, her stepmother, and a self-styled Mafia Queen.

"It's a risk," he said, "but we're under no illusion now that Dad knows where we are, so we're going to play along for a while. Ariel's going to demand to know where ye are as you've lost contact with her, and that will get back to your aunt and uncle. With any luck, it'll throw them off the scent for a while, giving our expert in protection time to do his thing."

He meant Ben. I glanced over. Ben watched me for a beat

then looked away. I could read nothing in his dark glower.

Maybe he was already fed up with me.

Maybe he was so horny he couldn't breathe.

Either way, I had to find out.

The helicopter chopped up the air, carrying us north, over the border from England and into Scotland. In my ear, Gabriel and Raphael advised on landmarks to find out of the windows. Morning changed to noon, and the ground turned more snowy the further we went. I was fascinated with the view. Thrilled at the journey I'd made and the fact I was now among friends.

My fear almost left me. Enough to chat and relax a degree.

The brothers had even thought to bring along snacks for the trip. I had my first ever helicopter picnic.

Ben drank coffee from a flask, refusing my offer of the British candy I'd found in the pack. He made factual statements only, answering questions on his role in rescuing me.

I wanted him to myself. It probably wouldn't happen again now.

Then finally, we were closing in on the McRae estate. Not that I could tell.

This far north, the weather had worsened. Wind buffeted the craft, and the skies darkened. Then a snowstorm hit, icy flakes swarming us in flurries, completely obscuring our visibility.

The easy conversation ceased.

Gabriel murmured quiet commands to Raphael, both men watching the instruments.

A savage blast from the gale thrust us off course, and I squeaked in panic.

A warm hand closed over mine.

Ben didn't look my way, but between us on the seats, his fingers laced through mine.

God, but that made my belly tighten more than the storm.

"The plan is to deliver ye to the cabin and for Ariel to get there on her own," Gabriel announced over the headphones. "It could be rough going touching down in the forest, but I promise we'll get ye there safely."

"Thank you," I almost whispered, then closed my eyes once more, feeling only the warmth of Ben.

Gabriel hadn't been wrong. Gusts of wind shook the aircraft. I peeked once and instantly regretted it. The tops of trees came into view below, so close it felt there was no way we could avoid them.

But somehow, we did.

The helicopter settled, and the engine sound changed. I opened my eyes again to see our pilots flicking switches. Both twisted to face us.

We'd landed on a snowy clearing.

I exhaled relief along with admiration at their skills.

"The cabin is along that wee path there," Gabriel informed me. "The door is unlocked, and last night we equipped it for a few days' stay. I'd hurry if I were ye. It is nae far, but this storm is getting worse. With any luck, Ariel will already be there. We're a couple of miles from Castle McRae, and I know how much she's gunning to see ye."

I followed his gesture to a track that curved through the woods. Tree branches quivered in the helicopter's downdraught, snow falling in an almost magical way, though growing heavier by the second. I had neither the coat nor boots for this, but I was ready to take on the elements to find a little slice of sanctuary.

"Thank you both so much," I said. "And Raph? You're a badass, sitting up there behind the controls. Just saying."

They both gave the same easy grin, looking so similar with their dark hair and eyes and matching quiet confidence.

"Ben, are ye coming back with us?" Raphael asked.

I turned in surprise to my bodyguard. This was it? He'd been my shadow since... I had no clue how long ago. Time had become a blur.

The only constant had been him.

I didn't want to say goodbye like this. I wanted to hug him and have his public demeanour fall away and for him to press his lips to mine again, rekindling the attraction he'd hidden so well.

What could I offer with people looking on? A handshake? Thumbs-up?

But yet again, Ben saved me in his own perfect way. "I'll escort Daisy to the cabin, just to be safe."

He opened the door, admitting frosty air, and put a hand out for me so I exited that side. I hopped down into the snow then copied him with keeping my head down. Ben led me to safety. I planted my feet in his footsteps, blindly following while fluffy snowflakes pelted my face. Once we'd reached the cover of trees, Ben dropped his grip on me, and the helicopter lifted and veered away. Snow dusted us from the disturbance, but all of a sudden, I could hear again.

The whine of the storm was nothing to the helicopter. Snow fell in clumps, deadening every other sound. I laughed and spun around.

It was beautiful. Freezing as well. Even though before my near abduction, I'd replaced my ballet shoes with my only others, a battered pair of Converse, they were no match for the Scottish Highlands in winter. Likewise, my hoodie and leggings were doing a poor job of keeping out the chill, but my mood didn't sink. I was here. I'd made it.

I practically danced after Ben who lumbered on like a bear in his element.

We wound down the track through thick evergreens until ahead, a small log cabin rose from the hillside. It was single-storey with a stonework chimney, pretty windows, and a pitched roof. Snow lay against it in drifts.

I rubbed my eyes, not quite believing the picture-perfect cabin was real. "Please tell me this is it."

Ben glanced back and gave a nod. I gave a squeal of delight.

If I was a cartoon bunny, I'd have heart eyes right now.

"Home sweet home," I uttered.

We reached the door, and Ben kicked away the snow that almost reached the handle and shouldered it open. He stomped his boots then toed them off in the entryway. I did the same, pushing the door closed behind me and shutting out the weather.

"Hello?" I called into the depths of the little house.

Ben flipped on a lamp, illuminating the hall. A door to the right opened onto a wide living room with a sofa, a thick, woven rug, wood stove, and the end of a big bed just in view. A picture window interrupted the log wall to display the view. Down the flagstone hall was a bathroom, and that was the whole of the space.

Two rooms, plus the corridor with built-in cupboards. Beautifully simple and so cosy.

I drifted into the main room. "Ariel?"

No reply came, and I glanced back at Ben. "She isn't here

yet. Which is good because I wanted to talk to you. Alone, I mean."

Ben passed me and knelt in front of the stove. The door creaked as he swung it open, and he collected a handful of kindling from a basket. "I won't be staying long. I'll get ye set up then leave."

I knew he'd do that, but nerves still gripped me. "Are you okay?"

"I'm fine."

"Can I ask you something?"

Ben inclined his head, still not looking at me.

This was worse than I thought. It wasn't just being with other people that had changed his attitude towards me. Something else was at play.

From now on, I needed everything to be upfront and direct. No being outside of the conversation. No more allowing others to keep secrets from me. "Do you regret what we did together?"

"Do ye want honesty?"

My heart constricted. "Always."

"Yes."

Damn. Damn that horrible answer, and damn myself for my sharp stab of hurt.

He struck a match and set it to the paper he'd bunched up.

It flared, lighting the fire and casting a warm glow over his face that was entirely at odds with his words.

"I've overstayed my welcome," he muttered. "I'll call Ariel to check where she is then be out of your way."

His welcome? The phone was in his hand and the call tone trilling before I had a chance to question him.

"Hey, dammit," Ariel's voice came over the speaker, the gale blasting her mic. "Ben? Please tell me you're still with Daisy."

"I'm here," I replied in a rush. "It's so good to hear your voice. Are you almost at the cabin?"

"I can't make it. I tried, but not even a quarter of the way up the track, I spun out and couldn't be sure I was even on the trail anymore. I didn't want to dig myself out of a drift but luckily managed to reverse out of it. The storm is hitting hard." The sound changed as if she'd gone indoors. "God, I can hear myself think now. Right. I can get skis and go cross-country."

I moved to the window and peered outside. Nothing apart from snow on top of snow filled the view. Total white-out.

"No," I breathed, picturing my friend lost in the snow-storm, or worse. "That would be so dangerous. Please don't."

"But that means not getting to you until tomorrow at the earliest. It's meant to last all night and through to mid-morn-ing." Ariel sighed. "This is the worst. You're within a couple of miles and I can't reach you."

I wrapped my arms around myself, miserable for too many reasons. "All I want is you to be safe."

"Same." Then Ariel cemented the deal. "Ben, can you stay? I won't cope if I know Daisy's on her own. You've al-ready done so much, but I have to ask."

I didn't check his expression. No need to rub salt in the wound of his rejection. I'd planned to get him alone and steal a kiss, then work out how to blow his mind in the way he had mine.

But instead, his words had stopped me short.

He regretted me. One more person who didn't want me

around.

"I'll stay," he replied, but his dour tone told me exactly what he thought of the plan.

The problem was, I didn't buy it.

This dismissive routine, his blanking me. He'd been the one to tell me of his attraction. On the plane, he'd initiated the kiss and everything after it. He wanted me. I just needed to decide if I cared enough to call him on his attitude problem.

16

Ben

I had an issue. Something that had never once in my life happened before. After Daisy and I had disembarked the plane in Manchester, I'd read the messages on my group chat with the Gordonson siblings. Ariel had teased Raphael about a crush he'd had on Daisy.

A crush.

I was friends with Raphael.

Giving serious consideration to employing him as a member of my crew.

Didn't stop how I'd wanted to rip his fucking arms off as he'd bundled Daisy in a hug.

The brutal emotion had taken me by surprise and knocked me off my game. I'd never been possessive over any girlfriend. Not that she was that. I barely knew Daisy and had no claim over her. No reason at all for the violent thoughts that had me balling my hands into fists.

Touch her and die, my ape brain had grunted.

It was my only explanation for why I'd hurt her feelings afterwards. I hadn't lied—screwing around with her had been unprofessional, even if I wasn't strictly working, so I should regret it. Even if every other part of me contradicted that. Better to have her tell me where to go than entertain such ridiculous feelings any further.

Across the cabin's living room, Daisy drew clean clothes from her bag then threw me a baleful look. "I'm going to take a shower."

She left the room without another word.

I watched her go and held in a sigh. Despite only three days in each other's company, I knew enough to tell how much I'd pissed her off. I bet she'd had to bite her tongue to stop from asking me if I wanted to take my turn in the shower first.

Polite and giving to a fault. She'd make an excellent girl-friend to some deserving arsehole.

I grumbled at the surge of yet another possessive wave and pulled out my phone. While we were waiting for our flight in Seattle, I'd started a number of lines of enquiry, mostly via Gordain, and information had started to come back in.

First, I'd checked out Daisy's aunt and uncle's business. She thought them well off, and from an outsider perspective, they appeared to be doing well. The problem with their kind of dealings, those linked to organised crime, was that I needed to dig deeper to understand them as any official reporting such as their public accounts was for shite. Usually this meant finding someone who would investigate for me. The best contact I had for that was Daisy herself. She'd worked for them and then lived with them. If anyone had access to the type of data I needed, it was her.

Next, I had a weird gut feeling about her ma. She'd reacted strangely to Daisy telling her she'd left their relatives' home, then her friend had revealed a possible debt to the uncle. It was a channel worth following.

The basic person report onscreen gave me little more than I'd already guessed. She moved from job to job, and state to state, barely paying taxes, and had been growing a list of minor debts along the way.

I scrolled through the data, considering my next move.

I also needed a record of the party attendees. I wanted to talk to Ariel about her stepmother, Willow, who'd been there. I wanted to create a longer list of people who had any interest in Daisy.

The one thing I was certain about was that Daisy wasn't safe. Somebody wanted her enough to trace her and attempt to kidnap her. Maybe the men she'd overheard talking at the party, but they were probably only lackeys.

There was an ex-boyfriend I needed to know more about, but I'd drawn the line at accessing any of Daisy's personal information without her permission given first, and I'd wanted to get her to safety without scaring her.

We were stuck together in a storm, but I'd use the time to work out what had happened to her. And *not* the other activities my body wanted to indulge in

I'd likely done enough to kill off any attraction she had for me. It was better this way.

Still, I hated that I'd hurt her feelings.

The sound of the shower cut off, and I set aside my research with an idea of how to proceed next.

Despite the raging battle outside, and the icy snow hammering at the windows, we had a well-stocked and cosy cabin to enjoy. I'd feed her, make her smile again, then we'd continue the detective work together.

I knelt in front of the wood-burning stove, putting on another log to generate enough heat to cook by. It was rudimentary, but I'd make it work.

Daisy stepped back in the room, finding me on my knees. Dressed, she towel dried her hair, her cheeks pink from the hot water. Her gaze coasted over me. I did the same to her.

Over her flushed skin. Down to yet another strappy, thin top which showcased her tits to the point where I could make out her nipples through the fabric. She'd gone without a bra.

Holy fuck.

In a hot rush, I realised my mistake. If I'd thought it possible I could ignore the attraction or downplay it in any way, I was fucking dreaming.

17

Daisy

Ben valiantly dragged his focus to my eyes then stood from his crouch by the stove. "Food. I mean, I can make something?"

I raised a shoulder. "No, I'm good from the snacks in the helicopter. Maybe in an hour or two?"

He held his phone out between us like a buffer. "Take this."

I did then angled my head, waiting for an explanation.

The bodyguard warred with keeping his gaze off my nipples.

I knew exactly what I was doing. There was nothing wrong with me going braless. If any guy had a problem with prominent outlines, that was his issue, not mine. Boobs weren't deadly weapons.

Except in a way, that's how I was using them.

In the shower, I'd veered between hurt and annoyance, finally settling on owning this thing. He still wanted me. There was no hiding it. The tent in his jeans showed exactly how much.

But he was struggling over his words, his gaze sinking to my breasts again.

"What do you want me to do?" I asked with a chirp in my voice.

Ben snapped his attention to where I waggled the phone. He closed his eyes for a second, then centred himself. "Flowers."

"Come again?"

"I wish I fucking could," he muttered, then said louder, "Ye wanted to order flowers for Mrs Jessie and my mother. I found an online shop that will deliver to Olympia and Falls Ridge."

I blinked at him in surprise.

Ben reached over and pressed a button on his phone then tapped in a code. Sure enough, pictures of bouquets filled the screen. He gestured at a lovely display of white carnations with bold-coloured flowers studded throughout. "Ma likes carnations. She says they're the underdog of flowers but just as pretty as roses. I always send them on her birthday."

He was too cute. I swallowed against the little zap of poignancy I really shouldn't feel for a man who knew his mother's favourite bloom. "We'll send them to both."

A few clicks later, and settled on the comfy sofa, we'd entered the addresses and the timescales for delivery. Ben insisted on paying, which I had to accept, being penniless and all, then the flowers were ordered. I offered back his phone, but he shook his head.

"In case ye run out of reading material, I set up an audio-book account. My phone is totally untraceable, by the way. No one can find it, even if ye go on your social media, though I'd recommend not doing that, or at least being offline and not leaving a likes or comments trail. Ariel's ploy with her stepmother is that you're missing and she's demanding to know your whereabouts. But I didn't want ye to get bored, so go ahead and download something to listen to. There are credits on the account."

I just stared at him. From the cold, dismissive profession-al to this sweet, giving man. He was back. The Ben I liked the most. It seemed like he had a lot more to say, and even more that he wanted to do, but abruptly, he jumped up, keeping going until he was at the door to the hall.

"Need to do a workout," he mumbled then shut himself out.

"You've left me with an unlocked phone," I called after him. "I could do anything with this."

"Have at it," came the muffled reply. "If it locks again, the code is three-two-four-seven-nine-four."

That was a bold move.

At college, there had been a running joke amongst the guy I'd dated and his friends that women were never al-lowed to get hold of their phones. Like they were players with side chicks. They went to great lengths to extend the joke, diving to intercept any unattended phone from a pass-ing woman. It was eye-wateringly embarrassing.

Ben's cool maturity was yet another nail in the coffin of my attraction.

I carried the phone to the nightstand where I'd left my bag, hunting out a hairbrush. In the depths, I touched the case that contained my vibrator.

The shower I'd taken had been quick and for cleanliness' sake only. I really should have used the time to take the edge off my neediness, too.

With the brush located, I sprawled out on the rug in front of the log burner and combed out my long brown hair while flicking through the audio titles in the romance section. I found the one for the book Ben had bought me and clicked on it.

For the next hour, I laid out and listened, getting into the story. Also getting even more heated. Outside of the picture window, the day darkened. This far north, I imagined the daylight hours in winter to be short, though I had no real clue if I was right. Maybe the storm was worsening.

We were completely alone out here. Isolated.

Gabriel had said the place was stocked with food, and Ben's fancy phone still connected to the Internet. It was no trial being holed up.

But there was still the matter of the weird distance between us.

The audiobook reached the same sex scene I'd read out to Ben. I paused it just past the part I'd got to. In the motel, after Ben confessed his attraction, it had felt so simple. Both of us felt it, so we followed it. What was stopping us doing that now? Nothing had changed.

I wanted him more and more.

Even when he'd been in that distant state, I'd burned to break his control. To introduce a blink into that thousand-yard stare and bring his focus to me. I barely knew where the confidence was coming from, but I eased up to my feet and padded to the exit.

Hit play on the audio.

Opened the hall door and closed it behind me.

My grumpy bodyguard sat on the cold stone floor, half-way to doing a sit-up, his knees bent, and his hands behind his head. For his workout, he'd stripped to his boxer shorts and T-shirt, and in the lamplight, I took my fill of his long body. His powerful thigh muscles. The tattoos that climbed his arm and disappeared under his sleeve.

He went to speak, then stopped as the audiobook narrator read out a particularly dirty line.

Yep. That's what was going down.

I held my breath and walked the short distance to stand by Ben's feet. Then I set the phone down on a shelf and sat cross-legged right in front of him.

Ben regarded me.

I raised a single shoulder and gestured for him to continue.

Still watching me, and with a wry smile I really wanted to trace, he resumed his position and commenced his sit-ups. God, he was fit. His biceps bulged either side of his head, and he breathed hard, the exertion letting me picture what he'd be like in another more fun exercise.

I'd half expected him to tell me to leave him alone, but his indulgence boosted my confidence all the more.

On Ben's next rise, I knelt up and ran a finger under the strap of my cami top. He groaned and didn't look away, continuing his routine. In this position, every time he sat up, he was face-on with my boobs, and I had an idea.

Moving fast so I didn't lose my nerve, I inched up the cami hem, folding it over until the underside of my boobs were exposed. Ben swore and jerked upright, his hands still locked behind him and his focus exactly where I wanted it to be.

"What are ye doing?" he demanded to my chest.

"Providing motivation."

He linked his gaze to mine. Heat flashed through me. It was like he was checking my intent. Where I was willing to take this. As far as I was concerned, I wanted it all.

I ran both hands up to palm my breasts, only the narrow band of the folded cami covering my nipples. My body was made of sparks, my skin sensitive to my touch. I was showing him without words where I wanted him.

Ben groaned. "Sit on my feet."

Yes, sir.

He stretched his legs out, and obediently, I knelt over his ankles.

"Put your full weight on me, I'm a lot heavier than ye," he added.

I did, and Ben rolled back again, this time coming up more slowly.

And with a smirk that sent spiralling lust through me.

"Be a good little coach and cup them again for me, aye?"

I curled my fingers around my breasts, plumping them together like an offering.

Ben continued his abs-crunching workout, each time coming up closer, and with that dirty smile in place. His gaze locked on my tits.

And with one huge erection from a glance at his shorts.

My mouth watered. Everything about this was turning me on. How I'd initiated it, but he'd added his own controls. I'd lost track of the story on the audiobook but tuned back in to boob play. Exactly what I wanted now.

I brushed my thumbs over my nipples, still hidden by the material.

Ben slowed his ascent, stretching to brush a kiss to my

cheek.

More. Lower. I shuffled further up his legs.

The next time he rose, he exhaled what sounded like delicious frustration. "Strip it off."

God. Game on.

I tugged the cami over my head, completely exposing myself to him. Ben swore, soaking up the sight of what I guessed was his favourite part of me.

"You can touch." I rolled a nipple between my fingers.

With his hands still behind him, propping him up, he nuzzled me, burying his face between my boobs.

I made some ungodly sound. Forget sparks and shocks, I was electrified.

And he seemed to know exactly what I needed.

Urgently, Ben stripped his own shirt. He used it to scrub away his sweat then tossed it down the hall. Then he slid a hand around my bare back and pulled me up to his thighs and laid a hard kiss on my lips.

In an instant, it turned erotic. He chased open-mouth kisses down my throat and to my chest, dislodging my hold so he could take over with my breasts. He licked me. Sucked my skin until he left a pink mark.

Then he settled his mouth over my nipple and took a hard pull.

This time, though almost mindless with need, I wasn't wasting my chance to get to grips with his body. I ran my fingers over his solid arm muscles. His strength broke my brain. Like I needed to mate now with this exceptional example of a man.

All the while, he played with my boobs. Switching from one nipple to the other, teasing me until I was half mad and so far beyond turned on.

In the back of my mind, I delighted over how this had worked out. He so easily could have refused me. Told me it was a bad idea. Faked not wanting it.

I needed to know why he'd resisted, but that was for later.

I could do nothing but live in the moment with him.

Like he'd done to me, I pressed my lips to his collarbone then sucked on a blank space of skin. Ben lifted his head and watched me. I kept up the action until I'd left a mark.

He growled approval then took my mouth with his, kissing me like his life depended on it. He drove me backwards, shifting us with a hand beneath my head until I was lying out on the cold floor and he was over me.

Then he sat up and curled his fingers into my waistband, not pausing before he yanked down my leggings, taking my underwear with it. Entirely naked, I should've felt awkward. About my belly rolls. About the curves that didn't quit. God knew I'd been made to feel bad about my body in the past.

But with this man, I didn't. The hunger in his gaze only grew.

Ben kissed my thigh then guided my leg over his shoulder and dropped another kiss right at my core. I moaned and arched my spine, tipping my head back because the visual of him right there was too much. I wanted to savour this. Draw it out in case this was the last time.

Ben licked me between the legs. His hot tongue slid over my clit and down. He gave up a sound of deep need and slapped the flagstone floor. "I could spend all fucking day between your thighs." But then he lifted away. "Up."

I squinted at him through hazy vision. "What?"

"This floor is freezing. I'll be the one to lie on it. Ride my fucking face."

I could have protested, but hell yes. On autopilot, I crawled over him where he laid out.

I needed this. Maybe because he'd been unkind, it felt so good to have him want me so badly.

"Hold the shelf," he ordered.

I gripped the wooden shelf in front of me, knocking over the phone I'd propped there, and lowered my soaking-wet core to Ben's mouth.

"Fucking smother me," he commanded, his fingers easing over my thighs to take two handfuls of my ass, bringing me down on him harder.

Then there was nothing I could do but hold on for dear life.

He penetrated me with his tongue, groaning again at my taste. I gasped and closed my eyes, losing myself to the long licks he took of me. How hard he sucked my clit and flicked his tongue.

Ben had skills. I'd had a small sample, but this was the full deal. He didn't hold back, touching me, teasing me, driving me wild in a way that clearly gave him pleasure, too.

I moaned his name. I gasped at every intrusion then went quiet when he delivered his killer move. Even pace. Constant pressure. Lick after lick after...

An orgasm crept up on me and struck. Hard.

The electricity in me crested. I'd been trying not to truly smother him, but I lost every sense in the glorious wave of one stunning climax.

He slowed, his attention turning languorous.

Then I was breathing hard, coming down from that staggering high. Ben lifted me from him like I weighed nothing, setting me on my knees. He crowded me from behind, no material where his boxer shorts had been. He'd taken them off, and I hadn't noticed. He slid his ultra-hard, thick dick between my legs.

Not pushing inside me, but close.

I would have told him to, but I'd lost all use of words.

In rough desperation, he took my hand from the shelf and laced his fingers through mine, clamping both of our hands to the juncture of my thighs. Then he fucked the gap, his forehead against my hair. His huge frame rigid around mine.

His other hand braced next to mine on the shelf, his knuckles standing proud. I knew if I peeked up, I'd see fever in his features.

Instead, I closed my eyes and just let myself feel him. Not quite fucking me, but enough that several thrusts later, he came over the outside of my pussy and onto our joined hands, spilling himself with a masculine growl.

And the single thought in my mind was how next time, I wanted him inside me and doing everything we probably shouldn't.

18

Daisy

By degrees, reality crept back in. Cool air from the draughty hall swirled around my naked body. Draped over my back, Ben stirred, pressed a kiss to my shoulder.

Withdrew.

In a long stride, he swung open the bathroom door and pulled the cord for the light.

Naked, he was gorgeous. Long limbs hard with muscle. Inkwork I wanted to explore.

Still clutching the shelf, I felt equally on display. I didn't want the comparison. Now our passions had been spent, I had the urge to cover up and be prepared for him to change his attitude again. Except there was the small matter of his cum dripping down my thighs and over my hand.

Water ran, then Ben reappeared with a washcloth. I took it from him in a hurry, not meeting his gaze, and swiped myself clean. Keeping my gaze on the task in hand, I snatched up the clothes I'd lost.

My panties draped over a ceramic water jug on the floor. The audiobook still played. Quickly, I shut it down.

"I feel like we defiled someone's pretty cabin," I mumbled.

"It's a safe house. We've used it for clients who needed a secure place to hide."

I peeked up, and he offered a hand, still naked and not hustling to armour himself like me.

"Callum's before that, I think," he added. "Used when he and Mathilda were dating and after when they needed a night away from the kids."

Dressed again, though missing a bra still, I stood.

I knew a lot about the McRae family, though I'd never met a single member. Ariel had told me everything about living here. The Scottish family had owned the estate for centuries and even had a couple of castles here, which I'd get to visit as my best friend lived in the tower of one. A fact that had been hard for me, a Californian, to comprehend.

I always imagined ancient buildings like that were kept as museums. Not homes.

Ben swatted my backside, propelling me to the living room. "I'm going to shower, unless ye want to go in first, then we have things to do."

I was good for a shower, liking the fact I probably smelled of him, but paused at the doorway to the warm room, a little spike of anxiety loosening my tongue. "Ben? Can we be straight with each other from now on? Don't go cold on me again."

Halfway to closing the bathroom door, he stilled, then gave me a single nod. "That's fair. While we're on the subject of sharing, I need ye to know that I'm clean. Regular health checks and testing come with the job, and I don't take risks."

He gestured down his body, and it took me too long to work out he meant his sexual health. Yet another thing no guy had ever bothered talking to me about before.

"I've never taken any risks and I got tested when I finished uni," I said in a rush. "All clear. Not slept with anyone since. Barely slept with anyone before that. Oh, and I get the shot so I'm covered for contraceptives."

He took in my babble, and I caught what looked like a flare of fresh lust before he gripped the door and shut me out.

Ten minutes later, he entered the room again, still naked and with his hair damp. He crossed to his bag and pulled out a clean T-shirt and grey sweatpants.

From my position on the rug, resting against the couch and with my hoodie on, I watched him, wondering how this was going to go down. Here felt safe. The fire warmed my toes.

He had the power to make it all cold again.

Ben exhaled and sat on the rug, facing me. "I didn't mean to freeze ye out. I can't do a good job protecting ye if I'm deep in lust the whole time. With ye, I keep breaking the rules."

I considered this, liking the fact he'd lusted over me but still confused. "Did you feel I was at risk once we'd got off the plane? Surely we were good with Raphael and Gabe there?"

He raised his gaze to the ceiling briefly, resigned to whatever he had to say next. "Something else was happening at that moment."

"What?"

He was killing me. I didn't know whether to brace myself

or reach for his hand. The man had me too mixed up.

"I was jealous."

He extended a finger and tapped under my chin to close my open mouth.

"Jealous of what?" I stammered.

"It's ridiculous."

"Spill it anyway."

"The fact Raphael has a crush on ye, and then ye were in his arms."

A smile curved my lips. I tried to stop it but failed. "Shut the front door."

Amusement crossed his features, and he was either blushing or the firelight was warming him like it warmed me.

"I can't explain it. I wanted to kill him. What the fuck is that about?"

I raised both shoulders in an exaggerated shrug. "I don't know, maybe you like me? God. Are you seriously telling me this is why I got the cold shoulder?"

He gave a baffled shake of his head. "That part might've been an overreaction, but I wasn't lying. I need to be able to do my job, so aye, shutting it down is the right thing." Then he exhaled and corrected himself. "*Was* the right thing."

There was so much more to say and to unpack. I couldn't get to grips with his confession. He obviously didn't understand it, so I had no chance.

But my pause gave him the opportunity to move the intriguing conversation on. Ben reached for the phone I'd brought back in with me.

"On the subject of doing my job, I'm going to call my team and Ariel so we can all talk through the mystery that is Daisy. I want updates and to have more minds thinking about what went down."

He unlocked the screen.

I pressed his arm to delay him. "One little thing first."

I knelt forward and kissed him, sinking into the hot press of lips. Happiness buzzed when he palmed the back of my head and returned my kiss.

We weren't done. Not by a long shot.

Then he hit dial, and we were back in action mode.

Ariel's voice came over the speaker. "Hey, I'm here. Raphael's with me. Jackson's dialling in."

There was an imperceptible strain in the way she said her brother's best friend's name that no one but her bestie could pick up. I knew all about Jackson, and not only from her. On the plane, Ben had asked my permission to include Jackson and Raphael on my case. Jackson was about to start working for him, a fact I presumed Ariel now knew, but we'd had no chance to talk about. Likewise, Raphael was aiming to take a pilot's role but had tests to pass first.

"I'm grateful to have everyone's help, particularly as I'm not really a client," I said.

"Jackson here," came a deep voice. "Client or no, we'll help."

"It's a good training opportunity," Raphael added.

"I hope you're not too bored, stuck out there in the snow," Ariel continued. "Wait till you get a load of my update about Willow."

"You got hold of her?" I asked.

"Eventually. I wish I'd come on the helicopter to fetch you rather than wait around, but it worked as I got to take the call. It was important as she always uses video and gets me to talk to our little brother. From my end, she could see my room looking its normal self, and I made the point to wander through the apartment and upstairs to the kitchen. Nothing to see here."

"Ariel, do ye mind holding that thought for a minute while I recap on the situation for the sake of everyone on the call?" Ben asked. "I want to lay it out sequentially so we're all up to speed."

"Go for it, boss man," she quipped.

In a succinct but thorough explanation, Ben covered over all that had happened, pausing to check facts and let me fill in gaps. From the time my family had invited me to stay, the removal of my car and phone, and then the appearance of the note. He had me fetch it and took screenshots, sending them to everyone on the call with my permission.

"Somebody knew and didn't agree with plans that had been made for you," Ben said. "We need a list of everyone who had access to your room on the day the note was left."

I cast my mind back. "That'll be pretty long. My aunt and uncle, of course. Then they have two cleaning staff, Mirabelle and Josie, and a housekeeper, Elaina, all of whom spend hours in the house most days. There's a personal chef, the pool maintenance guy who may or may not have been there, my aunt's yoga instructor, her PA, and security, but none of them generally go upstairs."

"Are ye particularly friendly with any of those people?"

I raised both hands. "I'm nice to everyone. But Aunt Sigrid had this real problem with me hanging out with the staff. Which was a contradiction as when I was younger and living there, she mostly foisted me off on them. It was different people then, though."

"So none have been around long or were close friends?" he pressed.

"Nope."

"Anyone show any animosity? The tone of the note could be taken as unfriendly," Jackson asked.

I opened my mouth to say no but then recalled one person who I'd missed from the list. "Actually, yes. My uncle's business manager isn't a fan. Camila was in the house several times over the holidays. I worked with her at their office for months as well, but she barely spoke to me unless she had to, and then it was never nice. I can't imagine her trying to protect me from whatever was happening."

Ben took her full name and some other details I knew about her.

We moved on, and Ben had me relate everything I remembered about the party.

"Your uncle introduced ye around, correct? Give me the names of the people he presented ye to."

I did, though a little warm from the fact I hadn't truly been paying attention to the cronies there. None had interested me, though I'd racked my brain since. Ariel chimed in, using her stepmother's private social media posts to identify people.

"Jackson," Ben said. "I'll walk ye through how to run a background report. First on Camila, then on everyone at that party."

I winced at how much effort they were putting into this.

I still had the sense that I wasn't important enough to be a target. I wasn't beautiful, wealthy, or a real asset to the family. There was something I was missing. A clue I'd overlooked.

Finally, we got to the attempted abduction in Olympia two days later.

"It was all so fast," I told them. "I was killing time until my bus. Freezing cold as the ground was snow-covered, so I fast walked along a road by the river, trying to stay warm. I'd just got on the phone to Ariel when a black truck stopped abruptly beside me. The cab door opened while the truck was still sliding on the icy road, and a man climbed out."

"Sure it was a man?" Jackson asked.

"Almost completely certain. He had a hoodie up and a mask on, the type they wear in the nurses' office, so I couldn't tell hair colour or see his eyes as the hood was pulled low. White guy, though. That I could tell. He had a good eight to ten inches of height over me, and a long reach because he grabbed at me. I pulled back. He slipped and lost his grip. I ran. He hunted me from his truck. Maybe Valentine and Ben scared him off, but I'm not sure. That was it."

"Not local, then," Raphael decided.

Ben squinted at the phone. "What makes ye think that?"

"Two reasons. The truck slid, suggesting no snow tyres, which you'd have if used to long winters of icy roads. Secondly, he himself slipped. Same argument. Wrong boots for the weather."

"Good analysis," Ben told him. "It doesn't snow that much there because of the proximity to the Pacific, but any local would be in the right shoes for the weather."

I pictured Raphael's shoulders straightening under the praise.

"Why didn't he catch Daisy?" Jackson asked.

His question silenced us all.

The weight of the words seemed to hang over me.

"He was bigger," he continued. "Most likely faster. Motivated enough to have followed her a significant distance to get there. That's an assumption, but he gave up the chase and returned to the truck. I get that he would have needed it to transport her away, but the opportunity was in the moment. He lost it."

"Suggesting inexperience," Ben concluded. "Not exactly in line with the professional who could track a phone."

"Or maybe someone saw and pulled over to challenge him?" Raphael supplied. "But why didn't they call the police? Ye said they didn't take Daisy that seriously, so it doesn't sound like there had been a report."

They discussed it, working through the possibilities.

For a moment, I got lost in my own thoughts.

What if he had actually captured me? Would I have been transported back to my aunt and uncle's house? Or on to some stranger's place—whoever wanted me at the party?

What would they have done with me?

Despite the cosy room, a chill slid through me, and I curled my arms around my legs.

"I hate the thought that someone tried to take you," Ariel said down the line, presumably having fallen down the same rabbit hole I had.

"I wish I knew why," I replied. "I wish I'd had any tiny skill in self-defence so I could've called on a technique to use rather than fate stepping in. It could all have gone so differently, and no thanks to me."

Ben's large hand took mine. I accepted the comfort, though his grip was fierce. I wanted to crawl into his lap. But the touch was brief, and he returned to business.

"Ariel, onto your stepmother. She's close friends with Sigrid, Daisy's aunt, is that right?" Ben asked.

My best friend gave a hard laugh. "Willow is a self-obsessed social climber, so the friendship is probably more based on the fact that they both run in the same circles. But anyway, I called her and got voicemail, then she rang back. I said I was really worried about you, Daisy, as you'd stopped replying to messages, and it was like you'd fallen off the planet. Want to know what she told me? That you'd run away with some guy and left your aunt devastated. Apparently, Sigrid had been thrilled you'd moved back in then stunned when you just vanished. They thought you'd been abducted. There was talk of opening a missing person's case, though I sincerely doubt any of them would call the police, so Willow was selling the drama there. Then someone thought to check the security videos. They saw you do a moonlight flit with some unknown male."

"Devastated?" I repeated. "Not angry?"

"That's what she said. Tears and heartache."

"Why is that important?" Ben asked.

I focused on him, trying to work through my thoughts. "Aunt Sigrid is a businesswoman. I've seen her lose her temper over deals gone wrong, but with family stuff, like her disappointment that her daughters weren't staying for Christmas, that just made her sad. If Sigrid had planned to sell me off, then the plans would be upset, not her. Do you see the difference?"

His shrewd gaze took me in. "Could she have been acting?"

I shrugged. "Possibly, though I don't know her to be sly. Ariel, did Willow say anything else?"

"No. I'll try her again in a few days and ask for an update. I can even try calling your aunt, if it helps."

"Maybe I'll do it myself," I replied slowly.

Except I didn't want to. Whatever they had to say, I didn't want to hear it. It could only make things worse.

Ben flattened his lips. "Let me investigate more first. It could be that Sigrid was in the dark about plans your uncle made."

"Meaning her reaction was genuine because she's attached to Daisy," Ariel cut in. "That makes sense."

But the wrinkle at his brow told me he wasn't entirely convinced of that option.

I wasn't sure either.

Briefly, he covered my mother and the likely debt she owed Uncle Paul, thankfully leaving out her topless cleaning endeavours, and instructed Jackson to look into that, too. I gave permission for them to do whatever necessary to get to the bottom of what was happening.

"With ye being here, Daisy," Ben said to me, but addressing everyone, "we're in a position of safety, and I intend to keep it that way. I'll walk ye through protection protocols, and it would be good to keep a low profile while we're in discovery mode."

I gazed at him. "You still think I'm in danger."

He inclined his head. "From what I can ascertain, ye were being manoeuvred into a position of use to your family. After your escape, someone tracked and almost abducted ye, which tells me there was some urgency to it. Whether those two things were connected or not, the loss is going to hurt them." His eyes flashed with pure determination. "I will get answers. I will find out what was going to happen, and why. I assume your relatives, at least one, were in on it, and I'll provide ye that name and their motivation. The business deal or personal benefit they'd gain. Trust me, lass. I'm good at my job, and I'll protect ye."

I couldn't help the thrill inside. All that strength and intelligence, dedicated to my cause.

Ben Graham. Top bodyguard. Entirely addictive.

Then a thought occurred to me.

"If you want to get under the hood of their business, I can help."

He angled his head, waiting for me to continue.

"I worked for them for months, covering for their book-keeper. They didn't trust anyone else to do the job because there's a lot of hiding information and concealing or faking of things like shipments. I guess you already know the kind of deals they're into."

"Officially importers of restricted goods," Ben confirmed. "I assume that's a front."

"No, that's true." A laugh bubbled up inside me. "They import materials that are tracked by the government and sell it on, but they've made an art form out of disguising quantities on invoices and shipments. In other words, hiding from the government chemicals and products criminals really shouldn't get their hands on in large amounts. Sigrid used to act like they were helping people get around tedious red tape, but when I was little my mom told me they were doing dodgy deals for big money and to keep my nose out."

With the benefit of distance, and all that had happened to me, the realisation hit me that I really shouldn't have got involved. Been stronger and walked away. I'd been so desperate to belong.

It wasn't normal. They were breaking the law, and I'd got swept up in their messy world.

I swallowed and continued. "As part of my degree, I was so determined to be useful to my family. So I introduced resilience into their business."

"What does that mean?" Ben queried.

I linked my gaze to his. Held it. "Every single one of their original and faked shipment invoices, I backed up to a se-cure online location. Right before Christmas, I told them

I was leaving the job and they had to find someone else to take it on. At that point, I was going to hand over the details of the secure files. As things stand, I'm the only person with access."

"And they don't know this exists?" Ben questioned.

"Nope. I never got around to telling them."

His focus turned hawklike. "What about the business manager, Camila. Could she have known?"

I hesitated. "I'm not sure. We didn't work closely together, and it's not like she had the view of my screen or what I was getting up to."

Jackson spoke up. "Access to that information makes Daisy a target. Maybe in the past but definitely now."

Oh shit. It did.

"Ben?" Ariel said. "Just so there's no ambiguity, the minute the storm is over and Daisy isn't snowed in, you'll be her official bodyguard, right?"

My amusement curled up, and my heart sank.

Ben had already made declarations about mixing business and pleasure. If he was on the books, he'd back up all the way from fraternising with me.

Even though it had just been a few days, our chemistry was only getting stronger. I'd loved giving in to it. Hadn't I just decided I wanted more?

"I will," the bodyguard confirmed. "Ye don't even need to ask."

A small flame I'd been nurturing in my heart guttered and very nearly went out.

19

Ben

*O*ff the call, I got to work setting up Jackson's contract and giving him an initiation in information gathering. Luckily he was available to start earlier than we'd originally agreed.

I'd interviewed him weeks ago and had intended to talk with him about a specific issue in his past. One that gave me pause when it came to the type of work I'd expect of him.

But my urgency to build my team had only increased.

Gordain's mandate, that he needed to trust our core members with his family's lives, was my final test. Jackson passed it, but in a way that worried me. We still needed that chat.

While I talked, Daisy busied around me.

The cabin had a cool box off the hall, and she found it and got to work making dinner.

I was hungry, only not for food.

Daisy had made the point multiple times that she wasn't

a client so I wasn't in conflict. That changed the minute we left this cabin. Ariel had unknowingly given us a time limit, and that clock was counting down.

Loudly. The ticking driving me to distraction.

With Jackson set to work, I finally got off the phone and joined Daisy by the fire. She'd made tacos, and the room smelled amazing.

"Best I could do," she said with a shrug. "I'm no cook, but it's edible."

I accepted one, unable to say much more than a quiet thanks for the food.

Daisy sighed and rested back against the couch, picking at her meal. "Walk me through Ben's life. You know so much about mine. I'm going to be staying in Scotland for at least a few days, I want to know about yours."

I wolfed down my taco, grabbing a second. "Ask a question."

"Where do you live?"

"Braithar. I have rooms at the back of the castle. Not quite an apartment, but it's private and I have my own entrance. I'm not there all that much. My office is at the aircraft hangar, and I travel a lot."

She tilted her head, considering me. "Why don't you have your own place?"

"Don't need one. No girlfriend. I don't intend to have a family. The space would be wasted."

"Okay. Work is your life. Tell me about that, then."

She'd asked me this on our road trip, and I'd blanked her. This time, I wanted to share.

"Gordain employed me five years ago to run a bodyguard service solely for Leo, his son-in-law."

Daisy nodded. "The rock star, Leo Banks. Ariel told me. He's so fine."

I stared at her, that same jealousy stopping me mid-chew.

A laugh flew from Daisy's lips, and she set down her food, grinning at me. "You are too easy."

"Don't make me want to kill Leo, too. I spend most of my time protecting him," I grumbled but carried on with my story. "For the past few years, Leo has toured regularly. I had a small crew employed on a permanent basis, then we'd bring in agency staff in whatever country the concerts were in. When Leo wasn't touring, I accepted work from other folk who needed close protection. Gabe worked for me in the past, as did a big lad named Sinclair who could stop a rabid fan with just one glance, but both moved on to other things. I've struggled to form a good team since. In the past year, I had to let go of one staff member for being drunk on duty. A second got poached by another, bigger company and left without a backwards glance. That left me with two. I ended up releasing both from their contracts."

"What did they do?"

"It was more that they weren't a great fit. With Leo stopping touring for a while, I had the opportunity to rebuild from scratch and better. One of Gordain's core directives for the service was that he needed to be able to trust with his life the individual looking after Leo, Viola, Gordain's daughter who married Leo, or Finn, their wee lad. With a diminished crew, I couldn't in faith put up either of those men for that specific job. An essential deal especially when they would need to lead a team of locally sourced bodyguards. It was time to reset."

She pondered this for a while, finishing her food. I expected questions on rock star gossip, or on the baby Viola was expecting any day—the reason they'd called off touring.

Yet again, Daisy surprised me. "That's a lot of responsibility on your shoulders."

"I can handle it."

"Sure, but how? What do you do to relax or nurture yourself?"

I opened and closed my mouth. Nurture? I had nothing.

Daisy arched her eyebrows, her lips set in a sympathetic smile. "Thought so."

My phone dinged. A message from Ma. She'd forwarded the picture she'd taken of me holding AJ on my very short visit.

I held it up. "My brother's bairn."

Daisy's eyes crinkled at the edges. "Oh my God. My ovaries just exploded with pretty blue fireworks. Gimme."

She reached for the phone.

Some strange feeling brewed inside me. Daisy cooing over my nephew was...cute.

"Want kids?" I asked, surprising myself with the question.

Daisy choked. "Weird way to propose, but sure?"

I pulled a face at her. "Eventually, I meant, and obviously not with me."

She sighed, handing back the phone. "Yes. A family around me is all I've ever really wanted. Probably why I was prepared to go along with my relatives BS for so long. First, I really want to give my cleaning business a try. When that's established, I'll sit back and let my employees do all the work. Use my time to raise babies."

She said all of that without looking my way, trained on the flickering fire. Free to stare at her, I took my fill.

I couldn't stop picturing her in the image she'd painted. Easy-tempered and warm-hearted, she'd be the perfect mother. Similar to Autumn in many respects. In ten years, Daisy would have a thriving business and a couple of pretty kids hugging her knees.

I'd hear about her from Ariel, if I was still around.

That clamping feeling in my chest intensified.

"What about you?"

I blinked and found her returning my scrutiny. "What?"

"You really don't want a family?"

"No." My single word came out hard.

"You'd make a great dad. You're responsible but fun—"

"I said no."

Daisy opened her mouth in surprise. I hadn't meant to snap, but then I was on my feet and clearing up the cooking mess.

"I'll get this clean," I muttered, grabbing the pan from the stove and stomping out the door to the bathroom. There was no kitchen here, so I did the best I could with the little sink.

All the while, unwelcome memories crushed me.

Tabby's behaviour to me, her rejection, if I had to name it, left a mark. I had a family I loved. Autumn, Bull, Archie, Valentine, and Merci. My siblings would have more kids. I'd visit. Stay well clear of their spouses.

But I'd never do the same myself.

I was made up of fifty percent of a woman who never gave a damn and the same percentage from my birth father who'd wanted nothing to do with me. I couldn't risk becoming a father who'd do the same to my kid as they'd done to theirs.

No son or daughter of mine would feel what I had.

I scrubbed at the now-clean pan, trying to rid myself of the wave of emotion. Autumn had mentioned coming here to visit Tabby. I had to find a way to put her off so she didn't give that woman any more of her time.

Warm hands glided over my back and around my sides. Daisy hugged me, her cheek to my spine.

"You're breathing too fast. See if you can slow it down."

She was right.

I was hyperventilating without even realising.

With her pressed against me, I forced myself to focus on the ins and outs of her breath, feeling her. Matching her. I had techniques for this. For managing stress, particularly while working. It came with the territory of needing to always be present and in control. Somehow, letting her show me was a thousand times simpler.

Which was another problem.

I was pretty certain I had the beginnings of an obsession with Daisy. She calmed my breathing but spiked my pulse.

Need grew.

Yet again, I was hard for her.

I abandoned the sink, turned, slid my hands under her thighs, and lifted her. The living room and the big, unused bed on my mind for what had to come next.

20

Daisy

Ben strode into the living room, holding me. Kicked the door closed behind us. Took me straight to the bed.

Talk of families had hit a nerve for him.

He'd walked away and freaked out all by himself.

It was fine. I didn't need him to confide in me. I wasn't looking for a proposal in the middle of the disaster of my life. If he wanted to distract himself using my body, I could help.

He set me in the middle of the quilt with a bounce and stepped back. "I really want to fuck ye."

Delight thrilled me. "Okay."

"I've been thinking about it non-stop. Ye make me fucking mindless."

Breathing in confidence, I reached back and stripped my

hoodie. "Let me guess. You still don't have any condoms because you were trying not to do this."

His darkening expression gave me my answer.

I palmed my breasts through my top, my breath hitching at how good it felt to do this with his gaze on me.

Ben's nostrils flared. "Ye still want me anyway."

I gave a slow nod, pulling the material tight over my nipples.

"Good," he replied. "Strip. Fully."

I eased up the top. On display for him and earning a groan. Then I stripped my lower half, too. "Now you."

He smirked, not coming any closer but letting his gaze take its fill of my body. "Go ahead. Own my cock, shortie."

I glowered at him.

Then I crawled to the end of the bed and beckoned.

He moved closer until I could reach his shirt.

"Off." I plucked his waistband. "All of it."

Ben gave me a cheeky little chin lift. "Didn't I tell ye to own it?"

The control freak bodyguard boss wanted me to undress him. I was happy to oblige.

Kneeling up, I collected handfuls of his T-shirt and peeled it off him. Ben dropped his head to help me but otherwise let me take my time, keeping his gaze locked on me.

In this position, I was face-on with his tattooed chest, finally getting the good look I'd wanted. I leaned in and kissed the pattern of black ink that swirled and blended, continuing down his arm.

Then I flicked my tongue over his nipple.

At the same time, I found his waistband and tugged his

sweatpants down. His dick sprang free, hitting his belly.

Ben groaned. "From here, it's almost right between your tits."

No one ever said I couldn't take instruction.

I took hold of his ultra-hard and intimidatingly large dick and encased it between my breasts. Instantly, Ben gripped me, jerking his hips to fuck my chest.

"Ye have no idea how hot that is. I've wanted to fuck your tits from the second I saw ye climbing out that window."

God. And I thought I was the one with the dirty mind.

I let him enjoy himself then dropped my head down, licking his end. His salty precum flooded my tongue, but it was his shout of surprise and pleasure that had me do it again.

I pulled back so I could properly take him in my mouth. Ben's fingers dove into my hair. He tugged my locks then wrapped the length around his fist, using the position to guide my blow job.

With my tongue flattened, I took him in as far as I could without choking. He was too big for me to take all of him, and thick, too. I fisted the base of him.

I sucked, loving how he pushed against me. How much it turned me on to give him pleasure.

Abruptly, he snapped back. "Up the bed."

He followed my scoot to the pillows, crawling over me. Kneeling between my legs.

"I can't take any more of that. Let me fuck ye now. I might be rough but I swear to the al-fucking-mighty that I'll make it good."

"I know you will. Feel me."

He grazed his fingers over my dripping pussy. Finding

out how much he turned me on just from me touching him.

Then his dick was right there, in position.

Ben touched his forehead to mine. I raised my lips to his. He kissed me as he drove into me.

My cry broke our kiss. He was so big. Stretching me wide around him, and he wasn't even all the way in. Ben jacked his hips until he was fully seated.

I knew he'd feel incredible, but I couldn't have anticipated this.

Maybe it was the fact we'd gone bare. Being together in the most intimate way possible. But my happy amusement turned to something deeper. Emotion built on lust. I needed him so badly. He was inside me, starting a slow rhythm. Hitting somewhere deeply pleasurable. And yet I needed more. I needed us both to feel good. For him to come in me. To bring an end to the longing and teasing we'd done with each other.

Draw a line under our attraction and end it in the best possible way.

Ben's jaw locked, and he braced himself over me, using just his dick to drive me insane. I ran my hands over him and then to my tits, loving the flare in his gaze. How he loved seeing me play with myself.

He sped up. Fucking into me with the same exacting control, the pace steadily increasing. He'd promised rough and brought it. His muscles shaking and the bed with it. The thick wooden headboard rattling. Furious passion.

I could hardly breathe, short pants giving me just enough oxygen. Matching his moves, I rose to meet him. Take him.

And inside, pleasure wound in a tight circle.

Everything we'd done had built to this. I'd propositioned him at the start. He'd distracted me with an orgasm on the plane. Our hideaway, our safe haven, witnessed us both moaning in pleasure. Clutching each other. Kissing.

I'd never get enough of Ben's kiss.

He sank his mouth onto mine, working his lips slower than his strokes. A full-body experience. He knew exactly what he was doing to me.

How hard, how fast. He watched me, learned, and delivered.

I was close. He stopped.

Sat up. Lifted my leg, wrapping it around his back and using the leverage of my thigh to go deep.

"Need to see ye come on my dick."

God. Another few strokes and his hand to my clit.

His actions drove me crazy, but it was his expression. His rapt focus, so intent on me. All humour gone, nothing there but need and something else. Unidentifiable as I'd never seen it before on anyone. But I didn't get the chance to analyse it as waves of pleasure crashed into me.

I broke.

Arched up, blinded by a stunning orgasm. It hit from deep inside and echoed out, continuing along my nerves and soaking me in satisfaction.

Almost the same moment, Ben gave up a groan and stilled.

Inside me, he pulsed, then he pulled out and finished on my belly.

His orgasm extended mine. Somehow, the knowledge of what we'd done, the no-condom deal, became even hotter. I'd never felt anything like this. Never wanted it until now. Until him.

There were no risks when the man himself embodied

safety.

Then he was gathering me in his arms and kissing me more.

It took a long, dizzying time to regain my mind.

Whatever that had been, I only wanted more.

For a long while, we kissed, then we just breathed together. Ben cleaned me up then lay on his back, cradling me on his chest. Under my ear, his heart slowed from a rapid beat to a calmer one.

"You," was the sole word I could manage.

Lazily, Ben took a squeeze of my breast then caressed my belly and finally down to feel over my pussy. I was soaked from him. Leaking the cum from him not pulling out quite in time.

"Mine," he said, then added, "fuck."

Like he'd surprised himself.

I laughed. "Jealousy and now possessiveness. You're on fire."

Ben groaned and rolled me back, kneeling between my legs. No pause, he gave his hard-again dick a stroke then rubbed the head over my core. Getting himself wet. Winding me up more.

"You're so fucking beautiful, Daisy. Particularly when you're wearing my cum."

"Just fuck me already."

"Aye, lass."

Outside, snow beat down and the icy wind blew. But in the safety of each other's arms, we saw out the storm.

Again, and again, and again.

*M*orning brought sunlight through the uncovered picture window. Along with a message from my best friend.

Ariel: Coming in hot on snowmobiles. ETA 30 minutes.

Ben read it out then hugged me. Delivered one last kiss.

Then he moved away.

He didn't need to say anything. I knew it already.

Ben's contract had begun, and our time was at an end.

21

Ben

*T*wo snowmobiles carved their way to the cabin, leaving deep tracks in the snow. Ariel drove the first, Jackson the second. Both carried a spare helmet.

Our rescue party. And not a minute too soon.

At my side, Daisy took a rush of breath, her fingertips to her mouth. The minute the first snowmobile stopped, she dove forward with a gasp that sounded like pain and happiness at the same time. She wrapped Ariel in a hug, her shoulders shaking.

Ariel embraced her then wrenched her helmet off and tossed it into a drift. Tears lined both lasses' eyes as they hugged again, their words tumbling over each other. Emotion poured from them.

It caught me in the throat. Daisy was loved. I was glad for her.

Jackson eased his helmet up and came to me. "Bitter storm last night."

The weather had escaped my notice. All I knew was the best night of my life. The heat. The endless need. How Daisy and I had used each other.

How it couldn't be repeated.

The last thought darkened my mood. "Aye. I appreciate ye coming out. We're good to go."

Our bags were packed. The cabin stripped down. After Ariel's alarm call, Daisy had rushed to clean it, but I'd taken over most of the tasks. Stripped the bed we'd rolled in. Packed away the food we'd snacked on in the middle of the night. I'd return later to fully clear up our port in the storm, ready for the next time it was needed.

Jackson reached for the bags I carried, strapping them onto the vehicles. A man of few words. Part of what I both liked about him and had concerns over.

Today, I'd spend time getting to know him more. It meant having a difficult conversation, but from the way his gaze left me and lingered on Ariel, his hand flinching when she adjusted something on her machine, we really needed to have that chat.

"All set?" I asked Daisy.

She pulled away from Ariel and wiped her eyes with the side of her hand. "I think so. Where will I be staying?"

On yesterday's call, we'd left that matter with Ariel and Gordain to sort out. All I knew was that I needed her away from me. Or maybe me away from her. A safe distance where I could protect her from afar. Only see her when other people were around.

Ariel spoke up. "Castle Braithar. Gordain's choice. He's picked out a guest room, so we'll head there now. Get you settled in."

Daisy grinned and accepted her helmet, sliding it into

place before the lasses climbed onto their snowmobile.

Fuck. Having Daisy under the same roof as me, even if it was a huge castle, would be a special kind of torture.

No, I checked myself. I could handle it.

But I needed to tell Gordain what had happened. The need for truth in our service was too important.

I'd just have to sleep at the office from now on.

We left the cabin behind, and the two women sped ahead of us, though Jackson kept up so we never lost sight until we delivered them to Gordain's castle home. With them inside, we transferred to Jackson's car. My 4x4 was still at Inverness airport, but I'd retrieve it this morning.

My new recruit drove us out to the hangar. On the way, he shared the process he'd started last night with Gordain.

"I have to admit, this isn't the work I expected when I first considered becoming a bodyguard. Fucking loving it. Don't get me wrong."

"Good to know," I replied. "I've got more of that for ye this morning."

We left the car and crunched through the snow into the draughty building. A soaring roof curved overhead, protecting the different structures and spaces inside from the elements. Helicopters were housed here. A flying school with rows of seats. The office block with the mountain rescue service and the bodyguard crew next door.

A couple of mechanics wheeled a helicopter across the concrete, Raphael pacing alongside them, talking with his instructor. He spared a short salute for us, but his focus was on the morning's training.

On the surface, Raphael, particularly around his family and friends, had an easy and open personality. Friendly and determined. Reliable. But beneath that, he ran deep.

Thought a lot. His killer instincts impressed me.

It made sense that he and Jackson had become friends at university, as Jackson shared many of those qualities. But all I'd seen was that surface level so far on my new recruit. A cool head. Obvious competence.

I needed to get under his skin.

I guided Jackson to my office and gestured for him to sit. When he'd come to me to ask for work, my interview had been preliminary because I'd needed to look into his past before really considering him. We'd never got into the details of an orientation. That changed now.

"Typically, a bodyguard would do exactly what the job title suggests," I started. "Stand in front of the person they're paid to protect and stop others from getting to them. Though we do employ people whose sole job it is to walk that walk, our service has another angle because of the nature of who we're protecting. Leo Banks, Gordain's son-in-law, has a wide and enthusiastic fandom. Most are reasonable people. Some are not. He's had death threats from individuals who simply disliked a song he wrote. Viola and Finn had them, too, just because they're Leo's family."

At the mention of Viola, Jackson sat taller in his seat. The foot he'd had resting on the opposite knee landed on the floor. "They threatened his wife and kid."

Not a question, but I answered it the same. "On occasion. It's our job to ascertain how much of a risk these people are, particularly when it comes to the family being on tour. Then we need to monitor them as the police will do very little without an actual crime. In some countries, they won't act at all. Think of us more as a personal protection agency with a specialism in risk management. Tracking individuals is part of the job. The work we're doing for Daisy is a good indication of what I'd expect from ye. The other side of it is on-the-ground coordination, protecting the asset in the field." I intensified my stare, watching his every reaction. "On that part, I need to understand how you'd handle a direct threat. Particularly to a woman."

Jackson steepled his hands, no immediate answer coming.

The summary I had of him included a report on a life-changing incident in Jackson's past. The kidnap and murder of a family member. He'd been a teenager, and I'd found a news report which detailed how close he'd been to the case. It included a photo of a fresh-faced version of the man across the desk. The same sharp, blue-eyed gaze and angled jaw but his expression open in panic.

Nothing like the closed-off version I'd offered a job to.

That level of devastation had ripples.

I carried my own demons. Knew how trauma could surface unexpectedly. What I needed now was a read on how badly affected Jackson was, and the steps he'd taken to heal from it.

I'd already recruited the man. His skills meant he'd be a good fit.

His honesty with me now would go a long way to letting me trust him.

Jackson lowered his hands. "Ye mean because of my sister. I haven't hidden anything. Your application form asked for any adverse life experiences, and I noted her death."

I tilted my head. "Her murder."

A muscle ticked in his jaw. I didn't want to cause him distress. I couldn't imagine the pain he'd been through. But this was important. I couldn't enable a loose cannon.

"Yes, she was murdered," he finally supplied.

I softened my gaze. "I understand ye were part of the

search for her. I'm sorry for how that turned out. I need to know what you'll do if I've placed ye with Viola, Daisy, or any other young woman under our protection, and someone makes a run at her. Or you're driving and an obsessed fan is in pursuit. Or it's the walk from the car to a hotel and some arsehole yells abuse about how he's going to hurt her, which they do in order to get a reaction. In a one-on-one situation, walk me through your mindset."

Jackson's gaze fixed on the point over my shoulder. I was pissing him off, but that was fine.

"In any of those circumstances, I don't doubt my capacity. I'm not about to confuse my professional life with my personal one. I can separate the two. If there was any issue, I wouldn't be here."

"The military rejected ye on grounds of mental health," I added.

"They did. Again, I didn't hide this from ye. It wasn't that long after, and I was a mess. I took some time off, picked myself up, and completed a degree since then. I've moved on."

"Did ye get counselling?"

"Grief and anger management."

"What about your personal life. Are ye seeing anyone?" I pressed.

"No."

"Have ye since your sister died?"

His gaze rolled back to me, uncertainty there. "No one long-term."

"And you're currently staying with Raphael and Ariel."

His eyebrows dove together. "What's Ariel got to do with this?"

I hadn't actually meant anything specific about Ariel,

though I'd noted his interest, but his response was telling. "A younger sister type," I commented.

Jackson inflated his lungs and sat taller, taking control of this exactly as I wanted him to. "Look, I get you're concerned. I have a fucked-up history and an axe to bury in men who hurt women. I can't change that, but I swear it won't bleed into my work in terms of loss of control. In your scenario, trust that I'll have a tight hold on myself—I always do. It's become innate, and I wouldnae be here if I couldn't handle myself. Flip this over and see how I'm an asset. I know the depths a depraved mind will go to. I won't underestimate anyone and I'll have the jump on them long before anyone else ye take on. I'm smart, and fit, and fucking determined. Are there any more questions?"

He'd impressed me, I couldn't deny it. I liked his fire and his restraint. I needed people onside who cared, and no matter my lingering concern about his history, I couldn't doubt he'd make a devoted bodyguard.

"None. Welcome to the team."

Jackson exhaled hard then slapped my waiting hand.

I got on with the orientation, tasking him with working through the list of Daisy's party attendees. If one of them was a groomsman-in-waiting, it would give us a clue of where to look next.

With Jackson busy at work, I left the office to take on my next task. Also uncomfortable, but with me at the centre of it this time.

As usual, Gordain was out in the hangar.

I located him. Requested a private word.

He asked me to give him a moment while he finished the conversation, and I strode to the open entrance and watched Raphael neatly pass in the helicopter he'd taken out earlier.

If Raphael was serious about joining my crew, I had the beginning of a new team. Valentine, my brother, would make a third. I'd have them trained up and ready for the next time Leo toured. Gordain had stated there was no one you could trust like family.

Jackson was starting to earn that. I'd been a friend to Raphael since he was fifteen.

I knew my brother and he knew me.

A fresh and tiny suspicion eked into my mind.

I couldn't shake the notion that Daisy's kidnap attempt might not be related to the issue with her family. Which meant an unknown third party was responsible. Someone present in the small Washington state town she'd been in. Following her.

Later, I'd meet with her to dig deeper into that, and maybe share the unhappy place my mind had gone, and the person I'd begun to suspect.

Right now, I had to get her out of my head. There was only one foolproof way to do that.

Hopefully one which wouldn't lose me my job.

Gordain joined me. He squinted at my expression, directed me to his office and to the visitor's seat. "Spill it."

"I want to formally take on the protection of Daisy. It's a good training opportunity for Jackson, not to mention personal for Ariel and her brothers."

Gordain inclined his head. "I agree for all those reasons, but ye don't need my permission. What's going on?"

I held his gaze, my heart inexplicably thumping. "There's something I need to tell ye. For the sake of transparency, Daisy and I had a short relationship. It's over now, and we won't be pursuing anything more."

He stared at me, surprise registering in his normally

friendly gaze. He took a moment, and I imagined him assessing what I'd done. The fact I'd not been under contract, so there was no breach. I readied myself to argue the point.

He chose his words carefully. "The relationship is over, ye say."

"It is."

"That's what ye want?"

"Yes."

"Then I trust your judgement."

That was it? I stared at him for a beat. Gordain woke his laptop, settling into reading something on his screen.

I'd been dismissed. Not even a warning over how to handle myself.

I left and got back to work, packing away every sliver of attraction I'd held for Daisy. This was necessary. I was her bodyguard, and she was my client, on the books and official.

Everything else was in the past.

22

Daisy

"This is yours. You have a private bathroom, and if you don't want to use the front entrance and the main staircase, there's another at the end of this hall that leads downstairs and to the back."

Ella, the lady of Castle Braithar, showed me and Ariel my room, a lovely bedroom filled with light and cosy fixtures.

I couldn't stop grinning, or my thanks. "I can't believe I get to stay in a real castle."

Ella returned my smile. "It's nice for us, too. Our daughter is due to give birth in a couple of weeks, so I'm stopping work for a while to support her. Usually, this wing would be filled with musicians, come to record in my studio downstairs. None of us really like an empty castle. It's far too big for our little family." She tipped her head to the end of the hall. "Plus Ben, of course."

"He lives here, too?" I asked, pretending that information

wasn't in any way vital for me to know.

Ella nodded. "Right downstairs, not that we see him much, but it's highly reassuring to have him near."

She rattled through other information I needed as a guest, waving away my protests that I'd be in the way. Then she was gone, leaving me and Ariel alone.

I closed the door. Turned to face my friend.

"Oh my God. I have so much to share with you. How long until you have to go to work?"

She groaned and slumped on the bed. "About twenty minutes. It's so busy with classes of kids from the local schools, but I'll try to finish early. How are we meant to sort through five years of face-to-face interactions without it descending into random sobbing?"

She rolled to face me, anxiousness in her eyes. "I'm not one for crying, but damn. I was so scared you'd be taken and I'd have no way to help or find you again. Then I was imagining you being taken by some awful old man."

"I bet that woke some shitty memories for you. You were fourteen when your dad pulled you from school and tried to sell you off. I remember how you couldn't trust anyone and thought even Gabriel was in on it."

Ariel ducked her head. "I was so angry for so long. I still am. It creeps up on me, and I find myself hating at random. I don't want that for you. That's why I sent Ben. If he'd refused, I'd have come myself."

I didn't doubt her. "You'd have stormed the house, you badass."

My friend took a steadying breath. "I would've. Now tell me, are you okay? The last few days must've been the worst."

I ambled over, faking nonchalance and also wanting to stop her worrying. "Oh, I don't know. I had a lot of sex. Definitely helped take my mind off things."

Ariel pulled a comically shocked face. "You're not joking. Who...? Wait."

I grinned, loving her reaction already.

"Ben?" She finally got there.

"I'm as surprised as you are."

A cackle came, followed by a hug. "Go you. I'm surprised you broke through his stiff outer shell." Her gaze softened. "Actually, I'm not. How could he resist you? You're perfect. It's so wild seeing you in real life after five goddamned years!"

I shook my head in disbelief, never a truer word spoken. "It's not weird for you? First time I ever heard of him was from you telling me how hot he was."

Ariel gave a delighted laugh. "Yeah, when I was fourteen. I never once considered Ben as a sex object. Only for kissing practice, and that's ancient history. Please give me the details. I'm dying to hear."

Taking a seat beside her, I got on with sharing the basics of my extended hook-up. Ariel and I had been friends since elementary school. Our families' dealings set us apart from other kids, and despite the small age gap, we'd been inseparable. Her moving away had been one of the worst things that had ever happened to me, even though I'd wanted nothing more than her safety.

Now I had her back in my life and able to share subjects close to my heart—it meant the world.

I snatched her into the fifteen hundredth hug of the morning. "Stop being so perfect or I'm going to cry again."

"Bring the tears. I don't seem able to stop mine." She sniffed and clutched my arm. "Just so you know, I'm now planning your and Ben's wedding. Mostly as a ruse for you to stay here. It was going to be Raphael, but Ben will do nicely."

My happy smile dialled back a degree. "Save your confetti. Ben and I are over."

"No! Your choice or his?"

"His, or maybe both? It's for the best. I already like him too much, and we live in different countries. Plus he's going to make a fuss about being my official bodyguard and not breaching that like it's a law punishable by death."

Ariel put space between us, curling a leg underneath her. Her gaze turned shrewd. "Has he hurt your feelings?"

Several times, but after I left, I wanted them to still be friends. "I'm fine. Honestly. I'm buzzed to be here and relieved not to be trapped somewhere. Forget Ben. I have you." I turned the tables on her. "Talk Jackson to me."

Horror flitted behind her eyes. "Oh God. Something terrible happened. Hilarious-terrible, but bordering on traumatising."

"Tell me immediately."

"I got home from work to an empty house. At least I thought it was empty. No one was meant to be there, and I called out just in case. There was no answer. I was in a rush, so I stripped as I went."

She paused for effect.

My mouth dropped open. "Jackson was there?"

Ariel's eyes rounded in outrage. Two spots of pink bloomed on her cheeks. "Not only that. He walked out on me in just my panties and socks, and I thought he was an intruder. I roundhouse kicked him in the gut. It couldn't have gone worse."

A stunned moment of silence held.

I spluttered, trying not to laugh. "Holy shit."

Ariel raked back her gorgeous dark hair. "Go ahead. It's hilarious, ridiculous. I've not been able to talk to him since. But do you know the worst part? He didn't even check me out."

"Is that a bad thing? Good for him for the self-control."

"I know! I would've judged him for staring. I can't make up my mind what to hate him for." She dusted off her hands, standing with a glance to the clock on the wall. "It's all good. The whole thing killed my crush stone dead. I'm over it. Just embarrassed about how I felt."

Despite the years of distance, I still knew Ariel better than anyone else in my life. She'd resented men for a long time. Each of her crushes left her conflicted. We'd had countless conversations about whether any man could really be good. Like deep-down decent.

I believed all humans had flaws, but selfless people with truly good hearts existed. Ariel's experiences taught her to trust few. She'd never had a boyfriend because she never believed the guys who asked her out were honest. Instead, she nurtured crushes while resenting the unknowing recipients.

It was easy to see through her bravado.

It was also easy to pick up something she'd overlooked.

"You know, people tend not to stare at those they're most attracted to," I supplied. "They actively avoid it because they can't hide how they feel. Jackson's lack of interest seems different when you consider it like that."

She groaned. "I don't want to consider it. All I know is I have to live with him. He's sleeping on our sofa until he finds somewhere more permanent."

"Stay here with me tonight. We can share a bed like we

did with teenage sleepovers. Snacks, gossip, the works."

It wasn't like Ben was going to come calling. Even if he did, tough luck. I wanted to hang out with my best friend while I had the chance.

Relief settled on Ariel's features. She entwined her fingers with mine and set her head on my shoulder. "Deal. Until then, don't go anywhere alone. Ben's orders. Oh—Viola mentioned a relative stopping by to take you for a drive around. She'll fill you in. Catch you this evening."

I waved her off, happy to stay put.

At last, I felt safe.

After unpacking my few possessions into the wardrobe and drawers, I wandered out into the hall. I needed to launder the things I'd worn over the past few days, plus I wanted to explore the castle. I headed right, in the opposite direction to the steps that apparently led to Ben's apartment, emerging onto a wide, carved-wood staircase with a balcony that led down to the castle's entrance hall.

Ancient stonework climbed to the roof. Stag heads decorated the walls here and there. Groups of sofas and comfortable chairs dotted the middle of the floor below with tartan cushions. I soaked it in, a little in awe.

"Hey!" a voice hailed me from the opposite side of the stairs.

A very pregnant woman waved. She had the same open and friendly expression as Ella. There was no doubt in my mind this was Viola.

"Ye must be Daisy," she said in a lovely Scottish lilt.

I joined her and introduced myself, feeling awkward about being in her home, even if it was the size of a hotel.

But Viola only appeared happy to meet me. "If it wasn't for the fact that I can't get behind the wheel, I'd give ye a tour of the estate. Instead, my cousin Isobel is coming over in a minute to do the honours. You'll like her. She's a bit nuts."

"Sounds like my kind of woman. That's really lovely of you to organise that for me. Congratulations on the upcoming new arrival."

I gestured to her belly, and Viola rubbed a hand over the swell, the other bracing her back.

"I can't wait. Never let anyone tell ye pregnancy is a beautiful thing. It's nice for a couple of months in the middle, but the rest of it is pure misery. All I want is for my little boy to be here safely."

"You're having a boy?" My heart melted. I loved babies.

"We are. We've already got a six-year-old, Finn, who you'll meet later. Ariel will bring him home as he's going straight from the village school to a skiing lesson with her and Jamie-Beth, Isobel's youngest." She grinned at me. "There's a lot of us McRaes. Be prepared for an information overload."

My smile broadened. There was something magical about the place already. Castles in the snow and a sprawling Scottish family who all supported each other.

Viola hefted a bag she'd been holding but had dropped to her feet.

I gestured to it. "Let me carry that for you."

"Ye don't have to. It's Finn's old baby clothes that I'd had packed away, plus a load more my cousins have donated. I need to put them away in the nursery, but there's another two bags, and the thought of it makes me want to cry."

"Oh my God. I'm an expert organiser. Lead the way, and I'll do it for you."

"Are ye sure?"

"I have absolutely nothing else to do, being on the run and all. Honestly, you'll be doing me a favour."

Viola gave me a soft smile. "I know a little about what happened from my da. You're safe here. Except maybe from putting these clothes away. I'm not about to say no to the help." She directed me along the hall.

While we walked, she pointed out her bedroom, and I stole a peek. Inside the big room, a bed had a bassinet beside it, and one wall was decorated with framed photos, interspersed with a couple of shiny guitars.

I didn't look too closely. This was their personal space.

More lined the hall outside. Family pictures, professional shots of Viola snowboarding, others of her husband, Leo, performing in huge stadiums or meeting other musicians.

How lovely. To build a life together and to have the cool things you'd done on display.

In the nursery next door, I emptied the clothes bag and packed away tiny romper suits and onesies into drawers. As I worked, Viola gave me a crash course in names, which I tried to keep up with, some already familiar from Ariel's stories.

Just as we were done, Isobel arrived. A tiny Englishwoman with big energy and mechanics overalls.

She guided me to a car outside, chatting easily as Viola had done, and drove me out on the estate. I'd seen so little of it and couldn't stop staring. At the loch with its silver water, iced over in parts, at the mountain that soared above it all and the surrounding hills. We trundled through a glen, passing a distillery, a village.

All beautiful, and all so distinct from everything I'd ever known.

I had a small pang of wishing Ben was the one taking me

on the tour, but I'd also had another idea.

"Isobel, I was thinking, while I'm here and with nothing to do all day, I want to make myself useful. Do you know of anyone who needs a cleaner?"

She cocked her head at me, petite in the driver's seat and super cute. "Is that your deal? I can ask around."

I found myself telling her all about my past work. The deep cleans I used to do. The satisfaction I missed from hard work.

"Hold the phone," she interrupted. "I've got a tenant exactly like that. An elderly gent who's lived on his own since his wife died. I maintain his car, but he's lost the ability to manage his home. Last time I went there, he wouldn't even let me in because he said he hadn't tidied up. I didn't know how to help."

My heart jumped. This was exactly what I needed. However long I was here, I wanted to be useful. I didn't even care about getting paid. Ella had refused to discuss me paying rent at Castle Braithar. I'd been provided with meals and transport without question. I wasn't the type to sit back and just accept it.

I smiled at Isobel. "Can you take me there? I want to meet your client and then persuade him to let me help."

"Let me call him to arrange it for tomorrow. I can safely say you'll have work on your hands."

She drove, and my excitement grew. I had no idea what was in my future, except for the next few days, I'd be here. Safe.

But that time had a limit. It wouldn't be forever.

My words to Ariel came back to me. I'd dismissed Ben's rejection as not mattering, but it did. I had the opportunity of a lifetime on my hands. A Scottish vacation.

A fresh burst of happiness grew in me. Ben the grumpy bodyguard put the edible in incredible.

He and I weren't over.

Not until I was on a plane returning to the States.

Maybe I was just addicted to breaking his control, because, oh God, when he fell, there was nothing better. From zero, I suddenly had two challenges on my hands. Life just kept getting better.

23

Ben

A small party greeted me at Braithar when I returned from work. In the hall's entranceway, I stomped the snow from my boots and scanned the faces. Daisy sat in the centre of a group, animated in conversation with Viola, Isobel, and Ella. Nearby, Ariel chatted with Gordain.

At something one of the lasses said, Daisy smiled.

It caught me unawares, and I stalled in my footsteps, watching her.

I had information to share. But seeing her here like this, happy, and in the midst of friends was messing with my head.

Leo emerged, strolled down the stairs, and joined Ariel and Gordain. I flicked my gaze back to Daisy, some odd feeling rising inside me that I didn't want to acknowledge. In a band shirt and ripped jeans, Leo was a good-looking bastard. After Daisy teased me about it, I didn't want to see her checking him out.

That was fucked up. What the hell was wrong with me? He was my friend as much as my responsibility to protect on tour.

Something slammed into my legs.

I peered down to find Jamie-Beth grinning at me. "Hello, grumpy bear."

I arched an eyebrow at the wee girl. "Hello, disturber of sleep."

She raised the foam sword she was carrying and held it out. "That's what my da calls me. A sleep thief. Now march! You're my prisoner."

I put my hands up and strode into the hall, the foam sword poking into my spine.

Finn, who was often knocking at my door for some reason or another, leapt over with his own sword aloft. "Ben! You're back."

JB whacked my back with the sword. "Don't try to steal my prisoner."

"Jamie-Beth, don't beat up Ben," her ma said with a warning tone, pausing whatever she was doing with Daisy on a screen.

It looked like they were ordering something.

I needed to mind my own business.

I gave a shake of my head, not staring at the lass I really needed to speak to. "Don't worry. I've got this pair of mini terrors."

With a low growl, I spun around and hoisted JB onto one shoulder before lurching for Finn. He gasped in delight and turned to bolt. I snatched him up, too, and bundled him under my arm, carrying both kids to a spare armchair. I dumped them into it, tossing the foam swords across the room. Then I moved as if to sit on them.

"No!" both howled.

"What was that? Weird, this seat is lumpy."

"Stop!" JB squealed.

"Hey, Leo," I called. "Ye need to replace these armchairs. Something's wrong with them."

The rockstar laughed. "You're not sitting down hard enough. Put your back into it. Tame those cushions."

I pretended to squash the two monsters until both breathlessly agreed to leave me alone, then I peeked back at Daisy.

No one else had batted an eyelid at me getting the kids. I'd known them all since they were bairns, and they didn't hesitate to mess with me at any opportunity.

But Daisy was watching me, softness in her eyes.

She stood and came to me. "You're good with children."

I raised a shoulder. "They're uncomplicated."

Her scrutiny took me to pieces. But if she was thinking about how great a dad I'd make, she didn't immediately say.

I pivoted, dodging the bullet of that conversation before it tore into me. "If you've got a minute, I have updates."

Daisy ducked her head and followed me into the dining room.

At the table, I brought two phones from my pocket and handed one to her. "This is for ye. It's like mine and cannae be tracked, apart from by me, and only with your permission. I'll show ye how that works. Do ye remember my passcode?"

She nodded, watching me, not the phone.

"Good. It's the same to unlock yours. Change it to something you'll remember." On my own phone, I sent a quick message. "Ariel now has your number."

Daisy gripped the phone. "Thank you. I didn't expect this."

I raised a shoulder. A surge of warmth flooded me that I had no business feeling. "Didn't want ye to be out of touch. I suggest staying off social media still and being careful over who ye contact."

"I can do that. I don't want to talk to anyone. Well, not anyone who isn't already here."

Did that include me? I wanted it to. "Next, your safety protocol. We'll follow a basic set of procedures. One, ye don't go anywhere alone. Two, keep your location hidden online, as we discussed, including not letting anyone upload a photo or tag you. Three, ideally, ye should remain trackable. Preferably to me, but we can switch it to Ariel instead."

Her lips curved. "So you're saying you want to know where I am at all times."

"Only to be sure you're safe."

"Sure, Ben. I believe you. Millions wouldn't."

I glowered at her and continued on, needing to get through whatever zone I'd put us in. "I've got something else. This is a list of all the eligible men at the party. Tell me if ye know any of them, or if the names are meaningful in any way."

I read through the short list of names. Charlie Ruffalo, Andrie Bastille, twin unmarried brothers from the Lucche family. Of the attendees we'd identified, most were older and long married, so it was their sons or nephews we looked at. None had raised my suspicions, and Daisy's expression remained blank.

"I don't know any of them. I know some of the families, but not the men."

"You've never been introduced to them or heard their names mentioned?"

"No. What does that mean? I've been trying to remember anything useful, but I've got nothing."

"Same. I searched through the records ye kept from your relatives' business. Tried to match them to these families. All have connections, but there's no money owed either way that I can tell."

Daisy dug her fingers into her hair, tied up in a thick ponytail. "If they'd really been planning to marry me off, wouldn't there be something, I don't know, more? It's two tiny clues, and I'm not sure they add up."

I exhaled frustration. "If you're right, that means there was another reason for ye being kept at your aunt and uncle's. Some other plan they had for ye."

If I could work it out, it would be a lot easier to keep her safe.

She sighed, twisting the phone in her hands. "I could just ring them and ask, but I don't want to. They need to sweat. Maybe even worry about me."

"I was going to suggest exactly that."

"Calling them?" She paled, her gaze flickering. "Please don't make me. If I know they cared and I've got this all wrong, I might lose my nerve. My heart could go out to them, and I don't want to agree to go back."

I didn't want it either. "Then let's ignore that option for now. It could work better. Let them make another move. If you're an essential piece in a chess game, it'll force their hand."

"Yeah, I see that. I need to message my mother so at least she knows I'm safe, whether she's worried or not. I can probably leave that a day or two."

"Would she keep your contact secret from her brother and sister-in-law, if ye asked?"

Daisy winced. "Unlikely."

That had been my feeling, too, especially if the woman owed them money. "Would they use her to get to ye?"

"I considered that. If they were planning to, why not do it already? She was always the one hanging off them, not the other way around. It doesn't feel like she'd be at risk in any way from them."

"Good. Then stretch out contacting her as long as ye can."

"I also need to text my housemate that I'm not going to be back for a while longer. Though to be honest, I can't afford my next rent payment, so it would be better if I let the room go. Would that be okay? They don't know any of my family. Never met them."

She tipped her head back, confusion marring her typically peaceful expression.

I forced my attention off the column of her neck. How it led up to her jaw. The place under her ear I wanted to kiss.

She'd asked me a question. But before I could answer it, she gave a short laugh.

"I don't know why that made me feel blue. I never liked the apartment I was sharing. It's a dive, and one of the guys let his creepy friend have a key, so I never knew who was going to be there when I got home. I only lived there a few months, but it was not great."

"What creepy friend?" I sat forward, locking on to this new piece of information.

Daisy had given me the name of her housemates plus her ex-boyfriend, but none of them had any red flags. The boyfriend had sent messages chasing after Daisy, but he was far away on the other side of the country when she'd nearly been abducted. I'd ruled him out, while trying to ignore yet more jealous rushes over the fact he'd had his fucking hands on her.

I wanted to erase every touch with my mouth.

Daisy tapped her lip, unaware of my struggles. "His name's Landon. I knew him from high school. He was in the year between me and Ariel."

My senses whirred, homing in on this new suspect. "Why was he creepy? Give me everything ye know."

"Ariel knew him better. He was obsessed with her before she left for here. That's the reason I thought him a creep. Let's ask."

Daisy went to the door and called for her friend. Ariel joined us.

"We're talking about Landon from high school," Daisy filled her in. "Ben wants to know more about him because he was at my apartment. Do you recall his surname?"

Contempt took over Ariel's features. "Landon Larson. He used to follow me around. Tried to put his hand down my shirt when I was thirteen. Why was he at your apartment?"

"He's friends with Justin. I think they work together," Daisy replied with a shrug. "In the week or two before I inadvertently moved back in with Paul and Sigrid, Landon was sleeping over on the sofa some nights. I never got a chance to tell you."

I took a breath, too many thoughts competing in my mind. At no point in my research into the Daisy situation had anything felt clear-cut. Her relatives were up to something, but I couldn't work out what. Someone had tried to grab her from the street, for which they'd have a motive if they worked for the aunt and uncle, but the sense of urgency around it hit a brick wall.

Somebody wanted her. I didn't know why. It was driving me nuts.

At last, I had a thread to pull on that had weight to it.

"Ben?" Daisy brought my focus back to her. "Is this meaningful? Landon wasn't interested in me. I never felt in any danger from him, hence why it didn't register as being relevant."

I sent the name to Jackson.

If he had any connection to Daisy's aunt and uncle, I'd be certain of his involvement.

"I'm not sure yet. I'll look into him. Can ye call your housemate now so I can listen in?"

She jumped up. "I'll grab my phone numbers list from my bag. I made a note of all the important ones before my phone took a trip to Canada. Be right back."

Daisy left the room, and Ariel's gaze burned into me.

"What?" I asked her.

Shite. She knew. I hadn't expected Daisy to keep what we'd done a secret. I hadn't, as I'd told Gordain for the sake of my sanity. Still, Ariel's opinion wasn't going to be great.

Ariel raised a shoulder, her expression knowing. "Daisy is one of the best people I know. She's kind. She does things for other people without considering how it will affect her. Expects nothing back."

I returned her stare. "Why are ye saying this?"

"I told you before you set out to find her that people see her as easy to use. She deserves only good things. Friendship. Kindness. Love."

Some dark emotion fizzed in my veins. A burst of it I couldn't hide. It stole my retort for Ariel to butt out of my business. My denial that I'd be anything other than a friend to Daisy, since we weren't screwing anymore.

Instead, I fought to let it subside, barely managing it before Daisy stepped back in the room.

"Got it," she sang, waving the piece of paper.

I cleared my throat. "Talk me through the house share. How did ye find it?"

She tapped the number into her new phone. "Zara is the person who manages the lease. I met her at UCLA, and she knew I was looking for somewhere to live. It was never meant to be for long, and it was cheap. Should I call?"

I took her phone and showed her the call recording function, then Daisy dialled the number.

Zara answered. "Yeah?"

"It's Daisy. Sorry I've not been around."

"Oh, hey. What's happening? You're not on your way back, are you?"

Daisy wrinkled her nose. "Actually, that's what I'm calling about."

"Shit," Zara uttered. "I'm real sorry. All your things are untouched, but the room was just there, unused."

"What are you talking about?"

There was a pause. "I swear it's only temporary, but I let my cousin sleep in your bed," Zara said with a strained laugh. "Like I said, the room was sitting there empty. I knew you wouldn't care."

Daisy and Ariel shared a glance. Ariel raised her arm to demonstrate biceps. I guessed prompting Daisy to be strong.

"I'm paying for that room," Daisy said. "I might not be there, but it's mine. You had no right to do that."

Ariel mimed applause.

"O-kay," the woman drawled out the word. "She'll be gone when you finally find your way home. It's a waste, but whatever."

A voice in the background said something. Male. I locked in on the sound.

Zara returned, her tone curious. "When are you coming back anyway?"

I pointed at the phone. Daisy looked at me and caught my meaning.

"Did someone just tell you to ask? Who was that?" she said.

"Only Justin. He says someone has been by, asking for you."

"Who?"

"They didn't leave a name. Some guy."

"Can he give me a description?" Daisy pressed.

"No. This isn't an answering service. Are you keeping the room or what?" Zara snapped.

I reached out and muted the phone. "We need to ID the visitor."

Daisy dipped her head in swift agreement. "Got it."

I unmuted it, and she took a breath.

"Justin, can you hear me?"

After a beat, a voice answered, the guy drawling like he was stoned. "Yeah, what's up, Dais?"

"Can you give me a description of who came by?"

"Jesus, I don't fucking remember."

"Do you remember how you owe me twenty bucks? Search your memory," Daisy snipped.

"Old. Dark hair with white at the temples. Stick up his ass," he said, faster.

"Glasses and a suit? And with another man behind him?"

"Yeah, what of it?"

She smiled and mouthed to me, "My uncle."

Louder, she changed tack with Justin. "Doesn't matter. Is Landon around?"

"Nah. Not seen him in a week."

"Any idea where he is?"

"Prison, probably." He burst out laughing.

Daisy grimaced at the phone. "Fine. Whatever. Zara, keep my things for now. I'll arrange to get them back in a week or two. Your cousin can sleep in my room, but consider us square with rent."

"You bet. Gotta go," the housemate said and hung up.

The three of us regarded each other.

"Well, at least we know what my uncle's up to," Daisy concluded.

I switched my gaze to Ariel. "Can I talk to Daisy for a moment?"

She gave me a dark look then pressed her friend's hand and left the dining room, shutting us in.

Alone.

I ignored how my body warmed. All the urges to collect Daisy from her seat and bring her to my lap.

"I'm going to run a search on Landon-the-creep, but there was someone else I wanted to talk to ye about. As a suspect, I mean."

Her gaze travelled up from my collar to meet my eyes. "Who's that?"

This wasn't comfortable, but I forced out the name. "Valentine."

Daisy's expression registered her surprise.

"He was in the right area. He hates my guts for what happened with his ex. His vehicle is a black fucking truck, which only occurred to me today. On paper, he has the means, motive, and opportunity. I can't believe I didn't think of this before."

"He's your brother."

"I know. I can't rule him out."

"But he didn't even meet me until after you got to Olympia."

"I mentioned your name when I met him, only to make conversation about why I was in town, but that could've put ideas in his head. Maybe he even saw us arrive in Falls Ridge and thought we were a couple."

Though we'd discovered a new suspect this evening, my suspicion over Valentine couldn't be overlooked. I hated the realisation. I despised how I could've been the one to bring this onto Daisy by way of what I'd done to my family.

"I can't let my heart get in the way of my head," I said louder than I meant.

That was the case in all things. Daisy's safety was all that mattered. Including protecting her from me.

24

Daisy

Across the bed, half under the covers but with her socked feet poking out, Ariel slumbered. After dinner, we'd hung out with the McRaes, then returned to my room and watched a movie on Ariel's tablet. But my friend's very physical job exhausted her, and she was asleep before we were even a quarter of the way in.

Not that I was watching it either.

Ben hadn't reappeared.

It was no good me lying here thinking about him. He'd made his grand statement about his heart and his head, but it had come after a series of heated glances.

We'd barely started to get to know each other, but the way he stared at me warmed my whole body. I knew that look by now.

Needed to see it again.

I rose silently from the bed. Crossed the room.

But I was torn. I didn't want to force a man to break his moral code. Or his employment one. Which meant either backing away permanently or changing things up.

I'd decide which route to take when we were face to face.

Out of my room, I sloped down the hall. Quietly descended the back stairs.

In a narrow corridor with a door to the outside, I stopped by another in the left-hand wall, a slice of light underneath it.

Ben's door.

I was certain of it, as on the hook beside it, his coat hung. I'd seen him in it earlier in the evening.

I gathered my nerves and tapped.

After a moment, a lock clicked, then the door swung open. Ben loomed in the gap.

"Daisy," he said in a way that scratched an itch deep inside my brain.

To my surprise, he stepped back and made room for me to enter. I moved inside, soaking in his space while he shut us in.

I wanted clues from how he lived, but this laughed in the face of sparse. A big bed, a long desk, a computer monitor and a laptop providing the only sources of light. Pieces of tech equipment around. No photos or personal effects beyond a few items of clothing and his boots. A hanging rail for suits I guessed he wore on the job. Nothing like Viola's room upstairs with her dedication to family.

"I'm surprised you let me in," I said.

Ben returned to his desk, clicking something on the screen. "Why wouldn't I? I was just going through your relatives' finances."

Oh, the ice man was back.

I narrowed my gaze at him, though he kept his on the data.

"Find out anything new?" I ambled closer.

He raised a shoulder, clicking away from the data and bringing up a new tab. "This."

Onscreen was a photograph of an invoice that had been uploaded in the files I'd stolen, notes scrawled on it. I squinted, not following his thoughts.

"Who's handwriting is that?" Ben asked.

"Camila's." The office manager handled more invoices than me. I'd just been responsible for totalling them up.

"Look at what's underneath it."

Around the edge of the picture, on two corners, a yellow pad was just visible.

The same shade and lined like the paper used for the note left in my room.

I goggled at it, leaning in. "This is the same as the warning letter. Isn't it?"

"I'm pretty certain it's a match. Was Camila responsible for cataloguing her own invoices?"

Slowly, I nodded, trying to remember ever seeing her with a notepad. It wasn't out of the question. "She didn't trust anyone else. Only I got to see them besides her. And she was there in the house that day. Why warn me? What was in it for her?"

Ben tapped away. "She's probably the only person who can tell us that. It backs up our theory that the arrangement your relatives were entering ye into was well premeditated and not universally agreed on."

I exhaled, relieved in a way to have one small answer,

even if it didn't help overall.

"Tell me something," Ben asked. "I've been cataloguing everything in these invoices. Working out what the bigger players are into, by which I mean how dangerous they are. Ammunition and bomb manufacturing. Drug production."

I popped a hip to rest on the desk. "And worse."

He pulled back to grip the arms of his office chair. Slowly, his gaze travelled up me. "Want to know what I don't get? All of that—those criminal families, doing whatever they like. Socialising with each other while openly running destructive organisations. And then there's ye. How do ye, Daisy Devereux, come out of a place like that?"

"I'm not so special."

He didn't answer, just held his attention on me.

Amusement curled inside me, mixing with my relief that while he'd been sitting here trying to carry out research, he'd instead got stuck on thoughts of me.

What should I do? Seduce him? There was no end to the attraction between us. Here, in the intimate space, we wouldn't be disturbed.

A new realisation came to me.

The old me would've been hurt by now.

I liked him. I wanted him. But he was holding back from me. In the past, I would have taken that as rejection and hidden away to lick my wounds.

Guys always made the move. Except where we were concerned, I'd owned that.

Something new was blooming in me. Ben made me feel powerful.

He was waiting on me to speak, not challenging me, not trying to get his time back. Just existing next to me.

"I'll be out tomorrow morning," I found myself saying.

He blinked. Sat a little taller. "Where?"

"I've got a cleaning job. Isobel is taking me to pick up some equipment we ordered. Ariel loaned me the money. I'll be tackling the home of a man who lives on the estate."

His lips almost formed a smile.

Pride bloomed in my chest.

Yes, I was finding a way to be useful.

"Good. Where are ye collecting the equipment?"

"From the village on the other side of the water."

"What time will ye be done? I'll pick ye up."

It was my turn to be surprised. "I'm not sure. Perhaps about three? But you don't have to worry, Ariel will collect me."

"We'll arrange to meet her. I've got an activity planned, but it'll work to have ye both there."

"What kind of activity?"

"A self-defence lesson." Still, he gripped his chair. Like if he let go, he'd have to grab me instead. "It drives me mad to think that if that man hadn't slipped on the ice in Olympia, he could have taken ye. I'd have no idea where to find ye."

My heart clenched. I'd said on the call that I wished I'd had defence classes. And here was Ben, not only remembering but delivering. If I'd realised something about myself in coming down here, I'd also got a new lesson in all things Ben.

He cared about me.

Not just professionally, but more than that.

And for some reason, the teasing I'd half decided to do turned to something warmer.

I pushed off his desk. "I'll text you the address. See you tomorrow."

Then I leaned in, put my lips to his forehead, and left a kiss there as I walked away.

*E*arly the next morning, Isobel drove me out once again. Fresh snow had fallen overnight, but the day was clear, the sun even peeking through.

I was stupidly excited to get to work. Also for Ben's lesson later. Ariel said she'd had a text from him, ordering her presence. But if things were looking interesting between us, she'd skip out.

"Mr Campbell is the tenant in question," Isobel was saying. "He used to be a ghillie here, taking visitors deer stalking, and he must be ninety. He's a widower, no kids, and his only company is his dog, Dougal. When I met him, he had a different dog, also called Dougal, so he's a creature of habit, which is why I think he'll be really unhappy right now. Nearly every day, he would drive to the village or take a long walk around the estate, but this winter has taken its toll, and I don't see him around as much. Be aware that he can be a little morbid, though it's meant with humour."

She drove me through a wide valley she named as Glen Durie, and into the forest. We pulled up in a clearing outside a pretty cottage. It reminded me of the log cabin Ben and I had stayed in, but better. Bigger, and more of a home.

Isobel hopped out, and I followed.

"It used to be a lot more isolated here," she told me, opening the trunk. "But my place isn't far, and my husband's brother, Blayne, built a house just over there with his husband and wife. They have three kids."

She pointed out a rooftop, visible beyond the trees.

"Did you say his husband *and* wife?" I asked.

"Yup. They're a throuple. A three-adult committed relationship. Brodie, his male other half, tells people Blayne is big in all ways. His height, his heart, and then people yell at him to stop talking."

We both snickered at the innuendo.

The cottage door opened with a creak.

Isobel had already called ahead to arrange my visit with the tenant, so I collected my bucket of products and brushes, my mop, and the vacuum I'd borrowed from the castle. At the door, Mr Campbell waited, stooped over and with an expectant expression. Dougal the dog yapped a couple of times by his feet.

"Yes, yes," he said to his dog. "We have visitors. It's all right." Then he raised his gaze back to us.

"This is Daisy?" he said to Isobel.

"Pleased to meet you. I'm happy to help," I replied.

"Are ye crazy?" the old man uttered.

I blinked at him. "No, sir."

"Grand. I was just checking because ye might be by the end of it and the fault will be mine. Now the worst of it is the kitchen, so you're to stay downstairs. When I'm dead and gone, someone will need to fix all this. Might as well make a start now."

"We want it nice for you," Isobel assured him.

"Whatever ye say. I'll be in my chair. If I fall asleep and

don't wake up, it was grand to have met ye. Come now, Dougal."

He ambled back inside, not waiting for me to wrangle my items to the door.

Isobel turned around and helped. "Do you need me to stay? I can hang around for a bit."

I shook my head. Through the door, I could make out a dark hallway that led to a big kitchen. Food containers and plates covered each surface, but this wasn't anywhere near the extremes I'd dealt with in the past.

"No need. I'll get to work. Thank you for this."

"Thanks to you. You're an absolute saint."

She closed me inside, then she was gone.

I breathed in slightly dusty air then tracked Mr Campbell down to the living room. "Hello," I said loudly. "I'm going to make a start. Is there anything you need right now?"

He gave me a wheezy smile. "Look at that, I'm still alive. Meals on Wheels will bring me my lunch at eleven, so if ye hear the door, it'll be them. Good luck to ye out there. I haven't seen those countertops in at least a year. Can't manage it anymore."

"That's what I'm here for."

His little white dog poked its nose around the side of his chair.

I crouched and put out a hand. "This is Dougal? Hey, puppy."

"Dougal the third. Or maybe the fourth."

The terrier was a youngster but clearly not used to strangers. He gave my hand a sly lick then hid back behind his master's legs. I left them alone and travelled back to the kitchen.

It was a good size, with a solid oak table and heavy chairs. The huge, ancient range cooker delighted me—I'd never used one before and had always wanted to. But every single surface was covered with grime, spills, and sticky messes. The only clean spot was Dougal's food and water bowls.

For some reason, the thought of the elderly man using his small amount of strength to look after his pet got me in the gut.

This was why I loved my job. I could do for Mr Campbell what he did for Dougal.

With that motivating me, I snapped on a pair of cleaning gloves, popped in a headphone, one ear only so I could stay alert for any sounds, and pressed play on the audiobook I'd transferred to my new phone. At the last second, I texted Ben my address, not getting an immediate reply.

That was fine. Right now, I had this.

Later, I'd have him.

Ben wanted to teach me self-defence. He really had to watch out for himself.

25

Ben

little before three, I rolled up to the address Daisy had given me, Jackson alongside in my car.

I climbed out and jogged to the door. Knocked.

It opened under my hand, and laughter came from inside.

"Hello the house," I called.

A small white dog scampered down the hall, barking at me. I stooped to stroke its fluffy head.

"Who is it, Dougal?" the homeowner called, on a slow amble after his dog.

I'd seen the elderly man in passing but had never spoken to him.

"Ben Graham," I introduced myself.

"Here for Daisy. I know. We're expecting ye. Come in, see what she's done," he ordered, ushering me into the house and towards the kitchen.

In the bright and clean space, the air scented with cleaning products and every surface glistening, Daisy stood with her back to me, taking something from the oven.

I narrowed my eyes at the bone-shaped treats on her baking tray. "Are those dog biscuits?"

Daisy turned and grinned, setting the tray down on a board. "Correct. I had some time left over and offered to bake. I'm no good as a chef, but I can make treats. Mr Campbell chose these for Dougal rather than something for himself. They're peanut butter dog cookies."

The old man shuffled past and peered at her efforts.

"Leave them to cool, then box them up in a container," she ordered and took off her apron. "According to the recipe, they'll store well for a couple of months."

"Longer than me. I'll be in my grave by then," Mr Campbell mused. He picked up a cookie and snapped it in two, waving both halves in the air to cool them.

His dog drooled.

Bringing my attention back to Daisy, I almost did the same. Her cheeks were pink from the work, but there was more, too. Happiness shone from her.

She chattered away with the homeowner, collecting together her bucket of cleaning goods. I grabbed the bigger pieces of equipment and carried them out to my car, returning to take a few bin liners of rubbish, too.

With Dougal the dog snarfing down his cookies and Mr Campbell thanking Daisy quietly while she promised to return for a service clean, if she was still around in a week, it took a minute to get her outside, too.

There, she showed me her phone screen. "Before."

I glanced at the picture. The same kitchen but a real mess. Junk everywhere.

A chill slid over me that had nothing to do with the snowy day. "Ye cleared all that up? It's unrecognisable."

Daisy beamed. "I did. It definitely helped having a romance story to listen to. Gave me an idea or two as well."

That, I could focus on. Thinking of things I wanted to do with Daisy, though I'd sworn off trying. Not the familiarity of having to visit with someone who lived in a worse state than Mr Campbell had been.

The smell. The rage that went with trying to help.

"You're amazing," I finally managed.

Daisy squinted, apparently spotting Jackson in the car. "Are we still having a lesson?"

"Yep. Jackson's your trainer. He taught self-defence so knows his stuff. I'm just there to practice your moves on."

"And you still want to pick up Ariel?"

"I thought you'd like her there."

She tilted her head, amusement flirting with her lips. "Should be interesting. Let's go."

I drove us to Castle McRae, having arranged to use the open space of the great hall for the lesson.

Daisy wandered into the ancient space, her eyes wide. "I haven't been here yet. It's different to Castle Braithar."

I tried to see it from her view. I'd been here so often, I got used to it. The stone floor and walls that led up to an exposed beam ceiling like the skeleton of a Viking ship. The huge fireplace where a blaze always burned. "It's older. Braithar was built because twin brothers split the estate centuries ago. Gordain told me the story once."

"Holy cow. I can't believe Ariel lives here."

On cue, the lass in question trotted out from an almost hidden corridor that led from her tower to the back of the great hall.

Ariel's gaze shot straight to Jackson. His, likewise, trained on her.

"What are you doing here?" she asked.

"I'm your instructor," he replied.

Ariel worked her jaw. "Is there anything you can't do?"

Daisy's *interesting* comment made sense. I knew Ariel was partial to him, but I'd assumed Jackson had her in his sights in a protective mode. Now, I wasn't so sure.

At her back, Raphael appeared. "All right if I sit in? I've been in a cockpit all day. I could use something more physical."

Daisy held her gaze on me for a moment, then stepped purposefully towards Ariel's brother. "Awesome," she chirped. "You can be my sparring partner."

Tension tightened my belly.

It was fine. Daisy needed the instruction. It didn't matter that she'd be grappling a man who had a crush on her.

Jackson shucked off his jacket and took his position. "Right, everyone ready? Back in university, I taught a class in self-defence. Not just for women, but for anyone who, like Daisy said on the phone, felt they needed tactics to be able to escape an attack."

Daisy tilted her head at him. "Did you have guys on your course?"

He dipped his head. "Sometimes. Not every guy is an alpha arsehole. Men fear men, too."

Ariel snorted and looked away.

Jackson gave Ariel a quick glance but started the lesson, first giving a thoughtful walk-through of how to avoid confrontational situations that Daisy complimented him on for being non-patronising. As an assessment of his leadership skills, I liked what I was seeing.

But knowing what I did about his past, I picked up the edge of need in him to push certain ideas. About being cautious with trust and not putting yourself in a vulnerable situation. He gave his examples then paused, his mind seeming to go elsewhere for a moment.

If I'd blinked, I would've missed it. Jackson was driven by his demons, though I appreciated the method he'd found for exorcising them.

Then he directed the two lasses to stand before him.

"Daisy, Raphael is going to act as your sparring partner, as ye put it. It's important to remember that this is just practice, with the objective to gain the ability to get free and get away, not to fight. If any part of it feels alarming, call a stop and he'll instantly disengage."

Daisy grinned. "Don't worry. I'm looking forward to this. Bring it, Raph."

Raphael moved in front of her, and a winding sense of urgency built in me. So much that I missed Jackson's next words, only tuning back in when Daisy spoke.

Raphael held her by the wrists, her arms raised in front of her.

"I can't get free," she said, wrestling him, her cheeks pink. "This is exactly what I've been imagining. Any guy who does this is stronger than me. Tell me how to free myself."

"Ye can, I promise. Get your elbow above his wrist," Jackson instructed. "Bring his hand down towards your belly and get your elbow into that higher position."

Daisy obeyed, getting Raphael's hand down. He put up some resistance but let her manoeuvre him for the sake of the lesson.

"Good," Jackson said. "Now's your chance. Bring your elbow down sharply and twist his arm to break his grip."

Daisy did exactly that, yanking her wrist free. "I did it!"

Raphael gave a playful growl and snatched hold of her again. "Ye missed a crucial element. Do it with both arms then run."

Daisy laughed, not showing any signs of distress at the reminder of her near abduction. They started over.

Meanwhile, I was descending into a far worse state.

Practically seething.

That ridiculous jealousy was back, but stronger. More urgent. Perhaps because of the reminder that someone had tried to take her, but I was rigid with it.

My hands balled into fists.

Raphael was touching her skin. *Laughing* with her. She was beaming at him. And instead of being happy that she'd gained a skill that would help her, I was...furious.

"Ben, will ye buddy up with Ariel?" Jackson asked.

It was a reasonable request, but I couldn't stop the feelings. If any of them took too close a look at me, they'd see. I needed to get out.

"I have things to do. Show her yourself," I grumped. "Ariel, will ye take Daisy home?"

At her nod, and a glimmer of amusement I had to ignore, I left them to their fun and got the fuck away.

26

Daisy

Ben stomped out of the hall, pulling the heavy oak door closed behind him. I shot my delighted gaze to Ariel, finding her already grinning at me. She lifted her eyebrows once, and I gave her a nod that said we'd talk it through later.

There was no doubt over what had just happened.

Jackson continued the lesson, Ariel insisting on her brother taking up the role of her attacker.

After a few rounds of escape, we called it quits.

"Good work," Jackson said. "Ye now have an action to practice. If you're still here in a few days, Daisy, I'll find time for a second lesson."

I thanked him, then he and Raphael left the castle, heading off somewhere together.

Ariel snatched up my hand and tugged me with her, guiding me through the hall to the doorway. Together, we climbed a spiral staircase into her tower.

I'd made this trip on video chat countless times but cooed over every bit of it.

"We have way more interesting things to cover than that," Ariel said when we reached the top floor and her living room.

A wide sofa curved against the tower wall, narrow windows behind it. At the end, a pillow and neatly folded blanket showed me this was where Jackson had been sleeping.

Ariel sat at the other end and patted the cushion. "Time to dissect how Ben reacted to my brother touching you. Like, damn. That grown-ass man turned into a hormonal teenager in front of my eyes. He was seething. Steam coming out of his ears."

Warmth flashed through my veins, and I perched beside her. "Do you really think that's what happened?"

"Oh my God. Without a doubt. The question is, what are you going to do about it?"

I took a deep breath and slumped back. "Honestly? I'm not sure. He made it very clear we were off. That he couldn't do his job if he's seeing me. And then he goes and acts like that." I gestured up and down my body. "And I look like this. I've been cleaning all day. I've washed up, but my clothes are gross, my hair's a mess, and I'm sweaty again, too."

Ariel gave a happy sigh. "You're missing the bigger picture."

I pondered that. "That it isn't just physical."

"No, that you're irresistible to him regardless. I'm not saying break him, lock that down, and move here permanently, though that would be sweet. I'm just pointing out that Ben isn't treating you like a hook-up he's lost interest in. He had to walk away or else lose control. Feel the power of that?"

She jumped up. "Now go take a shower. I'm going to cook us dinner over which we're going to talk about anything other than men." She raised a hand to stop me interrupting with a Jackson-shaped question. "After which, I'll drive you back, and you're going to Ben's room to have a conversation. Decide when you get there exactly how that's going to go down."

A few hours later, I was back at Castle Braithar and in my bedroom. It wasn't late, only a little after nine, but the place was quiet. People off doing their own things in their own spaces.

I didn't even know if Ben was downstairs. His car was outside, but that wasn't a sure thing.

All evening with Ariel, I'd forced him out of my mind. My best friend and I had endless things to say to each other. The conversation never stopped. Raphael had returned, and we'd started all over again, catching up, sharing memories of being at school together. The major and minor life events we'd been through. Everything I'd wanted for such a long time.

Now I was alone, my mind switched back to the grumpy bodyguard.

To the bolt of lust I'd felt then concealed when his dark eyes had flashed with jealousy.

As a minimum, I needed to call him on his behaviour.

That didn't explain why I was opening my top drawer and taking out pretty underwear to change into. Extracting my vibrator and bundling it in a shirt. Carrying it with me from my room and downstairs.

That same slice of light was under his door, and when I knocked, he was just as quick to answer.

"We need to talk," I announced, strolling in.

The same severe grouchiness hung heavily on his brow, the room shadowy like before. He didn't reply, just closed us in and sank back into his office chair. But he turned it to face me. I took a perch at the bottom of his bed, a couple of feet from him.

Expectation held the air tense. My body alive with it.

This was my decision point. Demand more from him or cut him off.

But then he spoke, stealing my initiative. "Don't ask for an apology for earlier. I can't give it."

I rested back on one hand, the T-shirt-wrapped vibrator on my lap. "I didn't come here for that."

Ben's gaze soaked me in. I'd changed clothes into a close-fitting blouse and a high-waisted skirt. More my style, but not suitable for cleaning work or cold wintry days. Nothing like what he'd seen me in before. Underneath, I'd chosen lacy black panties with a matching bra.

All of it flattering. Making me feel more worthy of the emotions I'd sparked in him.

"Then ye want an explanation," he concluded, his attention lingering on the concealed object in my hands.

"Not that either."

He linked his gaze to mine. "Then what?"

I took in a steadying breath. "You're getting it the wrong way around. I came here to fill you in. Or at least check you knew what was happening."

He didn't answer. Just continued watching me.

That heady focus boosted my confidence. I could almost feel his touch on my skin.

I scooted back on the bed. "Your jealousy returned in force this evening. It must be driving you insane. But I know what's behind it and how to solve it."

I plucked the T-shirt from my lap and discarded it. Ben took in my vibrator, his expression shifting from that grumpy coolness to one less certain. I flicked the switch to turn it on, the hum filling the room.

Then I ran my hand over it, my breathing hitching. "The problem is that you like me, and that's a big deal for you. I wonder if it's ever happened to you before. When we first hooked up, I had the once-only speech, but we broke that over and again. Then you had this whole deal that you couldn't protect me and sleep with me, but that theory was blown out of the water today because you were so distracted you had to leave. So, I'm here to tell you that you're wrong. And I'm asking for you to admit it."

As I spoke, I moved the vibrator to my chest. Between my boobs.

Ben's gaze sank to follow the action. He'd listened to me, and there was no immediate denial.

God, maybe I was right.

Emboldened, I glanced it over my nipple and gasped.

With his back to the monitor, the sole source of light in the room, Ben's expression was half in shadow, but I felt the weight of his stare.

I inched my skirt up my thighs, lying back to bring my feet up onto the bed. In this position, all I had to do was open my legs to be all but bared to him.

He shifted in his office chair and adjusted his dick.

A smile caught my lips, so I tipped my head back to hide it and ran the vibrator down my body. With my free hand, I inched the tight skirt higher until it was under my ass, then I drew the toy down my leg and underneath my hem.

Ben growled something I couldn't make out.

"All you have to say is that you like me," I told him.

Then I parted my knees and touched the toy between my thighs.

It hit my clit through my panties. I hissed in pleasure.

I'd never once done anything like this. A full-on seduction, though I didn't expect him to join in. If anything, I knew he'd be holding his position. Breaking his chair in the process.

But he wasn't stopping me. That denial wasn't forthcoming.

I shifted my feet a few inches wider apart, running a finger under my underwear. Then I pulled it aside to expose myself, picking up on yet another pained sound from Ben.

"What are ye doing to me?" he asked.

I grinned. "Pretty sure I'm doing this to myself. The question is how far I take it."

I ran the vibrator over my skin again, this time dipping it into my wetness. I pictured myself from his perspective, laid out for his viewing pleasure. My legs wider still and a clear line of sight to my glistening core.

Did he want to jump up and join in?

More, I hoped he wouldn't. I needed those words more than actions this time.

"This feels so good," I informed him. "Let me tell you how much I like this toy. It really does the job. Not that I've tried many. I saw one that simulates sucking your clit while it fills you, that looked cool." Another pass up and down. "Ooh, there's a type that sticks to the wall of your shower so you can fuck yourself under the flow of water. I really like that idea."

Ben growled out in agony.

Gathering even more courage, I reached for the elastic and stripped my panties off entirely, tossing them his way. Then I returned to my position and sank the head of the vibrator inside me.

My moan sounded loud in the room.

I'd only meant to tease myself, but it showed how ready I was. Ben's dick was bigger than my toy. It was him I wanted. Still, not yet. Not without that confession.

Pulling it out, I glided it from my entrance and back to my clit, touching lightly before easing it back down. As I played, I reached under my blouse to caress my nipples.

"Fuck," Ben muttered.

This whole scene was deeply erotic to me. The control I had. How each time I pushed the toy inside me, Ben gave me such delicious reactions.

And I was so turned on. If I'd lingered over my clit, the vibrations would send me over the edge. I didn't want that. It was too soon. Instead, I thrust it deeper and brought my free hand to make slow circles over my clit.

I had it on the lowest setting, but God.

"What do ye want me to do?" Ben asked. "Take over and fuck ye? Suck your tits? Tell me."

I shook my head, urgency building, though I kept the pace exact. "Stay right there. You know what I want. Tell me you like me."

"Christ, woman."

"I'm not going to come until you talk."

A pulse jerked me. *Not yet.* I flicked the vibrator's switch off, now just fucking myself with it.

Something cracked, then Ben was looming over me. I peered up to see his seat tipped over on the floor. His gaze ardent and on me.

He didn't touch me, as if knowing I'd tell him to stop. Instead, he took in my expression, the stretch of my blouse over my breasts, then he prowled down the bed, settling by my feet.

"Make yourself come," he ordered.

"Say the words."

A long pause came. I continued fucking myself, getting closer with every pass. I was barrelling towards the finish whether I liked it or not. Stopping would be a punishment.

I wasn't sure I could do it.

Then just as I was closing in on the path of no return, Ben's restraint broke. "Fuck. Fine. Ye want to hear it? Here it is. I'm fucking obsessed with ye. I think about ye every minute of the goddamn day, and I dream about ye in the night. You're always on my mind. I worry where ye are and what you're doing. I plan around where you'll be. I don't want to stop. Aye, I like ye, Daisy Devereux. Now fucking make yourself come and say my name as ye do it."

My chest heaved. I sucked in air.

Flicked the switch.

A few hard circles on my clit, the vibrator plunging in and out of me, and Ben's words were all I needed.

I came, pulsing hard. Blissful abandon reached.

Just as he ordered, I said his name, several times, the climax spectacular. The relief instant.

Then I killed the vibrations and pulled the toy out of me, my eyes closed and nothing but happiness chasing the pleasure. I panted, steadily coming down from the high.

And when I finally cooled and opened my eyes, I didn't linger.

Ben had backed to the wall, his hands behind him, every visible muscle strained. I leapt up, straightened my clothes, and bundled the vibrator in the T-shirt again. Then I wished him a smart good night and slipped back to my own bed.

27

Daisy

Bright and early, Viola knocked on my door. Finn stood beside her in a school uniform, and I grinned at how cute he was.

"I come with a message," Viola said. "I hope I didn't wake ye."

"Yes, but I'm grateful. I needed to get up."

After my experience with Ben last night, I'd crashed out and slept hard. Ten hours, from a quick glance at the clock.

"Mr Campbell drove to the village last night and talked ye up to everyone in the pub. You've got customers. People who want to pay ye to clean their homes."

My jaw dropped. "You're kidding."

"Nope. Leo's taking Finn to school, but afterwards, he's available as a driver. That's if ye want the work," she added.

"I do," I said, fast.

My day unfolded around the new bookings. Chauffeur driven by a rock star, no less, I headed into the town on the other side of the loch, taking care to text Ben my whereabouts. The first job was for a woman with three kids under five. The oldest attended preschool, but her two-year-old twins were home all day with her, her husband working away on an oil rig.

She almost cried with relief when she returned from putting her girls down for their morning nap to find the downstairs spick-and-span.

"Please tell me we can make this a regular thing," she begged. "When I heard about ye last night from my da who'd been in the pub with Mr Campbell, it answered all my prayers. We don't have anyone close by who will do work like this. Believe me, I've tried."

"I'm not sure how long I'll be staying," I admitted.

Her hope dissolved into a slump of shoulders. "I understand. You're a long way from home. Well, I hope to see ye again before ye leave."

Ben waited for me outside her house.

I blinked. "I was expecting Ariel."

He shrugged, hands shoved in his pockets. Snow drifted around him. "She's busy, ye needed transport to the next place. And I don't know if ye noticed, but it's lunchtime."

I squinted at him, but he passed me and picked up my cleaning goods then loaded them into the car. Once I'd climbed into the passenger seat, I realised what he meant.

A brown paper bag waited on the dashboard, and a Thermos in the drink holder.

Ben had brought me lunch.

He clipped himself in beside me, sparing me short glances. I peered into the bag.

"A grilled cheese and tomato sandwich. How did you know I liked these?"

He wouldn't meet my eyes. "On our West Coast drive, ye ordered it. Figured it was a safe bet."

I could kiss him for noticing. Remembering.

Instead, I grinned big and tucked in. "Even more proof of how much you like me."

Ben didn't answer but drove me up the hill to the next house. Here, I had a bigger task on my hands than surface cleaning as with the last place.

"I'll be done around six-ish, I think," I told Ben, finishing my last bite and dabbing my lips with the paper towel he thought to include.

"Ariel will come. I'll be out this evening, probably until late. I'm taking Jackson to meet a contact in Inverness. Someone I occasionally work with."

Which meant he wouldn't be in his room if I came down. I watched him for a moment, just letting the simplicity of what he'd done today sink in. Then I unclipped myself, turned in my seat, and pressed my lips to his.

It was quick, no time for him to kiss me back, and as I got on with the afternoon's work, I wished I'd given it another half second. Just to see if he was going to meet me in it. But that was a question for another day. We both had work, and I'd stopped feeling like the clock was ticking down so aggressively.

Ben wasn't going anywhere, and for now, neither was I.

The next day, I had another cleaning job lined up for an elderly person who lived on the estate. Ariel had a day off so drove me there.

Outside the cottage, she held up her phone. "Go do your thing and call me when you need collecting."

"I feel bad that we can't hang out together all day."

Ariel shrugged. "Don't be. You're thriving at this. It's a pleasure to see. You always wanted to run this kind of business, and in a matter of days, you've got customers and a reputation. You're amazing. So I am very happy to play protector and drive you around."

"You make a very pretty bodyguard." I hugged her then got to work.

At this property, the homeowner followed me around talking non-stop. I didn't mind. I found people endlessly interesting, particularly the older generation who had countless stories to share and didn't shy away from spilling the tea. It meant I didn't check my phone until I was packing away, and I had a message from my grumpy bodyguard.

Ben: I found out something I need to share with you. Can I see you over lunch?

Daisy: Meet me at Castle McRae in an hour.

He sent back a short agreement, and I loaded the waiting car in a hurry.

"Where's the fire?" Ariel asked. Her cheek had a rumpled line in it like a pillow mark from napping.

"Did you go home and get back in bed?" I asked.

"A little bit. Jackson had the morning off, so he was in the tower. It was either lounge in my room or hang out with him. If you hadn't messaged me, I would've missed my lunch with Effie. By the way, do you want to come with me?"

I pulled a face. "I can't, but I need to ask a favour. Can I borrow your car over lunchtime? I want to take Ben on a date."

She lifted her eyebrows. "Of course you can. Effie's going to pick me up anyway. Question is, will Ben actually go?"

"I'm not going to give him a choice."

As fast as I could on the snowy road, I drove back to Castle Braithar, dragging Ariel with me to help me pick an outfit. Then it was back in the car to drop her off at Castle McRae. She wished me good luck, and I sat and waited for Ben.

On the dot, his car cruised around the corner.

I sent him a message.

Daisy: Follow me.

Then I pulled away in Ariel's little Mini. Within seconds, his much bigger 4x4 loomed in my rearview mirror.

A thrill ran up my spine.

On the passenger seat, my phone buzzed. I answered it on hands-free.

"Hey, Ben."

"Where are we going?" His voice sounded loud in the close confines of the car.

"Somewhere."

"Stop and I'll drive us."

"Tempting, but no. Sometimes, you're going to have to let me decide what we're doing."

"Daisy—"

I hung up, cutting him off. Then I concentrated on the route in my mind. I wasn't down for taking any risks or worrying Ben in any way. Instead, I drove uphill on the winding road that climbed the mountain. We passed signs on the way for our destination, so it could be no surprise when we finally emerged at the snowboarding centre, high up on the mountaintop.

Ariel worked here, though not today, and had told me about the café with big wraparound windows that looked out on snowy slopes and a gorgeous view.

I climbed from the car and instantly regretted my decision.

Ben paced over, his collar turned up against a flurry of snow.

"God, it's freezing up here," I stated the obvious.

The corner of his lips curved. "There's a reason everyone else is walking around in skiwear. What are we doing here?"

I started moving, because if I didn't, I'd freeze on the spot. "You have information to share with me, and I'm taking you on a coffee date."

He paused in following me.

I turned to see his expression flatten.

For a horrible moment, I thought he was going to refuse.

In my head, this had been a cute gesture. A way of showing that I liked him, too. I wanted to do nice things for him that weren't just appearing in his room for sex acts. Though I had that in mind, too.

I'd misjudged things badly.

But then he moved again, reaching for me as he passed. He laced his fingers through mine and tugged down his sleeve to cover my hand from the chill.

Time sped up again, and my heart thumped.

Every little gesture from him was somehow more poignant and meaningful than if he'd bought me diamonds or yelled to a crowd that he thought I was beautiful.

It meant more because he gave up so little.

Maybe because he felt less, or because revealing anything was more difficult for him than most. I didn't know, but I was only getting more desperate to work him out.

Inside the centre's entryway, a couple of people called out a greeting to him.

"Hey, Blayne, this is Daisy," he said to one—a huge man I remembered Isobel talking about.

He repeated the introduction with the second person, another McRae. We passed a shop with brightly coloured ski and snowboarding clothes, then entered the café. It was busy, but not so much that we couldn't find a table. Ben guided me to a seat but remained standing. He read the choices from the board for me and took my order, disappearing to place it.

On his return, he carried a tray, his usual frown still there.

I wanted to congratulate him on his date etiquette. Introducing me around, managing the food order. All green flags. But I also wanted him to smile. To relax.

We tucked into the food, snow obscuring what I guessed to be a pretty view, but that was okay. I only had eyes for Ben.

"Business first?" he asked once we'd finished.

I wondered what else he had in mind for our conversation. "Shoot."

"I found out something more about your relatives this morning I thought you'd like to know. Does the address Madison Heights mean anything to ye?"

I searched my memory. "Only that it's a highly exclusive apartment block. Mafia families live there. Why?"

"I've been following the flow of money and discovered your aunt recently made two very expensive purchases. The first was jewellery, and the second was an apartment in that block."

His words painted a gloomy picture. "And you think it was for me, right? I was to be sold off as a bride and kept in a gilded cage."

He twisted his lips, some darker thoughts haunting his

eyes. "Perhaps. It's not clear-cut, but if they were seeking an alliance, that might be a clue as to who with."

I exhaled disappointment. For the past couple of days, I'd tried to forget my life in California. I wanted to enjoy my time here. But I couldn't pretend it hadn't happened. Particularly when it was still an active threat against me.

"The only real way to be sure is to talk to my family," I concluded. "But I still don't want to. I really don't want to know their explanation. They'll lie and try to manipulate me."

The last thing I wanted was to hear from Paul's or Sigrid's lips that they'd planned to use me. Or worse, to be persuaded to see it from their point of view. Despite everything, I loved them. They were family, and I'd known them all my life. They'd protected me when I needed it, and even if they didn't love me in the way I'd loved them, they'd still been there. More than anyone else in my life besides Ariel.

Their rejection would break me. It had already started. I could feel the edges of the tear. I didn't want it to rip right through.

"Is there anyone else who'd know?" Ben asked.

"I'm not sure. Maybe their daughters, or perhaps Camila. I'm not sure I'd trust her to be honest, even knowing what we know."

"Talk to me about the daughters. Ye said they were no longer close."

I gave an unhappy laugh. "They're clearly smarter than me. Got away and never looked back. Gianna probably wouldn't take my call, but Luna might. She lives in London."

Ben tipped his chin at my phone. "Text her. Just be cautious about what ye reveal."

Robotically, I brought out my phone and searched for

Luna online. I'd been following her, though we never talked. I tapped out a message. She'd know it was me from my account.

Daisy: Hey. I need to talk to you. Are you around for a call? Please don't tell your mom and dad.

It didn't light up to show as read, but Ben's phone rang. He apologised to me, and I waved him to go ahead. While he spoke, I clicked through to my mom's profile.

She'd shared pictures from her new business venture, now named Daisy's Delights. In every pic, she had her boobs out with star stickers providing the tiniest bit of dignity. In one, a mop handle stuck out from between her legs.

I didn't want to judge her, but damn, Mom.

She definitely didn't seem like she was missing me or in any distress. I shut it down.

Ben ended his call. His expression softened. "Ruined our lunch by talking about that first, didn't I?"

Lunch. I'd been corrected. Not a date.

"It's fine. I need to get the car back to Ariel anyway."

The urgency was all mine, but misery had swarmed me, wrapping around my emotions.

I didn't want to share this side of me. The unhappy version. If anything, I wanted to curl up in a ball and hide.

Ben seemed to understand. He cleared our table and walked me out.

In the cold fresh air, I made a decision. I'd take the afternoon to sulk, cry on the shoulder of my best friend, then be done with it.

"I'm coming to your room tonight," I told the man I wished I could do it all with.

He held my gaze, even if he didn't want to hold my heart.

"I know."

28

Daisy

Ben's door opened under my fist. He regarded me, his only clothing the pair of grey sweatpants I'd seen him wear before. Tonight, a lamp graced his desk, the warm glow illuminating his bare chest.

"Hey, shortie."

I stepped inside. He locked the door.

I could ask about the new lamp, or maybe just assume he'd suddenly realised he needed better lighting in here. But I wasn't in the mood for chat.

He moved behind me, not touching but close enough to give me shivers. "Why did ye run from me earlier?"

I turned. Pressed my fingertips to his chest. "Get on the bed."

If he thought my lack of conversation rude, the impression didn't last. Ben watched me for a second then prowled to the dark-blue bedspread. He reclined, clearly waiting on my next move.

I'd spent hours thinking about this. About his rules and responsibilities.

I'd considered all the ways a bodyguard wasn't allowed to fraternise with a client and rejected them out of hand.

I closed in until I was standing right in front of him. This evening, I'd chosen a purple bra, my only other decent piece of lingerie in the small bag of clothes I'd brought, no panties, covering up with another high-waisted skirt and a long-sleeved flowing top. None of it would stay on me long. Not if I played this right.

Ben's appreciative gaze soaked me in. "You're beautiful. Ye were fucking gorgeous making yourself come on my bed."

A little tremor ran through me. His compliments meant more than I could say. I needed to know he wanted me.

"Move back," I managed, though my voice was tight. "All the way up against the pillows. Then hold the headboard."

He obeyed, until his shoulders were against the heavy wooden slats. His hands loosely cupping the square corners.

I exhaled, scared but excited more. I needed him to let me do this with no objection. So far so good.

I knelt at his bare feet and ran my hands over the upper side. Big feet, unsurprisingly. But this was something I'd never done. Explored all of him in the way I wanted to. I had pieces of Ben. Snapshots of his body and his mind. It was impossible to think I could have it all, but I inched my hands up his ankles all the same, sliding over his taut calf muscles, his rough leg hair tickling me.

"These need to go." I tugged on the legs of his sweatpants.

Ben's chest rose and fell. "Undress me then."

He lifted his ass and let me slide them down. Underneath, he was naked. His dick already hard and springing free.

My mouth watered, but I wasn't going there yet, no matter how tempting.

I continued my perusal, feeling the thickness of his thighs and the power within them before straddling them and grazing my fingers over his hips, the V muscle I could never remember the name of.

Ben was beautifully made. His waist leading to tensed abs. His chest broadening, and all that ink mine to lay tracks over. Avoiding his dick, I bent to press a kiss to his shoulder. Another to his collarbone.

Even with boyfriends, I'd never done anything so intimate as this. The mapping of a man, the layering of information on his perfect form.

Until now, he'd let me explore, shifting slightly underneath me but simply tolerating me taking what I needed, but then Ben brought his hand to my loose hair, fallen forward to cover my face.

He twisted it round his fist, muttering, "In the way."

I held his gaze for a second then nodded, taking the tie from my wrist and whipping up a quick ponytail. "Better?"

He didn't smile. "Better."

Like me, he needed to see. I was a little bit in love with that.

Next, I collected his hands in mine, releasing them from the grip he'd returned them to on the bed so I could detail his strong fingers and thick wrists. Toned forearms and rounded biceps.

He flexed.

I gave a short laugh.

"Grip the posts again. Don't let go."

At last, I could centre on his face. I knew this best of all. The solemn expression he typically wore and how the smallest change to his features expressed great emotion, but only if you were really looking. No one could ever accuse him of wearing his heart on his sleeve. Ben's heart was buried deep down.

I doubted I'd ever catch a true glimpse of it.

Though he let me take control now, it was still on his terms. Everything was.

I traced over his jaw, then pressed his earlobe between my finger and thumb. Just lightly.

He groaned. Under me, though I wasn't putting any weight on him, his dick pulsed again. Fascinated, I repeated the action with his ear, tugging gently.

Ben closed his eyes for a second, his mouth open on a breath. "How is ye touching my damn ears so erotic?"

I didn't answer, instead grazing my fingernails into his hairline, lightly scratching his scalp.

This time, his groan came louder.

My breath hitched. Erotic didn't even describe it. Between my thighs, I was so wet. My body humming with need, the edge of it urging me to speed up, to abandon the slow tease.

Ben clenched his jaw. "Strip for me."

"No." But then I made a concession, opening the first three buttons of my blouse.

His gaze sank to my tits, pushed up in the pretty bra.

"I need you to know I respect your professional vow," I told him, even more shaky but determined in what I had to do. "Not the one about never sleeping with the same person twice. That doesn't work, and you already abandoned it, but your job is your life. I don't want to do anything to damage that."

Ben's eyes flashed with a dark light. "Fuck my job."

I nearly laughed but held it together. Kneeling in, I touched my lips to his.

Instantly, he kissed me back, shoulders straining forward. The need to connect desperate.

But too quickly, I broke away. Drifted down his body, trailing kisses as I went. Then I took hold of his dick and sank my mouth over the end.

Ben gave a shout of pleasure, his hips punching up.

I got off him. "Don't let go of the bed."

He swore and tipped his head back, submitting to me.

This time, I traced my tongue down his thick vein then back up to enclose him once again. Taking him in deep, I sucked, then began moving. Gliding up and down his length, loving how he thickened even more in my mouth. The taste of his precum on my tongue.

He kept to his restraints. The tension in his legs and each pulse of his dick showed me how he loved my attention.

I experimented with slow licks and deep sucks, working him out. Driving myself as crazy as him, my breasts weightier, my body alive, my core soaked.

Then his breathing changed, shorter pants coming.

I'd teased him to the edge. But we weren't done.

There was more I needed from this man, but I had to take because he wasn't prepared to give.

With one final, hard suck, I got off him and crawled back up his body.

The desperation was right there in his gaze. Hunger I

adored and felt just as strongly as him. Ben's lips met mine in deep, wet, open-mouth kisses. I positioned myself on his lap, driving his hard length over the outside of my pussy. Soaking him in me.

His mouth curved, and I knew he'd finally discovered my lack of underwear.

But I gave him no time to revel in it.

Kneeling, I let his dick do its job in rising to the right position, then I notched against him and impaled myself.

For a heady moment, I lost my mind. Even maybe my consciousness. He felt so good. His sound of sheer pleasure added to my waves of scorching heat, then his mouth sought mine. His branding kiss prompting me to start moving. Riding him.

I sank down, easier than the first time, despite his size.

I adored the stretch. Impossibly, I'd missed it, though we'd only had one night of doing this. It was like he was built for me. Every hit inside sent blinding spirals along my nervous system. A storm building created by how well we fit.

I fucked him. Keeping inside the lines with my technicality of him not sleeping with me. I was taking what I wanted from his body. He could've stopped me, but Ben needed this just as much. His kiss told me everything. If he slowed, I eased up my pace. He set the rhythm with the slide of his tongue.

It was dirty sex, bare to each other, and unlike anything I'd ever experienced before. Or even knew possible.

So quickly, under our rhythm, I was barrelling towards a climax. I broke the kiss and palmed my breasts, peeling back the bra so I could touch my nipples.

"Ye are so. Fucking. Beautiful," Ben gritted out.

His praise was my undoing.

A few hard hits later, and I stilled, a stunning orgasm sending fireworks throughout my body. I dropped my head back, letting the joy wash through me.

I laughed, too happy for this to be real, then I came back to earth, opening my eyes to find Ben's expression savage. Dangerous.

I'd stopped moving and left him hanging.

I let the happiness turn to a devilish grin. But he had a choice to make. In the snowed-in cabin, he'd pulled out at the last minute. Not all that successfully, but the intent had been there.

In that, I wouldn't take away his choice.

"Tell me when to stop," I said.

He gave a short nod, muscles bunched with the tension throughout him.

Now I was on the other side of my pleasure, my full focus was on his every little sign. I didn't take my eyes off him, and his gaze locked on me. On my chest, exposed to him, down to where we were joined, but back to my face. Keeping the eye contact that was doing so much for me, too.

I rode him hard, placing my hand on his chest to brace myself. Ben's heart raced. His breathing sped.

But he didn't tell me to stop.

Inside me, he thickened more. Pulsed. Surely the sign that he was almost there.

Keeping up the pace, I waited on his word, ready to climb off him. Finish him with my hand or mouth.

Yet still he kept his fevered gaze on mine. No words forthcoming.

Then abruptly, Ben tipped his head back and gave up a

growl of pure masculine pleasure.

He came, deep inside me.

I eased up, surprised but deeply in lust with the moment. Somehow it triggered a second climax from me, too. I gasped and draped against him, shocked, pulsing around him.

God, nothing could ever beat this.

Against his chest, I caught my breath, happy but confused. This wasn't how I'd expected it to go. At least not at the end.

A hug would have been perfect, but also too far. I withdrew and climbed from the bed, shuddering with the effects still dancing through me. At the feeling of being well used and soaked.

"Are you okay?" I asked, needing to be sure.

Spreadeagled against his sheets, Ben brought his gaze to me, arms still outstretched, and a grin creeping onto his lips. "Never fucking better."

It was all I'd wanted.

That smile... It meant the world.

I held his gaze for a second, breathing deep, then left his rooms for my own.

Sneaking back upstairs, I kept my footsteps light. The benefits of being in a castle meant not once had I seen anyone on this trip between the two floors, and I returned to my room undiscovered.

I intended to get straight into the shower, but my body had other ideas. In the cabin, we'd had sex all night. It was like I needed to relive that, though I hadn't wanted to take more from Ben than he was willing to give. Him saying no would hurt too much.

Plus I'd never expected him to come inside me.

It did something to my brain. I needed more, but I'd have to deliver it myself. Taking my vibrator, I sprawled out on my bed and fitted it between my legs. Switched it on and pushed back in the cum that had leaked out.

I orgasmed again. Then a fourth time. Taking him in deep. Obsessed with it, like he'd confessed to some form of obsession with me.

I had the feeling if Ben knew what I'd done, he'd lose his mind.

And the worst part? That he'd cut me off altogether if that feeling went too far.

29

Ben

"Daisy Devereux," Jackson said from across the office.

I lifted my gaze, frowning, like my obsessive thoughts had put words into his mouth.

And fuck was I infatuated. Last night, Daisy had come up with her perfect solution. I'd been close to breaking anyway, but her ideas had beaten out any of mine.

She'd owned me, and I loved it.

All morning, I'd been remembering every second of what we'd done.

How she'd touched me. Fucked me.

How through all of it, she'd kept her goddamned clothes on, and for some reason, that had been so sexy.

I'd badly wanted her to spend the night in my rooms.

Tonight, maybe she would.

I tuned back in to Jackson. "What about her?"

He drew his eyebrows in. "I was telling ye about that apartment her aunt bought. Weren't ye listening?"

I scrubbed my hands over my face, needing a cold shower. "No, sorry. Repeat it."

My new recruit gave a patient sigh. "There's an anomaly with the apartment. The residential record doesn't contain the aunt's or uncle's names, which indicates to me they never planned to live there. Today, I finally got the update I've been looking for. Daisy's name was added to that register the day of the party."

I ticked it over in my mind. "That confirms they bought it to keep her in, or perhaps as part of the marriage deal. I'll tell her later."

I had the feeling she wouldn't like the news.

"Good work," I said. "Anything on the uncle's office manager?"

Jackson returned his gaze to the screen. Unlike Raphael, he didn't respond to praise. Maybe because he was more confident, though the younger Gordonson brother didn't lack that, or he had greater faith in his abilities.

I still couldn't work Jackson out, and I needed to.

"Camila Garcia," he read. "Thirty-five, married, no kids, born in LA and never left from what I can tell. She's worked for Daisy's uncle for over a decade. Always in the same role, which is bothering me."

"Why?" I asked.

He rubbed his jaw. "Typically, people change jobs every few years, even if they stay in the same organisation and progress up the corporate ladder, unless something gets in the way of that, like having kids might do. She started as his office manager at age twenty-three and is still doing the same work now. No career break. No change in responsibilities."

"Many people stick to the same job for the security of it," I argued.

"How much security can there be in an organisation like his?" Jackson returned. "I'm not saying there's anything in that, but it doesn't feel right."

"Maybe she's in love with the uncle. Or even his mistress."

Slowly, he nodded. "Perhaps that's why she was warning Daisy off. Jealous of the attention. Can ye run that one by Daisy as well?"

I agreed, picking up my phone as he got back to work.

Already this morning, Daisy had texted me her whereabouts—Ariel had taken her back to Mr Campbell's. On her first visit, he hadn't wanted her to go upstairs, but he'd since relented, giving her free rein to straighten out the rest of his house.

I knew she'd be delighted. She didn't shy from hard work.

Like everything else about her, I admired that.

I wrote out a text.

Ben: What time will you finish work? I'll come pick you up.

Daisy: I wouldn't say no. Is three okay? I'll be done earlier but I just uncovered some photo albums, and Mr C wants to go through them with me.

Ben: Anything you say.

There was a pause, like she was reading into my reply. I didn't flirt. Barely knew how. But that last message had felt like I was trying.

Daisy: Anything, huh?

Ben: At all. Name it.

Daisy: Last night didn't scare you off?

Was she joking? I gave up a truth.

Ben: After you left, I fucked my fist, thinking about you.

Daisy: God. I did the same on my bed, using you as lube for my vibrator.

Under my desk, my trousers grew uncomfortably tight. This was a bad place to have a conversation like this, but I was hooked.

Ben: From now on, all your orgasms belong to me. Either I'm in you or watching you.

Daisy:... Well, now I'm hot and bothered at work for all the wrong reasons.

Ben: Same, shortie.

Daisy: With a dick as big as yours, guess there's no hiding it either.

A snort of a laugh burst from me. Jackson raised his head in surprise. I locked my phone and put it facedown on my desk, overheated and surprised at myself.

Counting down the hours until I got to see Daisy.

An unreasonable number of hours later, it was time to leave. I sped too fast over the snowy roads, finding her emerging from Mr Campbell's. I leapt from the car and jogged up to help her with her kit. Dougal danced around our feet, and we both stooped to pet him.

Daisy called a quiet goodbye and shut the dog in, lifting her pretty gaze to me. "It's been such a good day. You should see the upstairs of that place. Three big bedrooms and a family bathroom with the original fittings. It was thick with cobwebs and junk, but I sorted and tidied it all, then found that stack of albums. We both sat there and cried at how beautiful his wife had been at their wedding. Honestly, it's been such a joy to work here. I love this house."

It was on the tip of my tongue to say she suited life here.

In front of Mr Campbell's house, in jeans and an old shirt, she looked like she belonged.

"You're amazing for doing all that," I told her instead and packed her cleaning supplies into the back of my car.

Then I handed her into the passenger seat and jogged around to take my own.

"If I could run a business in this way," she continued, "with a balance of regular paid work and doing jobs like this where it really helps someone in need, I'd be happy." Then she slid her gaze my way. "On the subject of being paid, I've earned a little this week. I figure I owe you."

I scowled, getting us on the road. "Don't talk ridiculous."

"You paid for food, fuel, rescued me, got me to another country and then here."

"Daisy," I warned. She owed me nothing. "Stop talking."

She folded her hands in her lap. "Well, okay. But I bought you something. It'll be delivered in a few days. As a thank you and to remind you of me when I leave."

My eyebrows dug in. "You're not going anywhere."

Daisy paused, her gaze on me.

"We still can't be sure you're safe," I added. "For all I know, the minute ye return to California, they could be waiting to lock ye in that apartment."

I filled her in on what Jackson had discovered. Unlike in the café, she took this one on the chin. Next, I asked about Camila.

Daisy shrugged that off as well. "I remember her wedding. Her husband used to work for my uncle as a fixer, which means a violent thug in a suit, so clearly they made a good pair as she's pretty vicious. They were genuinely in love. Paul and Sigrid were guests of honour, and I often saw him at the office, coming to collect her. If she was in love with my uncle, or even just sleeping with him, it wasn't obvious either from her or in the state of her relationship."

Which got me no further with that line of enquiry.

As things stood, we knew of no further acts against Daisy, which meant poking the beast ourselves.

"Did ye hear back from your cousin?" I asked.

"Not yet. But the message was read an hour ago, so we'll wait and see." She took in our route then turned to me. "Where are we going?"

I pressed my lips together. "At our lunch date, the weather denied ye a nice view. I'm taking ye up to a lookout point."

A quick glance over had me staring at her soft smile.

She tilted her head. "Alone together in your car and no one else around. I wonder what we might get up to in front of said gorgeous view."

Aaaand I was hard again.

She'd read me like a book and matched exactly where my mind had gone.

I put my foot down and continued up the mountain.

The place I'd chosen to show her was the opposite side from the snowboarding centre and high above Mr Campbell's place and the deep glen it sat within. A thick evergreen forest muted with snow spread out below us as I parked by the side of the track and turned off the engine. I'd been coming out here for hikes but rarely saw anyone else aside from the occasional paraglider.

Daisy climbed out.

I joined her, circling the car to stand at her side. Though it was cloudy, we could still see for miles across stretches of the Cairngorms. Daisy gazed at it.

Then she brought her attention to me. "Beautiful."

"Yes, ye are."

Her cheeks pinkened. "Charmer."

"I never say anything I don't mean."

If she had an opinion on that, she didn't reply, only paused then reached out and cupped my face. Brought my lips to hers for a kiss.

I was playing with fire. I knew it, and I didn't care. Hooked on that get-out-of-jail-free card she'd given me.

Daisy pressed my chest, separating us. "Back of the car, jeans off," she ordered.

I moved faster than I knew possible.

More slowly, she hesitated at the door, scanning our surroundings, then climbed in after me. My car was a good size, a high enough ceiling and seat depth for her to be on my lap.

Without her even ordering it, I gripped the two headrests either side of me, waiting on her. "I need ye naked."

Daisy's eyes widened. "No way. Not outdoors."

I shrugged, already desperate for this. "Then later. Right now, I'll take ye however I can have ye."

She unbuttoned my jeans then hers and tugged them off, her face reddening more as her underwear went with them, discarded to the floor. "Isn't that the theme of us?"

I didn't get a chance to analyse her words, because she was on my lap and kissing me. Last night had been the slowest tease ever, but the effect of her exploration had blown my mind. She'd wound me up until I could feel her everywhere, and the last part, the way we'd finished, I needed that again. Often.

Luckily for me, Daisy didn't wait around. She rubbed herself on me, one hand gliding under my shirt to feel up my muscles—something that seemed to work for her—and the other gripping the base of my dick. Then her tight heat enclosed me, and I was mindless for it.

She sank down until we were as close as we could be, my dick deep inside her. My new happy place. Her fingers strummed her clit.

"This is going to be fast, because if anyone sees us, I'll die," she whispered.

"I'll kill them for ye, save any embarrassment."

She gave a laugh that turned into a gasp, then all words were gone.

Daisy rode me and played with herself, giving me my sole actions of driving our kiss and keeping myself from coming until she had. Not that that was an issue. Though she drove me crazy with lust and need, I'd never leave her wanting.

Yet her moans did something to my mind.

Some kind of animal instinct to fill her over and over. Getting her to orgasm after me so my cum was inside her. Jesus, fuck, that image was everything.

From believing myself completely in control, I silently urged her to reach the finish line faster.

The windows fogged.

The car rocked.

Out here, neither of us tried to contain our sounds of pleasure. Pretty quickly, Daisy's moans were all I could hear, but mine were louder.

"So perfect," I chanted. "You're so tight around me. Ye drive me wild."

She clamped down on me, and my control broke. I lost it, an almighty climax tightening my balls, electrifying me.

We came at the same time.

Pleasure cresting, taking over, wringing us out.

Daisy collapsed on me, her pulses around my dick the sweetest feeling ever.

I kept my arms where they were, gripping the seatbacks like my life depended on it, but still, I nudged her face to find her lips. Needed her kiss more than air.

"Stay in my rooms tonight," I asked.

Or maybe commanded.

Daisy searched my expression then finally nodded.

For the first time in my life, everything felt right.

30

Daisy

Dinner with the McRaes was a lesson in happy families. Gordain and Ella, despite years of marriage and being grandparents, were my new couple's goal. If Ella was out of the room, Gordain threw glances at the door until she returned. He smiled at her in a way that I both loved and which hurt my heart. Likewise, Leo and little Finn gravitated around pregnant Viola, barely letting her lift a finger.

I'd been living here for days now and had got used to the routine of the place, helping out and pitching in. Everybody was busy, but they always had time for each other. Their jobs and lives circulated around family, relatives often being in Braithar.

It was a life I was desperately learning from. The kind of family I'd wished I'd had. That I'd worked towards but had never been met even halfway.

Across the table, Ben talked to Viola while idly wrestling

with her six-year-old. Every now and again, I sensed the weight of his stare on me. It lit me up with a promise for later.

Finally, dinner was over, and I called an early night. Ben did the same, and if anyone suspected us, they didn't say.

After a couple of minutes lingering in my room, I went to leave, but my phone lit on the dresser. A message from Luna. She'd finally replied.

I hurried down the stairs, Ben's door already open for me.

In the middle of the room, Ben was glowering at his own phone. To his left, a two-seater sofa nestled against the wall. It hadn't been there before, and I squinted at it.

"Is that new?"

He followed my gaze then locked us in. Then his lips were on mine and my question forgotten. His kiss devastated me. His taste, the pressure, all so perfect. Eventually, he broke away, hauling in a breath.

"I realised my room was a little sparse, so I asked around if anyone had a spare." Then he held up his phone. "Valentine messaged."

I lifted my own. "Luna replied."

Ben pointed to the sofa, and we sat side by side.

"Ye first," he said.

I unlocked the phone, still using the same passcode as him, and read.

"It's short. She says she'll talk to me, but not over the phone."

Ben scowled. "How's that supposed to work? For all she knows, you're still in the US."

He was right. I stared at the message then hit the little

button to call her. I was taking a risk, but it sounded like she had something to say.

After a beat, she answered. "Daisy? What are you doing?"

"Don't hang up. I know you don't want to talk on the phone, but this is important. It's about our family."

Luna gave a short laugh. "Yours, not mine anymore. I told you, I'm not prepared to have a conversation this way."

"Please," I said. "Just listen to me. I'm not with your parents any more. I left them. Did you already know that?"

She hesitated. "No. At Christmas, I told them that was my last visit. There's...reasons why I never want to go back there again. Where are you, and why did you leave?" Then she made a sound of frustration. "Don't answer that. Shit. This is why we can't have a conversation like this."

She was worried about being recorded, had to be.

"You're in London?" I asked.

"No. That's just what I told them. I'm in Edinburgh for a few days right now but I don't live in this city either," she said.

I raised my gaze to Ben's. Luna could be an ally, if she was being real. I didn't know her well, but it was true that she barely visited, and my aunt had been devastated over her last visit.

Plus Edinburgh was only a few hours away.

Ben read my mind. Gave me a slow nod.

"I can meet you in Edinburgh," I uttered.

Luna took an inhale, presumably working out that I really had left the family. "If you do, you're coming alone. I'll choose somewhere open and public, and if I think you're up to something, I'll walk away."

I swallowed, dropping my gaze from Ben's. "Likewise. Is

it okay if I have my boyfriend with me?"

Another pause, then, "Fine, but only him. My man will be there, too. Tomorrow midday, central Edinburgh. I'll send you the exact location just before."

The call disconnected, and she was gone.

I took a breath. "God. I wasn't expecting her to be so scared. I'm dying to hear what she has to say." Then I winced. "Sorry I called you my boyfriend. If I'd said my bodyguard, I wasn't sure she'd agree."

He lifted one shoulder in a shrug, but his gaze distanced, as if his mind had gone into work mode.

Then I asked the question I should've already. "You'll come with me, won't you?"

That full beam of attention fell back on me. "As if I'd let ye go alone."

I breathed a sigh of relief and laughed. "Let?"

He wrinkled his nose like he was reconsidering his words. "From a professional point of view."

I relaxed on the cushions and slipped off my shoes, poking his leg with my toe. "What does Valentine have to say? Are you still worried about him?"

I didn't believe that Dan's brother had anything to do with my attempted abduction. I understood the rationale, but it just felt off. The motivation was weak when the guy had years to get his revenge.

"Not sure. I just saw his name on my screen when ye came in." Ben thumbed open his phone and scanned the message. His jaw hardened. "He informs me that the logging job he took has fallen through, and he's available to come here and join my service."

As he spoke, his phone buzzed with another message. Ben groaned.

"That's from Ma. Oh, for fuck's sake. She's taking the opportunity to travel with Valentine and coming to visit."

"Isn't that a good thing? When will she be here?"

Ben exhaled and stared at the ceiling. "In a little under a week."

I didn't understand his sudden attitude change or the air of discomfort over him. Then our conversation from the plane returned to me. It felt like so long ago, but I hadn't forgotten anything he'd said. Slowly, I fitted together the pieces.

"Will she want to see Tabby?"

At the name of his birth mother, Ben shuddered, stifling it immediately, but there was no disguising his shock. "She will. So I need to first."

Which was obviously a problem for him. I reached for his hand, aiming to give him comfort. "I'll go with you, if that makes it easier."

But Ben had other ideas. Instead of answering, he dropped his phone and slid his arms around me, bringing me to his lap, my new favourite place. Our kiss was more of a clash. Something in the news he'd had put him on edge.

Whether he'd noticed it or not, Ben was breaking his rule.

He stood, taking me with him, and carried me to the bed. There, he set me down on the cushions where yesterday I'd positioned him, his hands going to the hem of my shirt. He yanked it up and off me, reaching back to unclip my bra in a slick move.

But it was made of desperation.

He freed my breasts and palmed them, dropping his face to my cleavage with a growl of need. He kissed and sucked the swell, then curled his tongue around my nipple, grinning when I took a breath in pleasure.

His gaze found mine, fever burning within. "Get naked then lie back. This time, I'm in control."

I'd wanted this. I also needed to know his mind, but it could come later. When he'd burned up his emotions on my body.

Ben returned to sucking my nipple, getting it to a peak before switching to the other side, groaning as he stared at the effect he had.

I did as ordered and lost the rest of my clothes.

My self-consciousness at being fully naked with him again fled. He only made me feel good, his boob play winding me up in a way only he could. Serious, hard, fast, no messing around.

Abruptly, he tugged his shirt from his head, chucking it. His jeans and boxers followed. Then he was in the cradle of my hips, his dick between my legs.

Ben sank inside me with an exhale of utter relief.

Only then did he slow.

"Need this," he said. "I need ye."

"I need you, too," I confessed.

There was no smile. No joy in his looks. Only determination to fuck me.

Ben guided my legs around his hips, going in deep with each stroke. I had no problem with him getting lost in my body. I wanted that. I just wished I knew what had upset him. It was to do with Tabby, clearly, but was it seeing her? His mom seeing her? I wished he'd say.

Now definitely wasn't the time to ask. Not when he was hell bent on sending me crazy with his insanely talented dick.

Ben kept up a slow series of thrusts, his fingers landing on my clit. "I'm going to make ye come until ye beg me to stop."

I drew my arm over my eyes, but he snatched it free.

"No hiding from me," he said, the hypocrite.

Yet I obeyed, keeping my gaze on his. He built me up, keeping the same speed and pressure, hitting the same place inside over and again with his fingers strumming me.

In no time, the perfection of his touch and of how he filled me had me speeding towards the finish.

I gasped and came, easily his.

"That's one," he muttered, a dark amusement to his voice. "Keep your eyes on mine or I'll slap your perfect arse."

I blinked, my lips open on a protest that never came. I was pretty willing to try anything.

Ben smirked, then pulled out of me, lifting up onto his knees. "Get on all fours."

I obeyed, and he got behind me, two fingers sliding straight into me. He glided his dick between my legs, taking hold of it, wet from his precum and my juices.

"Your arse is a peach. One day, I'll fuck ye there," he warned.

He hooked an arm around me and pulled me upright, at the same second driving into me. We were both on our knees with him behind, but now he could twist me back to reach my mouth. We kissed as he fucked me, then he brought his fingers to my lips. Pushed them inside.

"That's what we taste like together," he said in my ear. "Fucking addictive."

I licked them clean then groaned and tangled his tongue with mine in another kiss, then he broke away and pressed his lips to the back of my neck, baring his teeth while he drilled me harder and harder. With both hands, he pawed at my tits. Playing with me, rough but deliciously. Rolling my nipples, lighting me up in too many places at once.

In a minute, I was moaning out again, spinning to a crash. Desperate to get over the edge.

"Ye feel so fucking good," he chanted. "Give me a second. Let me feel ye again on my dick."

Deep inside me, his dick pulsed, and I broke in my second climax.

Nothing beat that. Coming at the same time as him. My cries came over and over, matching the way I squeezed tightly around him.

Ben took us down to the blanket then moved onto his back, with me on his chest, looking to the ceiling.

"That's two," he said. Then he sucked my earlobe, earning another soft moan. "Now drop your legs down either side of mine."

I did, chest heaving, keeping my eyes closed because this was a full-body onslaught. I was completely exposed to his touch, and he was still buried hard inside me.

Slower now, he teased my body, his dick remaining still. He stroked my belly. My arms. Plumped my breasts. A casual exploration that brightened my senses.

Then it turned more purposeful. His hand made lazy circles over my clit. The other tugged lightly on my nipples.

No change in speed. Nothing but a constant tease of my body.

The way he filled me and touched me brought another orgasm in fast. I sobbed out soft moans, draped over him and lost to everything but deep satisfaction.

"Three," Ben muttered gruffly, kissing my hair.

Like last night, when I'd made myself come after we'd had sex, I was hooked on orgasming with his cum inside me. There was no risk of me getting pregnant, nor did I want that, yet if for a second I let myself pretend, it did crazy things to my mind.

Or maybe that was just Ben.

Being around him, sleeping with him, him making rules and breaking them, it mixed me up.

"Enough," I begged. Meaning of all things, him. He was too much to handle.

He turned us to the side and held me. For a while, as we cooled, I thought he slept, then his grumpy voice broke the silence.

"Awake?"

I lifted my head to show I was.

"I have some work I need to do."

Right. He'd wanted me to stay but got scared off.

I faced him and gave him a knowing look. "No biggie. I prefer my bed to your cold and empty one."

"Ye don't have to go," he said slowly.

But I did. Calling him out would get me nowhere—I knew him well enough to be sure of that. In the morning, we had a trip to make, and who knew what it would bring for either of us.

One thing was certain, if Ben was unwilling to let me in, there was nothing more to say.

31

Daisy

Through the dark of early morning, Ben drove me away from Castle Braithar. I'd expected to head out past the loch and onto the main road, but he diverted in the opposite direction.

"We need to stop at the hangar. Gordain wants a quick word."

It would take us three hours to drive down to Edinburgh and my appointment with Luna, but we'd started with plenty of time. From the monosyllabic answers Ben had given to my questions this morning, I had the idea conversation on the drive might be one-sided.

I gave an easy shrug. "I'd like to see the place you work."

His jaw ticked, but he didn't reply.

I gazed out of the window. His grumpy states amused rather than frustrated me.

The aircraft hangar loomed at the edge of an open valley

floor. A helicopter lifted off then peeled away, lights flashing.

"Was that Raphael?" I squinted after it.

Ben followed my gaze. "Not sure."

"Is he doing okay with his lessons?"

"I assume so. Haven't asked."

He strode inside the frontage, a quiet growl of my name commanding me to skitter after him. An office block was built into the back of the structure, and Ben took the corridor down the centre of it. I peeked in the first room. Some kind of operations centre with a map on the wall and whiteboards. A man in a jumpsuit with dark hair and a thick beard carried an armful of equipment out. Ropes and metal things. He gave Ben a nod and me a curious look.

"Daisy, this is Lochinvar," Ben muttered.

I gave a sunny smile to the man I guessed had something to do with the mountain rescue service from the logo on his chest, but Ben was still moving. I stuck with him.

He poked his head into further offices then entered a brightly lit room, a couple of coffee machines on the back wall, tall refrigerators, and tables for people to eat and drink.

In there, Gordain chatted with Jackson, the latter with a motorbike helmet in his hand.

Both looked up on our approach.

A sudden sense of awkwardness came over me. Gordain was Ben's boss and presumably set the rules of his employment. Though we'd been living in his castle, any fraternising we'd done had been strictly behind closed doors. But the past few days had changed something for me.

Ben might have been fully in work mode, but I was spanning a different place. One where I was comfortable with him. Where, grumpy or not, I'd reach for his hand without thinking.

I could lose him his job.

Deliberately, I left space between us and neutralised my expression.

"Thanks for stopping in," Gordain said. "I saw your message about Edinburgh after I texted ye. Later would have been fine."

Ben must've already told him the plan.

"It's fine," Ben replied. "I needed to talk to ye about accommodation anyway. Seems like my brother will be here earlier than planned. Jackson has been sleeping on the sofa. I want to get the bunkhouse back in use."

"We were just having that exact conversation." Gordain gave a head tilt to Raphael's friend. "While you're out all day, we'll get started on it. When's Valentine coming?"

"In a few days. He's bringing our mother for a visit."

"Autumn's coming? She's more than welcome to stay with us. Ella will get a kick out of seeing her again. We'll find her another room in the guest wing. The one next to Daisy's is free."

I blinked, surprised that Gordain knew Ben's mother. Small world, apparently.

Ben protested. Viola's baby was due soon, but I'd said the same thing over dinner last night, and the family had batted back my suggestion to find somewhere else to live. I'd offered instead to go onto meal prep duty, imagining the early days with a newborn to be fraught. It would do me good to learn how to get meals on the table for a family.

"Don't be daft," Gordain told him. "Your ma brought ye here as an infant. It'll be full circle if she gets to meet our grandsons."

Then his gaze turned speculative. With a quiet request,

he pulled Ben aside, saying something to him I couldn't hear.

"I didn't know Ben had ties going back that far," Jackson said from my other side.

I turned to see him set down the helmet then grab a coffee mug from a rack. He filled it and offered the mug to me. I shook my head, no extra caffeine required today. I was already jittery enough.

"I didn't either." Since the self-defence session, I hadn't really seen or spoken to Jackson. In my mind, he was Ariel's crush only, rather than a three-dimensional person, but like me, he was new here, too.

"How are you liking work?" I asked.

"Exactly what I needed."

"I guess you found out about it from Raph?"

He ducked his head. "A long time ago, Raphael told me he planned to join Ben's service after graduation. The idea of doing something like this took root in my mind. So far, it's challenged me in directions I hadn't even considered." He gestured to me. "The protection side of it is deeper than I imagined, though I'm gunning to get out in the field as well."

Everything I'd heard about my case had been filtered through Ben. Of course, Jackson had been working on it, too.

"Thanks for all you've done for me," I said quickly.

He flashed a short smile. "You're welcome. Like I said, I'm loving it. Even the idea of sleeping in a bunk room is better than I'm used to."

His gaze left me and landed on the two men and their quiet conversation behind us.

I used the opportunity to really look at Jackson.

Ariel was always discerning with her crushes, selecting only the most damningly attractive men. No one would ever have a patch on Ben for me, but I could see the appeal of this new bodyguard. He had dark hair and an unshaven jaw, but somehow not untidy, and his blue eyes stood out, almost startling in their intensity. He was tall and held himself like he knew how to use his strength. The closed switchblade sort of man. Where Raphael had a casual swagger about him, confident in his chat but with an element of danger to him—helicopters weren't his only deal, he'd grown up around guns and knew how to use them—Jackson seemed more reserved. Polite, but maybe because I was a client in his eyes.

I wondered what he was like among friends. Did he relax and smile? Ariel had bemoaned the fact that she still hadn't spoken to him after the half-naked dropkick incident.

An idea came to mind.

"Since I've been here a while, we should all grab a beer together," I said. Then my brain clicked in to where we were in the calendar. "Actually, it's Ariel's birthday soon. We can make it a party. She and Raph are really social, so I know they'll be down."

Instantly, Jackson frowned, his dark eyebrows pulling in. "When?"

I checked the date. "In a week. Holy shit. That snuck up on me. She'll be twenty."

He heaved a breath, some emotion breaking through his exterior that startled me in the effect it had on him. "So fucking young."

Then he downed the coffee, set the mug down, and stomped away.

I stared after him, wondering what the heck had just happened. But Ben was done with his conversation, and we were ready to leave.

Edinburgh, here we come.

In the car, as expected, my bodyguard kept up his grumpy routine. The sun still hadn't risen, but I wasn't going to let the dark day bother me.

"I'm going to organise a party for Ariel's twentieth, but also to get everyone socialising," I told him.

"I'll make myself scarce." He paused at a junction, his gaze not coming my way.

"Why?"

Ben shrugged. "I'm a lot older than the rest of ye. Nobody wants the boss around."

"Well, that's a stinking pile of bull. Do you see Gordain that way? He's got to be twenty-five years older than you, but you talk to him just fine. You're, what, five or six years older than Jackson? Ten for Raphael? They respect you. You can be friendly and their boss. Or is this a problem like at the self-defence class?"

He slid a dark look my way.

I beamed.

"I didn't feel so jealous when ye were talking with Jackson in the rec room," he slowly gave up, like he'd just realised it.

"Good. You're making progress. Want to talk about it?"

"No."

"Want to talk about anything?"

His lips formed a thin line.

Silence wasn't an option. I needed to not be dwelling on what we might find today.

"If you're not in the conversation mood, I'm going to put an audiobook on."

"A smutty one?"

I tapped the car's controls to hook up my phone. "Yep. Dirty as heck."

He rolled his shoulders. "Fine."

I *knew* he secretly loved them. I pressed play and let him drive me while we listened to other people bang.

We entered the City of Edinburgh with its busy streets and houses crowded together, the noise and endless traffic a culture shock after what felt like forever in comparative peace. I'd been raised in the sprawling metropolis of Los Angeles. Though my aunt and uncle's house was out in the hills, the city views were always there. Restaurants and bars minutes away. Any apartment my mother had for us was always in the busiest, grimiest urban areas. My own shared apartment was the same.

Staying on the McRae estate in the Cairngorm mountains had calmed a part of my brain I didn't know had been stressed.

Maybe I wasn't a city girl after all. The closer we got to the centre of town, the more I wanted to turn around and drive straight out again.

From Ben's increasing glower, he was feeling the same. His birth mom lived here. He was facing off with demons, too.

The video call came in from Luna just as we'd parked. I answered, and she peered at the camera.

"We're here," I told her. "This is Ben."

"Just the two of you? Show me the back of the car," she ordered.

I held up my phone then came back to my cousin.

"Okay, I trust you," she said. "Meet me at North Bridge Arcade. I'll be in the Scotsman café."

She hung up, and I searched for the address. A five-minute walk away.

I showed Ben. "Why is she so scared?"

"I guess we're going to find that out."

I held my gaze on him for a moment. "I'm surprised at how calm you are about this. Or maybe you even letting me come here."

All morning, Ben had barely looked me in the eye.

He did now, and I hitched my breath at the swarm of emotions I got just from the eye contact alone.

We connected, when he let us. Far beyond just the level of our bodies. It was entirely addictive.

"Do ye really think I'd let anything happen to ye?" he asked.

"Well, no."

"We have to find out what's happened with your family, and if ye don't want to talk to your aunt and uncle, this is a good option. I researched your cousin last night. She's married and has a job here. Pays taxes. As far as I can see, she's out of the family business entirely. But in case you're worried, mark my words. Nobody will touch ye. Not if they want to keep breathing. You're safe with me."

I'd no idea Luna had gotten married, but I was more caught on Ben's sudden and exacting defence of me. I was getting the measure of him more and more.

His quiet didn't mean he'd stopped caring. His grumpiness hid a beautiful heart. To some extent, it thumped for me.

I stretched across the car and pressed a kiss to his mouth before he could stop me. Then I climbed from the car, setting out to get answers.

In the café, I spotted my cousin immediately. Luna had always been a copy-paste of Aunt Sigrid. Except now, her style had changed. Luna rose from the table, a man standing with her.

My gaze instantly dropped to her baby bump.

"Oh my God." I reached their table, agog at the change in her.

I didn't go for a hug. That had never been a thing in our family.

"Hi, Daisy." Luna shifted her weight.

The man I guessed to be her husband automatically extended an arm out to brace her. With glasses and slightly overlong hair, he had a sweet and open expression. Like a scholar or someone who worked in a bookshop.

"Congratulations, I had no idea," I said. "How far along are you?"

"Six months." Luna's gaze jumped from me to Ben, her expression wary.

I imagined how he appeared from their perspective. Big. Strong. Probably scowling.

Then Ben mirrored Luna's husband and curled an arm around my shoulders. I concealed my surprise and peered up in time to see him smile and reach to shake the other man's hand.

"Ben," he introduced himself.

"Edward," the other man said. "And this, of course, is my Luna."

It was a role. Ben was just playing a role.

But a horrifying realisation hit me. My heart had accepted Ben's position and wasn't about to go back. I wanted him as my boyfriend. Permanently.

We sat, Edward darting away to fetch us tea.

I tried to shake off my realisation and centred on my cousin.

Luna anticipated me. "You're for real, then."

"I'm not sure what you mean," I replied.

"You walked away from them as well. They'd never let you be here otherwise."

I slowly caught up. On the phone, she'd been afraid. Her visit at Thanksgiving had been brief and clearly designed to avoid them paying too close attention and guessing. "Your parents don't know about Edward or the baby."

Luna shuddered. "No. I'm keeping that from them for as long as I can."

Her not wanting to tell them spoke volumes. Still, I needed to know. "Tell me why."

My cousin recoiled. "Why are you asking me that? For the same reason as you're here talking to me, obviously. They're toxic. I want nothing to do with them or their lives ever again."

Edward returned with a tray, and I glanced at Ben. He gave me a small nod of encouragement.

"I ran from them," I said on a breath. "They had plans for me. I didn't want any part of it."

"They had plans, as you put it, for all of us. Why do you think Gianna fled to the opposite side of the country? Why do you think I'm thousands of miles away, about to have a baby who will only ever know one set of grandparents?"

Gianna was her older sister. I knew her even less than Luna.

My cousin set a hand to her belly. "I need you to promise me you won't talk to them. I'm not even sure why I'm here, except I had an emotional response to your message and needed to see you were okay. I know we weren't close but I hated that you were still stuck there after Gi and I got away. I'm glad you're free, but please, swear it to me. They can't find out about my baby."

Edward poured us each a cup of tea, muttering calming words.

"I won't tell them, I don't intend to ever see them again," I promised.

Luna closed her eyes. I sipped my tea. It was piping hot, just like our conversation. I hadn't understood her absence in the family at all. I'd always been so much younger but clearly more naïve, too.

I leaned in. "What do you think they'll do? What exactly are you scared of? It's important that I know."

But my cousin switched her gaze to the street, something shuttering in her gaze. "Another chess piece, waiting to be used. All I can say is you're better off far away from them. Don't go back."

"I won't."

"If you're serious, I'm glad for you. If not, you should know I don't live here. I won't give my address. We'll be gone from the city today, so they won't find us."

Luna's cheeks flushed red. She stood and shrugged on a thick coat then reached for her bag. Her husband grabbed it for her so she didn't need to bend.

"I'm really sorry. I'm overwhelmed and I shouldn't have come. I'm glad you're out of there. It will hurt them to have lost you. My mother always praised you above either of her actual daughters. The job was a better fit for you, but I wish the business would die with them."

Then Luna swept away, her husband rushing with her,

leaving us in her wake.

32

Daisy

*I*n silence, we returned to the car. Ben drove us out of the city centre.

"A chess piece. A better fit for the job," he repeated my cousin's words.

My mind had lingered over those, too. The job... Did that mean the same as a marriage pawn? I wished Luna hadn't run, but there was no way I could have demanded she stop. Stressing out a heavily pregnant lady definitely wouldn't help things.

Besides, part two of our not-fun day out had commenced.

We cruised into a suburb, and Ben pulled over outside a tower block by a canal. The streets were quiet, but an elderly couple crossed the road together, hand in hand. Bird feeders hung in the trees and from railings. The much lighter snow this far south surrounded what must be pretty flowerbeds in the summer.

It was cute. Clearly a home loved by the residents.

Hiding a less happy side, too.

"Tabby's place?" I asked gently.

Ben stared forward, giving the smallest nod of acknowl-edgement. All last night and this morning, I'd replayed the story he'd given me on the plane. He'd handed over his his-tory in such a candid way, and I suspected that he regretted it.

He was the definition of closed off. Holding himself apart from people. Even those who cared for him.

This was why.

As a child, he'd been forced to visit Tabby, first in pris-on, then at her apartment. She'd used him to get this apart-ment. Showed no interest in him or his life. Selfish as she destroyed it. There were no happy memories here for Ben.

I knew how this was going to go down. He'd jump from the car and snap out an order for me to stay put, then he'd stomp inside to do whatever he needed to do. I'd wondered over that, as well. His visit had been prompted by his mom and brother coming here. Maybe he needed to prewarn Tabby in some way. Which logically followed as she wasn't taking his calls.

It killed me that I wouldn't know what happened when he spoke to her. There's no way he would tell me.

On cue, Ben drew in a deep breath and popped his door.

He didn't look at me or say a word. But to my surprise, he rounded the car and opened my side. Held out a hand.

"Coming?"

My heart squeezed.

Quickly, I unbuckled and climbed out. It was on the tip of my tongue to ask if he was sure, but I held in my words.

He needed me with him. He didn't say, but discomfort came off him in waves.

Ben locked the car and shoved his hands in his pockets, turning to march across the street and over the sidewalk to the block. I kept up. At the entrance, he pressed the bottom buzzer on a panel, no number on it.

"Hello?" a male voice answered.

"Ben Graham," Ben replied.

There was a pause, then the door buzzed and popped open. We entered a lobby, a janitor mopping the floor with headphones in giving us a cheerful wave.

Ben kept up his forward motion, no explanation as to why he'd needed someone else to let him in and not Tabby.

He stomped up the stairs, pausing at the first landing to make sure I was with him.

"Wait," I ordered.

He breathed out through his nose, tension radiating from him.

With my heart in my mouth, I grasped his wrist and drew his hand from his pocket. Laced his cold fingers through mine.

I was aulding for rojoction, but the fact he'd wanted me here, allowed me into his world, spoke volumes.

Ben stared at our joined hands then continued on, slower, and connected to me.

My pulse skipped a beat, every second of this feeling vital.

At the fourth floor, we left the stairwell and entered the hall, someone's TV murmuring in the background. Voices from another apartment exclaimed over something. Ben stopped at a door, then glowered at the number. Four one four.

A stack of boxes sat beside the door, dented cans spilling from one. A note had been stuck on the top, ordering the removal of the items from the public area.

Ben dropped his hold on me.

An odour assaulted my nose, seeping from out of the apartment.

Of garbage left out in the sun. Something rotten. Mould and grime.

I knew this scent. It was the sort I'd mask up for in a clean.

Ben raised a hand and thumped on the door.

From inside, something moved.

"It's Ben," he called. "Open up."

Silence followed.

A muscle in his jaw ticked. He thumped again. "Tabby, next week, you'll have visitors. Your sister will be here. Do ye hear me?"

If she heard, she didn't acknowledge. No further sound came. No rustle or movement.

Tabby was pretending not to be home.

"I'll text ye before," he continued. "Autumn will want to see ye, so be prepared."

Still nothing.

Ben glowered at the door for a moment longer, then grasped my wrist and yanked me away. Back down the stairs, across the lobby, and to the car. He didn't speak, and I didn't ask. Not until we were seated again, and he was gunning the engine.

"Does she ever answer?" I asked.

Ben rolled his shoulders, his most severe of expressions

firmly locked in place. "No."

I worked it through in my mind. His whole family had moved here. First when Valentine was born and Tabby had been using her son as a guilt trip for the parole board, then when Ben was a teenager and she wanted a nice apartment and had flexed her parental rights.

He'd stayed in order to facilitate this charade of a relationship.

Released the rest of his loved ones so they could lead their own lives.

All that time, she'd blanked him. Ben had learned to cope on his own, and now he was masking that from his mom.

My chest hurt, and I pressed a hand to the ache. How could a young teenager cope with that? Let alone make such a decision.

"Your mom will expect to see you and Tabby together," I slowly worked out.

Ben didn't answer, faking concentration on junctions and traffic.

After a while, he instructed me to continue with our audiobook. But I'd changed what we were listening to. Instead, picking a more emotional story, focused on the feelings rather than the physical side.

The story made up the backdrop to my tumbling thoughts. Of my family, using me. Of Ben's doing the same. Totally different in actions and impacts, but equal in that both were problems that needed solving.

If only I knew how.

33

Ben

*W*e'd left the Cairngorms in the dark and re-turned at sunset. The weather set in, a storm blocking out the last of the light, matching my mood.

Today had done a number on me. Taking Daisy to see Tabby had been purposeful. After spinning my story to her on the flight over here, I'd needed her to get the punchline. The clue that would get her backing away from me, as she should.

It shouldn't hurt. *It shouldn't fucking hurt,* any of it, but it did. And I needed to get that the hell out of me.

I'd also had an inkling from meeting her family member of just what Daisy's relatives had intended for her. Not as I'd initially thought. Something entirely different, starting with them losing two daughters—their heirs—and ending with them wrapping her up at the centre of their lives. If she'd reached the same conclusions, she didn't say.

Besides, talking was beyond me. I dropped Daisy back at Castle Braithar, almost growling how I'd be out working late and for her maybe to see Ariel tonight rather than come to me. If Daisy had anything to say, I didn't give her the space to do it, leaving before I said or did something stupid.

My windscreen wipers battled sleet on my drive out to the hangar. It didn't soothe me any, and by the time I'd parked and found Jackson, I was burning to use up my energy.

A few years ago, at the back of the hangar building, a group of us, led by Maddock, the flight school lead, installed a bunkhouse. A four-room structure made out of shipping containers with a boys' and girls' dorm, a communal bathroom, and a lounge. It even had a wood-burning stove and bookshelves, everything you'd need for an overnight stay.

The flight school ran intensive training courses, requiring short stays for the pilots who'd be in the air or in the classroom for several days together. Likewise, the mountain rescue crew used the space for power naps in the middle of rescues. Often, their callouts happened overnight, and crew exhaustion was a real thing. If a large-scale operation went into the next afternoon, Lochie would organise rest periods for crew to minimise sleep-deprived mistakes.

I'd used the space myself for my team on occasion, but six months ago, fire caught in the lounge room. A cigarette dropped by a careless guest burned the soft furnishings plus the wooden bed frames in one dorm, and put the bunkhouse out of action. We'd cleaned it out, but a busy summer had pulled us all in other directions, and work to revive the building hadn't started again.

Right now, I needed the hard work. To throw myself into something that wasn't my obsession with Daisy.

In shorts and a T-shirt, Jackson scrubbed the interior walls with a yellow sponge and a bucket of soapy water.

I scowled at him, planting my hands on my hips. "Ye

should be wearing protective kit."

He turned, noticing me, then held up his rubber-glove-covered hand. "The place is ventilated pretty good. These are enough."

I pressed my lips together, trying to rein in my bad mood. It wasn't fair to take it out on him, or anyone for that matter. I shucked my jacket and rolled up my sleeves. "That's the plan? Scrub it down?"

Jackson straightened and gestured to decorating supplies in the middle of the floor. "Clean up the smoke damage, prime it when it's dry. The first wall is looking pretty good, so I'll probably start on that this evening. If I'm to be sleeping here, I'd rather move in sooner than later."

A work ethic I admired. "Got another bucket?"

Daisy had told me to spend time with him. I wanted to quip how this was yet another task he hadn't expected, but I couldn't manage anything more.

Luckily for me, my new recruit accepted with a shrug. "Take this one. I'll make up another."

Side by side, we scrubbed down the metal walls of the dorm.

At six, Jackson took a food break. I didn't stop. Scrubbing, wiping down, my only company for an hour a dehumidifier rumbling away to dry it out. I accepted the sandwich Jackson returned with, washing it down with a beer he handed over.

Into the evening, I painted until my arms ached.

Then I slept in my office so if Daisy came looking for me, I wasn't there.

The following morning, she sent her message about a cleaning job she had that day, with Leo taking her, and Ariel picking her up. I replied with a thumbs-up. A dick move, but as long as I knew she was safe, it was for the best.

That evening, I worked again at the bunkhouse, with more painting then putting together new bunks. Jackson and I checked over the second dorm and decided to refresh it as well. In the day, I'd spent time with him going over a couple of previous operations. One for Leo, and the other working for another celebrity doing public appearances. I also organised an on-the-ground evening where we'd work together to help out a friend of Leo's. All good for him, all busy time for my head.

A message came in from the lass I was avoiding.

Daisy: I'm home. Are you?

Ben: Probably not tonight.

Daisy: I'm going to message my mom and tell her I'm okay. I'll be careful over what I say.

She needed to do this, but I didn't like it.

I sent her a refresher on no location clues, followed by a warning.

Ben: Your other relatives will likely know.

Daisy: Yup.

She didn't reply again. Neither did I.

"Question," Jackson said, a slice of white paint on his cheek like we were in some kind of couple's home renovation project. "For how much longer will Daisy be here? I don't mean that like I'm hurrying her return home, but we're tasked with protecting her. Here, she's safe. At least currently. Back in the States, there's no reason to think she'll be out of danger. Her relatives still want her, aye? The arsehole who tried to grab her into his truck is still out there."

I stared at the window frame I was painting. "I suspect now her aunt and uncle wanted her for another reason. One she might even be amenable to."

Jackson gave a low whistle. "Ye think? Will it protect her from the kidnapper?"

"You're sure it was an unrelated person." Not a question. Jackson had believed that all along.

"Almost completely. The evidence pointed to someone tracking her phone and pinpointing her. That same person lost the trail, but that doesn't mean they'll give up."

Ice slid down my spine.

"Recap on suspects."

"The ex-boyfriend," Jackson recounted, "who was the wrong side of the country to feasibly be chasing her. The creep who'd stayed over at her flat. I can't find out much about him, other than his school record and a previous address, which he and his mother no longer live at. Someone else in her life she hasn't considered. Her relatives and their people are an outlier. If she's thinking about going back soon, I want to get into that more."

Valentine made three names, plus the unknowns. I despised the thought of her returning. It intensified that awful fucking constriction of my chest.

She'd go. I'd miss her.

Least I could do was get to the bottom of this.

"I'll talk to her," I vowed.

But outside her bedroom, I stalled. If I knocked, went in, I'd want her. I wouldn't be able to hide it.

I sat on the cold floor, trapped by my own stubborn mind, protecting her. From me, as much as anything else.

I woke to footsteps approaching the room. Instantly, I was on my feet and facing whoever had come for Daisy.

Ariel blinked at me. "Ben? Why were you on the floor?"

I rubbed a hand over my face, a quick check of my watch telling me I'd spent the night here. "Shite," I grumbled.

The door opened, and the woman I'd played draft guard to stood in the frame. She looked from Ariel to me.

Fuck knew why, but I turned and stomped away down the corridor.

Rushed conversation followed me, then Daisy's voice came louder.

"Ben, stop."

At the top of the staircase, out of sight of Ariel, I waited. Daisy padded to join me, her warm brown hair loose and messy. Her sleepwear of shorts and a T-shirt was far sexier than they had reason to be.

She blinked. "Did you sleep outside my room?"

I controlled every urge to grab her in a fucking hug and just gave a gruff nod.

"Why? You've ghosted me for days."

"I've been busy."

She gave a short, unfunny laugh. "God. I can't believe you just said that. Tell me why. What changed?"

Frustration rose in a hot wave. "We both know what happened in Edinburgh. Both what ye heard and what I had to show ye. From my side of things, that isn't going to change. It can't. I need to get to work, but later, we need to start making the calls you've been avoiding. Pave the way for your return to the US. There, you're wanted."

A ripple of hurt passed over her expression. "My re-turn...? Fine." The upset changed to resolve.

But it wasn't fine. None of it was even close. Every fucking piece of it was entirely the opposite. And there was nothing I could do about it.

I turned to walk away.

Her voice chased me down the stairs. "If I need to go somewhere today, I'll take Jackson. Is that okay with you?"

That stung. Someone else protecting her other than me. But it was her right.

"All yours," I grouched back then continued away from her.

34

Daisy

Back in my bedroom, I closed the door, my brain ticking overtime.

"What was that about?" my best friend asked from her perch at the bottom of my bed.

"I'm trying to work it out myself."

Dozens of thoughts collided, the conclusion so huge, I needed a reality check. I turned to Ariel.

"I think Ben has feelings for me," I uttered slowly, the words so alien yet also right. "And the only reason I'm sure is because it works both ways."

Ariel's jaw dropped. She reached for my hand so I sat next to her. "Are you serious?"

"Deadly. I think? How is that possible with someone I've only known for a couple of weeks?"

"It's no good asking me. What do I know about real love?"

"I don't know anything either!"

"Wait, let me get a few opinions."

She took up her phone and started typing, determination and a touch of happiness in her expression. When I'd arrived in Scotland, she'd joked about me staying and pairing off with Ben or Raphael. Not that I was truly considering it. It had only just dawned on me that this was real.

"Who are you messaging?"

"My sister-in-law, Effie, her sister-in-law, Casey, Viola, and Isobel." She continued tapping her screen.

"Effie had a friends-with-benefits arrangement with my brother, which is gross if I think about it, but I'm glad, too, because she's the best. She's also very open and I can ask her anything. Casey is from the US, and she came here on a working holiday then bam, married Effie's brother, Brodie, and they have a three-person marriage with Blayne."

"I've heard of them," I exclaimed. "That's three people falling in love."

Ariel pointed at me. "Exactly. If anyone knows, it'll be her. Then we have Viola and Isobel. Both of them had false starts, meeting their husbands when they were young, I'm pretty sure sharing a first kiss then not getting together until years later. That's a whole load of testing feelings to be sure."

She finished writing her message, and I dropped back on the bed, swimming in emotion. For the past two days, I hadn't seen Ben at all, and I'd missed him. I'd lain awake thinking about him. Not just thinking about sex either. I'd wanted to fall asleep with him.

But it was his words in the hallway that woke me up to what I'd overlooked. He'd snarled about me going back to America.

I didn't want to leave him.

Even the thought of it sent panic spiralling through me.

Mother-loving hell. I was falling in love, and we were barely talking.

"Okay," Ariel said. "Answers coming in."

We crowded together and peered at her screen and the unfolding group chat.

Ariel: Talk love to me. How early in the relationship did you know you'd fallen for your significant others?

Effie: OMG. Give me his name. I need details.

Ariel: Not me. Don't panic.

Casey: Ooh, I love this topic. Bear in mind I was only meant to be in Scotland for a short time, it was pretty quick. My two boys chased me down to the US to bring me back. The rest is history.

Isobel: I hated Lennox's guts for ages. Then a switch flipped inside me, and I was crazy for him. Like legit insane. I threw an engagement ring into the sea because I thought he was going to propose to someone else.

Effie: Love that story.

Isobel: Ten out of ten would recommend.

Ariel: Go big or go home. Got it. Keep 'em coming.

Viola: It was more gentle for me and Leo. I was moping and recovering from injury, he was getting over the death of his mother. We kind of had to love ourselves again before recognising how much we were falling for each other. It helped that my da adored him first. Never looked back since. He's my other half. Also, pregnancy hormones have me weeping at all the love in this conversation. Keep typing, ladies.

Effie: Gabe says he knew before me. Which tracks because he told me first. He really wants to know who we're talking about with regard to you, Ariel.

Ariel: Tell my nosy brother to mind his own business.

Casey: I have a test you can try. How interested are you in this other person? I don't mean physically or in how well they treat you. What do you know about their life? Do you care about what they've been through and how that affects them? If someone contradicted, wronged, or even threatened them, how does that make you feel? Would you watch or stand in front of them? If any of those questions bring a strong response, like you want to fix their problems, or force others to go through you to protect them, that's love.

The conversation continued, and my friend grinned, tapping out replies. I was stuck on Casey's challenge. Ever since Ben had told me his background, I'd cared. During our trip to the city, I'd hurt for all he'd suffered.

For how it continued to affect him.

He'd snarled at me on the stairs that what he'd shown me wouldn't change. Maybe that was true. Maybe that was his reason for not loving. But it wasn't mine.

"There's something I need to do," I said on a breath.

Ariel lifted her head, her attention on me.

I grasped her hand, the picture forming so clearly. "We need to go somewhere. It could take all day and you'll need to spend time with Jackson. Oh, and we need a car. But I can't tell you exactly what I'm doing or why. That isn't my information to share."

She nodded, her cheeks flushing slightly. "I'm here for it. Whatever you need."

In half an hour, we were outside the castle, Jackson helping Ariel load my cleaning equipment into the back of his car.

Ben wanted to see me later. But it wasn't just my problems I'd be aiming to fix. I'd stand in front of him and take on his.

To do that, I needed to know the extent of the damage and how deep it ran. He'd given me one side to his relationship with Tabby, but there was more. Her existence hurt him. Going to her home had been forced by his family visiting. He was keeping up a pretence of a relationship to protect them, but she'd refused to open the door, which meant right now, he'd be stuck, maybe even afraid of what would happen when it came time to take his mother there.

All of this had been playing out in the back of my mind, but until I considered it an *us* problem, I'd had no solution.

Maybe I still didn't, but I had to try.

Just before we set out on the three-hour journey, I dialled his number.

The other thing that came across loud and clear from the group chat was communication. Talking about thoughts and motivations, and being upfront with the person you cared about.

Ben's voicemail kicked in. No surprise.

I left a message, my heart pounding, finishing with, "If you don't want me to do this, I won't. But I want to try. Please let me."

Ten minutes into the journey, I got the notification my voicemail had been listened to.

No message returned.

If he cared, he didn't say.

In Edinburgh, I directed Jackson to the right street. The right block of flats. The route memorised from the significance of Ben bringing me here.

Then like Ben had done just days ago, I sat and stared up at the windows.

My hands shook.

I'd done this so many times. Taken my kit and arrived at the home of the person who badly needed the help. But in every scenario, they'd been the one contacting me, or at least a relative of theirs had. It had always come with a conversation. A recognition that this wasn't a fix for everything wrong in their lives. Just a single aspect that gave them a better starting place to try again.

If I considered Tabby's journey, it included prison time. Making terrible choices. And losing access to her son. She'd missed out on him growing up. Maybe that was behind her hostility now.

Ben had come all the way here to warn her about Autumn's visit—it was important to both of them. There, I could help.

I sucked in a breath then exited the car.

35

Ariel

I twiddled my thumbs, waiting. Jackson had walked Daisy into the block of flats, though she'd said she'd go in alone. He'd insisted on escorting her, which I could imagine Ben ordering him to do.

It was better for him to stand guard outside of wherever she'd gone rather than sit in the close confines of his car with me. The pressure of not talking, or worse—needing to make small talk—would end me.

The door to the block opened inwards, and the man in question strode out, his gaze locking on to me instantly. Then he switched to check the road.

Strange. It had looked like relief in his expression, though there was no reason for him to worry about me. I wasn't in any danger.

He climbed into the driver's seat, shutting out the chilly January day.

"All okay?" I asked, dread swarming.

"Daisy told me to hold back and that she'd text me when she was done. I waited for a while but wanted to check on ye, too."

Instead of standing in the hall, he'd returned to me.

My fingers twisted into my sleeves. I was nervous. I didn't get nervous.

"Your protective streak is a mile wide," I commented, forcing my hands still.

Jackson raised a shoulder, nothing casual about his position, appearing as tense as me. "It's my job."

I'd met Ben's previous bodyguards. None carried themselves with the same alertness as Jackson.

"It's more than that," I muttered, just for the sake of having something to say. "Or maybe just a sister thing?"

He snapped his attention onto me. "Then your brother told ye about me."

"My brother?"

Incredulity flashed over his ridiculously handsome features. "Not Ben. Fucking hell."

I raised my hands. "Wait up. No one has told me anything. The most I had from my brother was your name and the fact he met you in a statistics lecture at uni. I didn't even know you were coming back until—"

I flushed hot and shut my mouth.

We hadn't addressed the fact he'd seen me undressed. Or the kick to his gut. Or the fact I'd been avoiding him, and he'd probably been avoiding me since.

"About that."

"Hell no. Forget I spoke. Forget the whole thing, in fact."

His phone rang over the car's entertainment system.

Ben, it read on the dashboard screen.

"Jackson," my unwilling car buddy answered.

"Is she okay?" Ben asked, brief but also hesitant.

"Daisy's inside the apartment. I walked her there and waited outside for a while. All is well. Ariel and I will remain here until she's done. You're on loudspeaker in the car, just so ye know."

There was a pause. "She actually went through the door?"

"She did. Like I said, I waited outside, but there were no concerning sounds. Want more intel?"

"No. Just do me a favour and let me know when she comes out and you're on your way back." The call disconnected.

I didn't know whose apartment Daisy had gone into, but I guessed it was connected to Ben in some way. If she wanted to tell me, she would, but I respected the fact that this was her situation to handle.

We both knew how dangerous secrets could be. Truths, too.

She was one of the few people I trusted with almost all of mine.

Jackson's voice broke into my consciousness. "Back to what we're not talking about. Just let me say this. I scared ye, and for that, I need to apologise. I'd been working nights and had crashed out after Raphael let me in. I didn't wake up until I heard footsteps in the hall. It was all my fault."

I winced, the picture seeming so different in retrospect. "It should be me apologising. I hope I didn't hurt you."

"I'm hard to break." He cracked a smile. It was gone as fast as it came.

I stared at him, my awful crush intensifying. Low in my belly, compelling feelings swirled.

Something was different. With every other guy I'd crushed on, I'd never wanted to get to know them. Always the opposite. It was like I knew I'd be disappointed when I got to the heart of the man. Jackson would be the same, surely, but he was also infuriatingly intriguing. There was clearly something about him that Raphael and Ben knew that he considered gossip worthy.

It would drive me nuts because there was no way I was asking.

"Should I be getting a complex from your scrutiny?" he asked.

It took me a long moment to answer, despite the fact I was making this weird. "Just trying to figure you out."

"It's better if ye don't," he muttered back.

Annoyance flared in me, carried on the wave of my inappropriate feelings. "Why? You're living in my home. Best friends with my brother. What possible reason could you have for creating this air of dark mystery?"

I hadn't meant to say that.

It came out like an accusation.

But the effect on Jackson was instant. "Just because I'm friends with Raphael doesn't mean I need to befriend his kid sister. There's nothing to tell. No mystery. I'm just trying to do my job."

I tore my gaze away, my pulse thundering. How the heck had this turned into an argument? Why had I snapped at him? And what right did he have to infantilise me as a kid sister in his retort?

That was a million times worse than being friend zoned.

I faced forward, faking interest in my phone while silently stewing. The damage was done. With any luck, my crush would curl up and die.

Jackson breathed out through his nose. "I'm sorry—"

I held up a headphone. Popped it into my ear. Did the same with the other side. Then I offered him a saccharine smile and locked my ridiculous feelings in a box for good.

36

Ben

How fucking long did it take to drive back from Edinburgh? I knew the goddamn answer, but that didn't help my pent-up state as I paced the hall of Castle Braithar. Nobody else was home. No need to check my behaviour or hide the obvious stress I was giving off.

Jackson had told me they were returning, and if I wanted, I could track Daisy's phone. Pinpoint her exact position. But that was a breach of trust I wouldn't make.

After this morning's message and her plan of seeing Tabby, I'd been a mess. This evening ended it. All of it. Daisy would leave, and I needed to facilitate that without any more delays.

At long last, tyres rumbled on the ground outside.

I stalked to the door. Swung it open.

Daisy hopped from the back of Jackson's car, her gaze instantly coming to me.

She was okay. No tears. I breathed out and stomped back

inside the hall, throwing myself into an armchair with my laptop open on the coffee table.

Daisy entered, Ariel and Jackson following.

She pivoted to them. "Could you guys give us a few minutes?"

I gave a single shake of my head. "No need. It will be better if they're here."

Her uncertain gaze returned to me.

"We have work to do," I told them all. Locking myself into business mode. No space for anything else. "First, Daisy, call your mother. Then the office manager. Confirm the things we suspect."

Slowly, Daisy approached me and took a seat on the sofa beside my chair. She put her cool hand on my forearm. "Ben..."

I withdrew from her touch. "Just make the calls."

Her stare burned into the side of my face. I clicked something on my screen.

"Okay," she finally agreed.

In my peripheral vision, Ariel and Jackson drifted closer, though neither sat.

"Should I hide my number?" Daisy grumbled.

"No."

A ringtone filled the air.

The sound of a party came over the line. "Daisy's Delights. Tell me what's dirty and how hard I need to scrub."

Daisy winced. "It's me, Mom."

A rushed intake of breath followed, the background noise quieting. "Baby, there you are. I've been expecting you every day. Where did you go?"

"I stayed with a friend," Daisy replied, no discernible tone to her voice. "I just wanted to let you know I'm safe."

"Safe? Are you joking? What good is that? I need you here."

Daisy gave a harsh laugh. "Sounds like business is booming. I won't be taking the job offer, though, as much as I appreciate the name of your company."

Her mother tutted. "Don't be petty. I told you to come straight to me, but you're off in the world, leaving us all hanging. Your family has been so worried."

"I didn't mean for that to happen. Can you do me a favour? Please don't talk to Paul or Sigrid about me."

"What? They have a right to know where you are. Family comes first. Tell me where to find you."

Her shoulders hunched, and Daisy squeezed her eyes tightly closed. "I'm not going to do that. I've got to go. I just wanted to say hi."

"Hi? Are you serious? After everything I did for you—"

The call ended, Daisy stabbing at her screen.

Mild fury swept through her gaze, and she glowered at me. "Happy?"

I gave her nothing. Her mother was now set up to show her true colours. Even the fucking name of her company showed how easily she used Daisy. "Onto the next one," I ordered.

She placed a second call with an angry pout. "Is that Camila?"

Silence held the other end, then the office manager spoke. "Holy shit. The prodigal daughter."

"The what? Never mind. I just wanted to say I got your note," Daisy snapped, her temper fraying. "Thanks for that.

It would've been nice if you'd had the guts for a face-to-face chat, but I took your advice. Mind telling me what was behind it?"

"You need to tell me where you are," the other woman said.

"Do I? Why?"

"Because of the panic you caused."

"Wait up. You wanted me gone."

"What I needed to happen," the office manager snipped, "was your swift exit from the family business. You didn't deserve what they offered you, and you don't have the balls to live up to their legacy. But you could've done it with grace. Instead, you stole away like a thief."

"A thief? They were holding me there."

"Yeah, a terrible thing, being given a roof over your head in a multi-million-dollar home while the rest of the world slums it. Poor you. Can you hear yourself over that entitled whining?"

I'd suspected this. The office manager wasn't trying to help her. Camila had been jealous. Daisy had said her dislike had been obvious, and Jackson's background check had shown how long she'd worked for the company.

She'd wanted the life Daisy had led.

I drew my fingers over my throat, indicating to Daisy that she needed to get off the line. We'd found out all we needed.

But the lass who couldn't be mine wasn't done. "For the record, Camila, I never asked to be part of this family. It doesn't work that way, and I never once tried to exploit it. I never wanted a free ride, though you bet I was grateful for everything they did for me. But trapping me? Denying me the chance to start off on my own? There was nothing graceful in that, as you put it. I'm hanging up now. I hope you have the day you deserve."

She killed the call then gripped her phone like she was about to throw it at me. "Is that what you wanted to hear?"

The phone rang in her hand.

Exactly as I expected it to do.

Daisy lowered it, staring at her screen. "That's Sigrid's number."

One of them, almost certainly her mother, had jumped straight on forwarding Daisy's new contact details.

"Answer it," I told her.

With a look of betrayal, she let the call connect.

"Daisy? Is that you?" an older woman's voice filled the room.

Daisy held my gaze. "It's me."

Flustered sounds came down the line. "Paul, it's really her," Sigrid spluttered, fraught. "Daisy-flower, we were so worried. Are you okay?"

At last, one of the people who was supposed to care about her asked the right question.

Daisy curled her legs underneath her. "I'm fine. I know I left in a hurry, but I've been safe ever since."

Sigrid gave a sob. "I'm so relieved to hear it. I've been out of my mind with worry. We tried finding out the identity of the man who came for you. It was only your call to your mother that let my heart rest that you hadn't been kidnapped." She took a deep breath. "This is all my fault. I came on too strong. Since you turned twenty-one, I'd been preparing so much for you, but I didn't tell you any of it because I wanted it to be a surprise."

"What are you talking about?" Daisy asked.

This was the heart of it.

Luna had sown the seeds. Sigrid was about to confirm it.

"The party was for you, my dearest girl. We were ready to introduce you. All the people you met were there to get the message out. To get your name on people's lips. We've been planning it for years."

The colour left Daisy's face. She opened and closed her mouth, starting but failing to find her words. "Planning what, exactly?"

"To put you where you belong. Right in the centre of our family as heir to the business."

Ariel moved to the back of the sofa and took Daisy's free hand.

Both women knew what it was like to be used by their families. This might not have been Daisy's vision for her future, but there was every chance she'd take it. That she'd walk away from her friends here, and memories of Scotland would be exactly that. A vacation while she was settling her direction in life.

"I had no idea," she whispered.

My fucking heart ached.

I leaned in to the phone, neutralising my Scottish accent to closer to English. "This is Daisy's bodyguard. Are you aware of the kidnap attempt Daisy suffered a couple of days after she left your home?"

Sigrid took in a shocked breath. "No."

"It wasn't you who sent someone after her?"

"Absolutely not. I swear it."

A male voice followed. "Paul Devereux here. I can assure you we would never act against our own family in that way. I'm pleased to hear Daisy employed a bodyguard, though. That shows the foresight I'd expect in the future owner of Devereux Family Holdings. If you make arrangements to bring her back, I will take over her personal safety as my utmost priority. Daisy, I will, of course, cover all expenses you've incurred during your...time away. We just want you back."

I linked my gaze to Daisy's, ignoring the shock of recognition I always got when we made eye contact. "Mute the call," I mouthed.

She tapped the screen, a myriad of emotions in her expression.

"Ye can return safely to them," I forced out.

"Oh, can I?"

I shrugged, well aware I looked like an arsehole. She was going to leave. Better for her not to regret me. "Ye said yourself that family was everything. All that's happened here is a misunderstanding. They love ye. They can protect ye. It's everything ye wanted."

"Everything I...? Are you sure about that?"

She peered back at Ariel who somehow read into her expression, as her friend turned, ushering Jackson with her out of the front door.

Purposefully, and with her glower locked on me, Daisy un-muted the phone. "Sigrid, what do you envisage me doing in this future role?"

"Why, running the business. You'll work alongside Paul and me and learn everything there is to learn until we can hand over the reins to you. First, with taking over management of our staff. Camila will report to you. She has ambitious ideas for expanding the business into new areas. You can do great things."

"What if I say no?"

Her aunt sighed. "I know you're confused. Your mother did a bad job in raising you to believe in yourself, which is why I took it upon myself to manage your education. To give you a home and to encourage you in healthier habits than the ones you picked up. I only ever wanted the best for you." Her tone changed, the upset falling away. "The decision has been made. You'll come home and take up the role. The gratitude, I'm sure, will follow."

An alarm bell rang in the back of my mind, buried underneath a day's worth of bullshit that had piled over my senses.

Daisy had never batted an eyelid at the type of business her family was in. The criminal aspect didn't seem to concern her, probably because she was immune to it. Immersed in it since birth. Their expansion couldn't mean anything good. She would be walking into a criminal role.

"I'm finding the gratitude part a little tricky right now," she snipped. "Again, what happens if I say I won't do it?"

"We've bought you an apartment. A signet ring that marks you out as on a tier with us. What possible reason could you have for refusing?" Paul asked.

His wife huffed. "I'm calling her mother back. With all she owes us, she'll be persuaded."

"So Mom *is* in debt to you," Daisy interjected.

"Significantly. You can protect her."

"From what?"

"Owing such a large sum of money is a dangerous game."

The colour left Daisy's cheeks. "You're blackmailing me? Seriously?"

"Without us, she'd be in jail," Sigrid suddenly shrieked. "Now listen here and don't you dare interrupt. You'd better—"

Daisy hung up, her breathing coming hard.

Her gaze held mine. "You absolute idiot. Stand up."

I climbed to my feet, not taking my focus off her for a second.

"Are you happy now? It's all out in the open. Is it everything you wanted to hear?" Daisy prowled into my space, her phone held out. "You said there's tracking on this phone. I want you to change who can find me to Ariel."

I worked my jaw.

"That wasn't a request," she added.

I took it. Made the change.

Daisy tossed it to the couch and kept coming, her finger to my chest and absolute fury in her snarl. "Paul and Sigrid are my family. I loved them. Now, I'm pretty sure I hate them. Consider for a second everything they did, not only to me but in whatever drove their daughters away. I *never* wanted to go back to them, but there's you, ready to throw me to the wolves. All because you got freaked out by your feelings for me."

I folded my arms. If I didn't, I was going to do something stupid like try to hold her.

"Now you listen up and listen good," Daisy continued. "Today, I spent an hour in the company of Tabby. I'm so sorry for how she's been with you. She was vile to me as well, but visiting with her was important. I got to understand so much more about you, you jackass. I told her I was your girlfriend—by the way, please don't make me into a liar, but also that I owned a cleaning company. I suspected after your visit that she'd be worried about her sister seeing the place, so I said I was there to help out. She let me in. It was clear before I even got into the place that she has some pretty significant mental or emotional issues. Likely both."

The last thing I'd wanted was for her to see that, but I

was hooked on what she'd done. What she'd tried to do for me.

Daisy's expression gentled. "For all the cleaning I managed, I barely made a dent. She's a hoarder. Which then made sense to me for why you live in two rooms with barely anything in them, collecting nothing while she has everything. For people like her, you can't just clear trash because it holds emotional value. She got angrier the more I touched things."

"If she hurt ye—"

"She didn't. I left when I could see she'd had enough. The woman needs help, compassion. From the very little I know about it, there's often a traumatic event in the person's past. Tabby has boxes full of baby food. But then I guess you know that."

I closed my eyes for a second. The boxes had been there for years. If they were linked to her loss of me, as she was deep in criminal activity when she'd fallen pregnant and perhaps anticipated jail, I'd never let myself acknowledge it.

"In the States, I was developing contacts with professionals so I could give referral information, but that kind of thing is rough going. Family members are not the people to fix it. You don't need to fix her. Nor do you need to hide her from your family. She isn't a reflection of you."

I swallowed. Swallowed again. Tried to find any of the right words. "She isn't worth your time."

"But you are. Despite how you've pushed me away, I still believe that. And do you know what? It isn't just me. You push your family away. You're clinging to a life with no change. Fixed with you here and your family over there. Safe so long as they stay away from you, right? Even with Valentine, you pieced together the most unlikely revenge story, painting him a suspect because he was at risk of getting close to you again. You don't want him here as you'll have to work through a functioning relationship with him. Instead, you practice this excuse that they're better off away from you. They aren't. They love you." Her voice cracked, her chest rising and falling. "You are loved."

My breathing came fast. "Daisy…"

She threw her hands in the air. "And then you go and say my name like that. I'm mad at you. So freaking mad."

The castle door opened, and Gordain ran in. "Ben, I need ye."

I didn't want to stop staring at Daisy. To end this conversation here. I dragged my gaze to my boss.

"Viola's baby is coming," he bit out. "We're going to the hospital. I need you to guard my family."

This was why I was here. My job. My role.

But the timing, fucking hell.

Daisy shoved my arm. "Go, you big ape."

I didn't want to.

Gordain jogged back into the hall, carrying a bag, urgency in every look. I had no choice but to leave with him.

37

Daisy

With Ben gone, my bravado evaporated. I sank to the sofa, dropped my head to my hands, and bawled. Then I pulled myself together and called my best friend. She returned in minutes, giving me the kind of hug I wished I could have taken from Ben.

"We argued," I sniffled.

"He deserved it," Ariel decided. "Honestly, what was he thinking?"

"Pretty sure he wasn't doing much of that."

He'd been on autopilot, following unchangeable rules and not letting anyone near his heart. I'd hated calling him out, but nothing I'd said was unfair.

"Want to talk family matters?" she asked.

"Not for a second. They had plans for me, just different to what we expected. I don't want to give any of them another minute of my time."

I pointed to the phone she'd set on the table. "Can you type this into your group chat? *What to do when he's the biggest jerk?*"

Replies came fast.

Isobel: How big?

Ariel: On a scale from keying his car to slamming his dick in a door, it's up there.

Isobel: Tequila shots. Stat.

Casey: I'm so down. We've been talking about making baby number four, so I could use a last blast. My place? My boys can entertain the kids and we'll take over the kitchen.

Effie: Hell yes. On my way.

Viola: This is Leo. Viola is currently busy giving birth, so she can't make it, but I'm sure she'll be with you in non-alcoholic spirit.

A flurry of messages responded, encouraging Viola and reassuring Leo.

Then Ariel put me into her car and drove me out to Casey's place.

At a large family home not far from Mr Campbell's lovely cottage, Casey welcomed us, guiding us into the kitchen where a number of women already waited.

"I added a few members to the party. We're all friends here, and everyone's had to deal with a stubborn ass of a man from time to time," Casey said then introduced me to Cait, Rory, and a few others.

A cocktail of some sort arrived in my hand. Minutes later, I'd finished it, cracking up at a story Cait was telling about her own flawed start to a relationship where she'd fled the country instead of facing the fact she'd had feelings.

Almost as bad as Ben's cold shoulder and betrayal, trying

to push me back with my relatives.

No one pressed me for information, though it was obvious they knew I was the source of the drama, not Ariel.

More, it was... Nice.

There was a supportive community here, ready to spring into action to help one another. They didn't even know me, but I'd already been accepted.

A grinning, half-drunk Ariel slipped back to my side and curled an arm around me. She pitched her voice lower, just for me, looking out on the sea of happy faces in Casey's bright kitchen. "If it's family you want, we have it. You've always been my ride or die, and I'm ready to throw down to get you to stay. Make a business here, find somewhere more permanent to live. Even if just for a trial. But if you decide that, let it be for you. For the first time in your life, it's entirely in your hands. Choose your own adventure. If Ben isn't it and here isn't right, I'll support you in whatever is. Just know you have the choice. And you've made that happen all by yourself."

She was right. There was nothing to influence my decision now but my own wants and needs.

"I think the tequila's gone to my head," I said on a shuddering breath. "Because all of a sudden I'm considering the impossible."

With an elbow on the kitchen island, Casey stared at her phone and snapped a hand to her mouth. "Viola's had her baby. Her little boy arrived safely."

Everyone cheered.

"Let's get drunk and toast the newcomer," Ariel cried.

The kitchen door swung open, letting in cold air from the outside. Isobel appeared in the frame, her cheeks wet and her expression cut up.

I'd noticed the Englishwoman's absence, but presumed she'd been caught in family matters, or something else to delay her coming.

Her gaze landed squarely on me. "I'm so sorry to break up the fun. Daisy, you need to come with me. Now."

38

Ben

The hospital corridor buzzed with life, medics busying around, escorting patients to or from the delivery suites, carrying equipment. All standard fare on the maternity ward.

I stood with my back to Viola's door, keeping any casual onlooker from trying to grab a peek or even a sneaky picture. The door opened behind me, and Gordain emerged. He sighed, his grin unending since his grandson had made his quick entrance.

"He's a bonny wee thing. Viola wants ye to meet him. I'll stand guard."

He folded his arms and faced outwards, releasing me to enter the hospital suite. In the bed, the lass smiled up at me, Leo beside her with Finn on his lap. I focused on the tiny newborn scrap in her arms.

"Ben, meet Torran, your newest little buddy," Leo said, his voice pitched low at snoozing baby level.

I tiptoed over as carefully as a man of my size could and stooped to examine his face. "He's braw. Just like Finn as a wean. Please to meet ye, Torran. Welcome to the world."

Promptly, Viola burst into tears. She handed off the baby to Leo and reached to hug me. "You've always protected us. I don't know what we'd do without ye as part of our family," she sobbed on my shoulder.

I patted her arm, warm emotion rushing in me.

Daisy's words returned to me. She'd accused me of pushing my family away. Keeping myself from them so I didn't have to handle relationships.

Standing on guard for another family, I'd had a whole lot of time to reflect.

She was right.

I used the disaster of Valentine's ex as an excuse, but I'd been doing it way before then. Starting with not fighting Tabby's demands, going into the military, then remaining in the UK. My brother had stayed with me, and I'd had the gall to put him on my suspect list.

"Here, cuddle time," Leo said. He circled the bed and held out the bundle of baby and blanket.

I cradled Torran, setting his face in my mind. In future, I'd be carrying him around at gigs or walking behind Leo and Viola while they showed their boys their da's world of a stage and crowds. Finn used to ride on my shoulders to do the same.

My thoughts arched in another direction. Tabby would've once held me like this, knowing she had to let me go. I'd considered it back at the castle, but now it sank in. It was impossible to hold a tiny baby and not want to protect them from the world. Whatever bond she'd felt had obviously cracked something in her if she knew it had to break.

Or maybe she'd always been that way. I didn't have to like her, but Daisy had helped me understand her. Equally, I didn't know if I could forgive or forget the way she'd treated me, but one stunning, life-changing fact slammed home.

I didn't need to let her trauma impact my life.

From now on, I wouldn't.

I raised my head to find Leo, Viola, and Finn all watching me.

"Got to say, you look at home with a baby in your arms," Leo said. "Maybe one day our positions will be switched and it'll be your little one I'm greeting."

I shook my head, tracing my gaze down the swoop of the tiny bairn's nose, trying to imagine having one of my own. Of their features being mine or my lass's. "Pretty significant missing element in that I'm single."

Gordain ducked into the room. "Really? How the hell did ye screw things up with Daisy?"

My mouth opened. "Ye knew we weren't over?"

Leo gave a soft laugh. "Of course we did. You're as subtle as a breeze-block. All those longing looks across the dinner table and watching her wherever she went."

Horror passed over me.

I'd broken a code.

"I didn't mean for it to happen. I never intended to be unprofessional," I swore.

Gordain scrunched up his nose. "What's that got to do with it?"

"The interviewee ye cancelled. The fact I've shown the same poor judgement."

He gave me a patient smile. "This is ye we're talking about, not some random who was after one thing only. I'm happy for ye. Or at least I was."

"You and Daisy? We're delighted for you both," Ella said, coming back from making a series of phone calls outside, sharing the news on her daughter's behalf.

"He messed things up," my boss snarked.

"Ben, no!" she whispered. "What happened?"

"I was the biggest moron."

"Can ye fix it?" Gordain asked.

Could I?

I handed Torran back to his ma, taking a second to ruffle Finn's hair, making sure the wee lad knew he was still my number one.

"I'm going to arrange for Jackson to take over as security until you're ready to leave," I said. "I don't mean to duck out on ye, but I need to do some damage control."

Leo squinted at his father-in-law. "G? He's waiting on you. Tell him to get going. It's a mission of mercy."

Gordain flapped a hand at me. "What are ye waiting for? Get going, man."

There was no telling me twice.

Outside the hospital, I called Daisy's number. She didn't pick up, which wasn't a great sign, but this was better dealt with in person anyway.

I ploughed on, driving into the night.

Half an hour in, my phone lit, but it was my mother's name on the screen.

She and Valentine were due to fly out in a few days, arriving in Scotland for a week for her and longer for my brother. I answered her on hands-free.

"Ma, is everything okay?"

I listened as she filled me in on their schedule, promising to collect them from Inverness airport after the transfer.

"Tell Val I'm looking forward to seeing him," I said honestly.

"I will. Other than you, there's one person I'm very much looking forward to seeing again, too," she replied.

"We can try to see Tabby, but I need to tell you something." I'd never done this. Not once admitted the extent of her neglect and rejection while maintaining control over me. "Tabby doesn't let me into the apartment, not anymore, and hardly ever when I was younger. During the holidays, I used to go back to school on my own. It was only if she had an official visitor such as the parole service that I was allowed through the door. I haven't seen her face to face for years."

Ma took a shocked breath. I found myself telling her everything.

Years of hidden history spilled down the phone line. My reasons for hiding it.

Ma sobbed, and emotion broke wide open in me, too.

"All I care about is your happiness," she uttered. "My sister was always such a selfish creature, but I gave her the benefit of the doubt time and time again for your sake. Because you deserve better. I'm sorry I didn't realise what was happening."

"Ye didn't know because I didn't say anything. I'm the one who's sorry."

"Well, we don't have to see her. I won't put you through that." Ma clucked her tongue. "I just realised. Is that who you thought I meant when I said I was looking forward to seeing a woman?"

"Who else?"

"Daisy, your maybe-wife. If she's there."

Unless I'd driven her away completely, Ma might even get her wish.

"I'll see what I can do," I offered, my heart hitching at a sound of delight from the other end of the line.

Then I told my mother I loved her and drove the rest of the journey in perfect suspense.

At Braithar, the hall was dark, and I jogged upstairs to Daisy's room.

Empty.

"Daisy," I called, striding back down to the kitchen then peering into every doorway.

Nothing. She wasn't here.

I tried her number again, but still she didn't pick up.

Outside the front entrance, someone had left a parcel with my name on it. I'd parked around the back so had missed it on my arrival.

An eerie sense of trepidation oozed through me.

We rarely had parcels delivered here. It was too remote. Most companies didn't come this far out.

I shook it, and something rattled.

My breathing sped up.

I tore into the cardboard.

A yellow piece of paper fluttered to the ground, landing on the snow.

Ignoring that for a second, I extracted a plastic-wrapped package.

I had no idea why, but I was getting the worst feeling from this. The ticking time bomb effect, though I had no reason for my premonition. Gingerly, I peeled away the plastic. A Swiss army knife was revealed.

My pulse skipped. I turned it over, examining the perfectly ordinary folded knife. Then I stooped to grab the paper.

It was an invoice, most of the details left off, but with a gift note label at the bottom.

To my favourite grumpy bodyguard.

Keep this as a memory of the help you gave me in your car.

Love, your Daisy.

A gift. I breathed out, scanning it again to make sure there was nothing I'd missed. She'd told me she'd picked out something for me. That's all this was. Nothing more.

Except the *love* part I couldn't dwell on.

Why did I still feel like something was badly wrong?

My phone rang, and I snatched it up. Jackson's name lit onscreen.

"Good to talk?" he asked.

"I am. Any idea where Daisy is?"

He paused. "No. I took Ariel back to Castle McRae, but a short while later, she got in her car because Daisy had asked her to return. That was the last I saw of either of them."

"I'm going to try Ariel," I bit out, urgency building within me.

"Hold on. There's something ye need to hear," he interrupted, freezing me halfway in my attempt to switch to another call. "Following what ye and Daisy worked out about her relatives, it's been bugging me that we still don't know the identity of the would-be kidnapper. I can't rule out that it's them and they're lying, so I had a second look through their invoices, cross-checking all the names we'd listed and hunting for clues. Hidden away in a section for contractor payments is a record of cash paid out to an L Larson."

"Landon Larson, the creep from school who showed up at her apartment?"

"Got it. There was a possibility of me being wrong, but the invoice had an address. From that, I was able to get his employment details for which he has mostly been losing more jobs than staying in them, but also his passport number."

Fuck. "Get to the point," I ordered. There was worse to come, I sensed it.

My premonition had been for this. It couldn't be good.

Jackson's tone darkened. "He left the US yesterday on the flight to the UK. Landing in Manchester."

My blood iced over.

"He took money from her family then came here, choosing the same city ye and Daisy landed into. That's no coincidence," he said with barely hidden anger.

"Daisy's not home. She's not answering my calls," I managed, my stomach clamping and my feeling of unease morphing into full-blown fear. "Where the hell is she? How the fuck did he find her?"

"I have no fucking idea. My guess from the fact he worked for her family is we're dealing with someone in the business. Maybe even a specialist."

I turned on the spot, jamming my fingers into my hair.

If he'd gone anywhere near her, I was going to kill him. I didn't care if she never wanted to see me again, I'd failed her both in my heart and in my protection.

My phone beeped, and I pulled it away from my ear. Isobel calling. I told Jackson to hold then switched to answer her.

"Ben, I know you're in Inverness—"

"I'm not. I'm here. What's wrong?"

She took a short breath. "Get in your car and drive to Mr Campbell's place. Daisy needs you."

39

Daisy

In Mr Campbell's darkened living room, the air still scented with the light polish I'd applied on my last cleaning trip, I knelt and picked up the photo album beside his chair. Dougal whined and nudged my hand, seeking comfort.

I collected the little dog onto my lap and opened the book.

Wedding pictures filled the pages. A beautiful smiling bride and her handsome husband. The pictures in a fading brown print. The precious memories of a man no longer with us.

On her way to Casey's, Isobel had stopped in to take Mr Campbell a piece of cake her husband had baked. She called in on him from time to time, just as I'd intended to start doing for as long as I was here.

The door had been unlocked, and he hadn't answered

her hails.

She'd found him asleep forever in his favourite chair.

Outside, an ambulance crew loaded him into the back, Isobel overseeing him leaving his home for the last time. A fat tear rolled down my cheek. I dashed it away so it didn't land on the wedding album.

In my short time of knowing the elderly man, I'd liked him so much. I'd also loved his stories. Tales of Highlands life. The happy marriage he'd had with his wife which had made me able to imagine what I wanted from my own.

Love. Mutual respect. Willingness to be there for each other in all things.

I'd wanted that with Ben, and I couldn't have it. He'd told me himself that he was closed off. He'd been that way for years and wouldn't change.

I'd yelled at him, thinking that perhaps he'd yell back. Set me right. He hadn't, and then it had been too late. He'd been back on duty, and I'd had a reality check.

Ariel had been right. My life was mine now, and I could choose what I wanted to do with it.

An engine roared outside, a door slamming. I stretched to peek from the window. Ben leapt from his car and stormed to where the ambulance crew closed their doors. Frantic, he said words I couldn't hear.

Then he spun around to Isobel.

The Englishwoman spoke to him, her hands out. His shoulders sank. His expression crumpled then reformed.

My traitorous heart ached.

His gaze found the house, then he was moving.

I dropped back to sitting, hugging Dougal close to me, my fingers buried in his soft white fur.

Ben entered the living room. I'd turned the lights off after the crew had wheeled out Mr Campbell's gurney, preparing to lock his house up until morning. It suited the mood now as Ben discovered me in the gloom.

He paced over, dropping down until we were eye to eye. His hand came out as if he wanted to touch me, his gaze fluttering over me.

"You're okay," he finally said.

Tension played out over him. I had the sense that he wanted to snatch me up. Carry me out of here.

"Not really," I replied softly. "Mr Campbell died."

Emotion rolled through me. My breathing shuddered.

Ben closed his eyes for a moment and nodded. "I'm so sorry. He was a good old boy. What I meant was I was scared for ye."

I stroked Dougal's shaggy fur. "Why?"

Footsteps came from the hall, then Isobel appeared in the doorframe. "They've taken him away," she said softly.

Dougal gave a small yap and wrestled out of my arms, trotting up to Isobel.

She bent and picked him up, holding him close. "My kids love Dougal. I'll take him home with me until we can find him another home. Daisy, if you're around tomorrow, can you meet me here? There will be some sorting out of the house needed, and I'd love your help."

I nodded. "I'd love to. Thank you for letting me."

As landowners, or future landowners at least, homes of tenants were her and her family's responsibility. She'd told me how her father-in-law, Callum, had gifted her the task. I couldn't imagine a nicer place to move where everyone cared about each other.

"Take whatever time you need and I'll see you tomorrow," Isobel instructed.

Then she left us alone.

I stood, taking the photo album with me. Of all Mr Campbell's possessions, this felt so special. I knew Isobel wouldn't mind if I kept it safe for a night. On heavy legs, I trudged outside. Ben followed.

At the door, he grabbed my hand, enclosing my fingers in his much bigger grip. Then he led me down the path, apparently in a hurry.

I lifted our joined hands. "What are you doing?"

Ben hauled in a breath, the cool winter's evening calmer than any other in the time I'd been here. "Everything ye said to me was right."

"Meaning...?"

"I've been a jackass."

He tugged me onwards, leading me to the car.

I stopped dead. Shook him off. "I'm not going to argue with your choice of words, but what the heck sort of explanation was that?"

"Believe me, I have more to say. I need to get ye behind closed doors first. Do ye trust me?"

There was more to what he was saying. This wasn't a grand romantic gesture. Ben was in his controlled action mode.

"Something happened," I guessed.

His phone buzzed, and he checked the screen. "Jackson's on his way to take care of Viola and Leo and their family. He confirmed that Ariel's safe in the tower. Let me get ye home and I'll explain."

A frisson of energy ran over my nerves. I gave up resisting, got into his car, and let him drive me back to Braithar.

Inside the castle, Ben kept hold of my hand while he performed a circuit of the place, locking doors and windows. He searched the entire building, checking security feeds that I hadn't been aware existed. Finally, he was done.

"Is it safe to go to bed?" I stared at him.

It was impossible. I was in love with this man, and he couldn't feel the same for me. I really, really wanted a locked door between us so I could nurse a disintegrating heart on my own.

Ben stopped in front of me. "Stay in my room."

"No."

"Why not? We need to talk, and I'll feel safer knowing exactly where ye are."

I made for the stairs, wedding album tucked under my arm. "Whatever you have to say to me can wait till morning. I assume the danger I'm in has passed. I'm slightly drunk, very miserable, and seeing you is only making it all feel worse."

"My family was big on telling each other we loved each other."

His words chased me.

I paused with my hand to the carved wooden stair rail. Listening but not looking around.

Ben continued. "At some point, I stopped saying it back. I can't remember the exact reason, but it was as if I felt set apart from them. Not through anything they did, but because of my own circumstances. How I had to lead a separate life to them if they were to be happy in theirs."

Slowly, I turned.

He scrubbed his hands through his blond hair, ruffling

it further. "Earlier, on the phone, I told Ma about Tabby. Everything. All the truths I'd been hiding because I didn't want her to share my burden. Then I finished the call by telling her I loved her. She'll be here soon and she really wants to meet ye again."

"I'm glad you told her. I'll happily see her, but I hope you set her straight on what we are to each other."

He didn't answer, but his gaze beseeched me. I had no idea where his mind was at. It was great that he'd gone on a journey of discovery. Realising truths about himself. Maybe in future, some lucky woman would reap the benefits.

For some reason, that last thought flashed new frustration in a fast surge. "You know what? This trip has been the gift that keeps on giving. I never left the US before, and I did it while escaping the control of my relatives and having my world turned upside down by the most infuriating man. If you have something to say to me, spit it out. You drive me mad. I never meant for this to happen. I never meant to fall for a guy so impossibly much I'd be willing to..."

"Willing to what?"

"It doesn't matter, because you don't feel the same. Correction, you won't let yourself feel the same."

"You're wrong. By which I mean I've been so fucking wrong to have made ye think that." Ben advanced to the bottom of the steps until we were at eye level. "Ye want a love story, I'll give that to ye. Those romance books we listened to are about more than people screwing. All those people had obstacles to overcome, just like us. Please hear me out before ye write me off. We've been living our love story. I just hadn't realised it."

A band of pain compressed my chest. Surely he couldn't be for real. "I don't know if I can believe you," I admitted.

"I know why ye touched my body," he went on. "Ye craved

intimacy I didn't give."

I took a quick breath. He wasn't done.

"I can see now that I left gaps in all the things I did. I let ye do the hard work. I pretended to myself I was just being a good protector, and that was why I obsessively needed to be wherever ye were. In reality, I just couldnae be apart for long."

My memory served a myriad of images that contradicted his initial belief. Ben bringing me food. Remembering my order. The little touches in his room were all about me and not him.

"What are you saying?" I pressed. I needed to be sure, because my poor heart had been through the wringer tonight. "Was I right? Do you think you have feelings?"

"No, shortie. I know it. I'm one hundred percent in love with ye."

I slapped my hand to my open mouth, my pulse racing and an explosion of joy replacing most of my hurt. This was everything I'd wanted, but somehow better. He seemed happy. Not grumpy about it at all, which was more than I'd pictured in my wildest imaginings.

Ben pulled my fingers away, cradling my hand. "Ye told me I had feelings and I was running from them. Completely correct. I didn't know what it was. Now I do, and it's changed everything. I'm fucking terrified."

"Why?" I managed, though tears threatened to clog my throat.

"Because I messed things up. I hurt ye, and that's the last thing I want. Please give me another chance." He swallowed. Looked around at the castle he called home. "I'll go back with ye to the US. I know I'm jumping ahead, but I'm fucking panicked at the thought of losing ye. I need to tell ye about what happened tonight."

I lifted our joined hands to set a finger to his lips. "Promise me this is real."

"I promise."

"You won't wake up in the morning and change your mind."

"I swear it."

"Then everything else can wait."

I leaned in and kissed him.

Ben met my lips with barely controlled hunger. I couldn't get over the change in him, but if I thought about it, he'd been almost meeting me at every stage. The barriers, first of his work, then of his birth mother, had needed to fall.

I broke the kiss. "What happens with your job? I'm still technically a client. Wait, you're fired. Why didn't I think of that before?"

He gave a laugh and ran his arms around me, collecting me from the steps bride-style. "Gordain already knew. The whole family did. They're rooting for us and were quick to judge me for screwing up."

Then he was moving, carrying me to the back of the hall and down the passage that led to his rooms.

Whatever we had to face next, I was ready.

Daisy

Inside, he shut us in and placed me on the bed. Soft light filled the room from the lamp he'd brought here just for me.

He took the photo album from me and set it carefully on his desk then prowled over, stripping his shirt in a fluid move.

Excitement tightened my belly.

I loved him like this. Focused on me. Intent on what he was about to do.

He sat by my feet and picked one up. I'd already kicked off my boots, and he drew his fingertip up the arch.

I shuddered and extracted my foot from his grip.

"Ticklish? Good. I'm learning. I'm going to take my time with ye, shortie. Explore every inch. Work ye until you're screaming my name."

I scooted up the bed and dragged my top over my head, my boobs bouncing as I threw it to the floor.

Ben's gaze sank to my chest, and he bit out a groan, obviously trying to restrain himself from leaping on me judging by his locked biceps and strained neck muscles.

I didn't want him to take his time. I wanted him around me now. Inside me.

"Am I in danger?" I asked. "No details, just answer that."

He worked his jaw. "Maybe."

"Then give me everything you've got. Don't tease. Fuck me until I forget both our names."

He swore then launched at me, bringing his arms around me and crushing me to him. Our lips met in a kiss built of furious passion.

Ben ran his hands up my back, caressing my skin. He unclipped my bra and wrenched it from me, tossing it in the same direction as my shirt. Then his hands were on my boobs, and his lips travelling down my neck until he bit and sucked my breasts.

I tangled my fingers in his hair, tipping my head back with a gasp at his actions.

He slowed, taking a hard pull at my nipple. Then he gazed up. "More than once, I've imagined ye pregnant with my bairn. I've no idea where the thoughts are coming from but I'm half insane with it."

"Slow down there," I answered on a breath. "You've only just realised you want me. Now you're talking babies?"

"No, I've always wanted ye. From the first second I saw ye, crawling out of a window in underwear that I was dying to get off ye."

His kisses descended to my belly, but I was far too in love now for any remaining self-consciousness. He loved me.

How did I get so lucky? Then Ben's fingers were at my waist-band, and the rest of my clothes gone.

With me naked, he blew out a breath and leapt up. "Follow me."

He stripped his jeans and boxers, walking into his bath-room. There, he started up the shower and stepped under the spray.

He set his back to the tiled wall, his dick bobbing. "Ye wanted to try out a shower sex toy. Go ahead. Use me."

I snickered and entered the stall, closing the door. There was barely enough room for us both, and the warm water sluiced over my skin, wetting my hair.

Ben held his position, his chest rising and falling.

I sank to my knees. Took hold of his dick and enclosed the end with my mouth.

"Fuck," he gritted out. "Pretty sure you're using it wrong."

I burst out laughing and swallowed him down, teasing him until he gripped my hair in warning. Then I rose. Turned.

To get him into position, I needed to go up on my tiptoes, but then finally I was able to sink down on him.

We both moaned. With my palms flat to the glass, I rolled my hips, taking him in deep.

"Good little sex toy," I gasped. "You fit so well."

"Little?" he gritted out.

I continued fucking him slowly.

"Okay, big. Really big. Perfectly shaped—"

Abruptly, Ben slammed his hand on the button for the water and withdrew. "This sizeable sex toy is taking over."

He hurried me out, bundling me in a towel. On the bed, he scrubbed the water from my skin and got between my legs.

He groaned, gazing at my pussy. "I've missed ye."

I laughed, about to ask if he meant just that one part of me, but then his mouth was on my most sensitive place, and all my words fled. He licked me from my entrance to my clit, muttering something about me being fucking delicious, then he set in with rhythmic sucks, and first one, then two fingers inside me. Driving me crazy.

This was the way sex went with him. Fun, easy, and with plentiful orgasms.

He sent me over the edge within minutes, pulling away for seconds that had me peeking at him through my delicious state. Ben crawled back up my body to hug me to him then rolled us over.

Him on his back, me astride him, my damp hair tumbling down my back.

I didn't wait. I rose up on my knees, fitted him to my entrance, and sank down once again.

Both of us gave deep sounds of pleasure. Ben pushed up on an elbow to watch, his free hand cupping and feeling my breasts. I eased him in and out of me, rising and falling slowly, loving the stretch.

There was nothing so intimate as this. The way we joined. The heat and perfect fit of our bodies. Ben stretched to bring his lips to mine, and I slowed, revelling in our kiss.

"I need you so much," I confessed.

"Hold tight to me." Ben clamped me to him and took over control.

He slammed into me, lighting me up in spirals of incredible feeling.

I clutched him, my face in the crook of his neck, breathing in his addictive scent. Loving every part of him.

Stroke after stroke, his passion intensified, until there was only us. Only this.

Then his dick pulsed, and Ben's rhythm faltered. His orgasm triggered mine. We fell together. Breathed together.

He took me down to the bed, holding on so tight I never wanted him to let go.

Maybe I never had to.

If I could have this forever, I would be the luckiest woman alive.

A little while later, Ben cleaned us up then arranged the blanket over my naked body before slipping in beside me. Had we done this? Just lain in bed together?

"I'm in love with you as well," I told him.

"Thank fuck for that."

I lightly elbowed him, peeking up to see his beautiful grin in place. "Say it back."

"I love ye."

"Again."

"Daisy Devereux, you're the love of my life. Marry me."

I cracked up laughing. Then I registered his expression. Deadly serious. My heart pounded, and I reached to cup his cheek. "Nought to sixty. This morning, we weren't even talking."

"This morning, I was still being an arse. It took ye yelling at me to realise all I'd been messed up over. I'm sorry I didn't get there sooner, but I'm deadly serious about making ye Mrs Ben Graham for real."

I took a deep breath, wildly close to just accepting. "Ask me again in a year, if you still want to."

"A whole year?"

"Prove you can be patient."

"Fine. I will. Be prepared for a proposal in exactly twelve months. It'll give me time to find out your ring size and what kind of stone ye like best."

He was too cute. "I'm not going back to the US," I said, fast. "Not just for you—I'd already decided when I thought you didn't want me. I love it here in Scotland. I love the people, and it's so beautiful. I'm going to give it a trial for as long as I can."

Ben gave a satisfied growl. He pulled my leg over his, then took my hand to his dick. Hard again.

"Feel what that did to me?"

In an easy move, he thrust against my core and pushed inside. Ben took things slow. He touched me, stroking my skin. Kissing everywhere he could reach while keeping us joined. He loved on me in the way I'd so badly wanted.

This time when we came, emotion swiftly followed, and I clung to him. Seeing out my throbs with the man I loved held tightly in my arms.

"It's okay," he said with a kiss to my hair. "Everything's going to be okay."

But I knew there was more to come.

The problem that followed our bubble of happiness.

Once we'd cooled, I dressed again. Armouring myself to hear the threat I'd asked him to hold from me.

"I'm not returning to my relatives," I said slowly. "But I know they won't let that lie. Is that what happened tonight? Did they do something?"

Ben sighed heavily then answered with a short nod. "Potentially. Landon Larson worked for them. At least once. Jackson found the payment. In doing so, he was able to trace Larson in the way we hadn't been able when we first looked him up."

A shiver ran down my spine. He was building up to something.

"Larson flew into Manchester airport yesterday," Ben said, his words clipped.

I sat up taller. "He came after me?"

"We think so. Considering that he was on your aunt and uncle's payroll, it makes sense that he'd be trying to retrieve ye on their orders. But that's not the only possibility. Considering his past, he could be working on his own."

My mind raced, travelling back to every interaction I'd had with Landon. The whole time, he'd probably been infiltrating me. Except...something felt off.

"I'm not sure it adds up," I said slowly. "My relatives hadn't enacted their plan to trap me at the time where Landon was coming to my apartment. What need would they have of him? They weren't expecting me to bolt."

"I'm not sure. All we know for certain is that they paid him for something and that he was hanging around ye."

"Show me the payment," I asked.

Ben found his phone. "Jackson discovered it this evening. Here."

I examined the picture. At some point, I'd processed this, and hadn't blinked an eye at the name. The payment was for five hundred dollars a short while ago. The only clue as to what he'd done for them was in the fact he'd been categorised as a contractor. For my aunt and uncle, that meant individuals who weren't affiliated with companies doing specific one-off services. Those could range from bribes to shipping officials to a gang they might use to threaten a rival.

"I just can't work it out," I said. "He didn't seem interested in me when I saw him. I didn't like him being there, but that was because of the past. It's not like I woke up with him standing over my bed."

"None of your possessions went missing while he was there?" Ben asked.

I shook my head. "Not that I recall."

It was a new mystery to add to all those we'd already wrestled with.

Then I took in a sharp breath. "Ariel. What if he sees her and tells her father exactly where she is? Is she—"

"She's fine. Jackson made sure she was in her apartment before he went out to the hospital to guard Leo and Viola. He'll keep her safe."

A rush of anger followed my panic. "This is so shit. What do I do, wait until he shows up? I won't go back with him to Paul and Sigrid."

"I'll kill him if he tries," Ben vowed.

"They must have done this," I decided. "My aunt and uncle hurt people. I realised it the other day when you were describing the people they fraternise with and do business for. They enable the sort of organisations who endanger others. My aunt always made out that they were just being helpful with the service they provide. The things they import that are meant to be controlled. That's a lie. People make bombs using those chemicals. They profit off misery and can't see how bad they are. I was too close to it for too long to really understand the impact. It was so normal. But I see it now. I can't live with that on my conscience." I stared dead ahead, an idea forming. "I won't."

"What are ye saying?"

"For my own sake and for anyone impacted by them, I want revenge."

To his credit, Ben just watched me, hearing out my idea.

It grew in my mind, taking shape into something real.

"I have evidence of exactly what they do in the data stash. Cargo manifests. Quantities. All the manipulation of figures from what they claim to import to the reality. The proof is all there. Maybe it's a drop in the ocean of the Californian crime syndicates, but I'm going to leak it."

My bodyguard boyfriend's eyes darkened. "There's risk attached to that."

"They already sent someone after me. I can't make things worse for myself."

He curved his lips. "It will be easy to make it appear to come from another source. Someone like, say, an office manager with an axe to grind."

Could I really do it? I sat back, working it through my mind. I didn't want their business on my conscience.

"Working this through, there's someone else to consider," Ben said, bringing me back to him. "They threatened your mother."

"They did." I exhaled the need to protect her. "Mom does whatever they want then runs and hides. Like the way she just handed over my phone number without any consideration for me or what I'd asked. As a child, she left me with them, despite knowing what they did. Probably what they planned for me, too. Now, I think I was there because they told her they needed me. Their own daughters wanted out. They asked for hers. She kept that from me."

"She gave you over to them and didn't look back."

"She did. It gives me a horrible feeling and makes me want to be uncharitable in return, but if they threatened her, that's between them. It's nothing to do with me anymore. I can't be responsible for decisions my mother made. If they suspect me of leaking documents on them, ones they knew I'd seen but not that I had any access to anymore, how does that make things any worse for my mother? It changes nothing, except they'll be busy trying to defend themselves. In that respect, it could even make things better. And I really don't think they'd hurt her—for all their faults, they took her back time and time again. It's a bluff."

I made my decision, heart pounding but utterly sure.

"I'm going to hand over the files to the authorities. Let them do what they want after that. Will you help me?"

"Do ye even have to ask?" Ben pulled me in for a kiss.

We sat up for hours, working out a plan, then transferred the documents to an untraceable file location but with several of the company's admin email addresses buried in the metadata as accessing the stash. Subtle, but easy to find for an investigator. Simultaneously, I sent the link to the Californian authorities and a newspaper group so it couldn't be buried.

Bridge burned.

There was no going back, not that I ever wanted to. Not now I'd lived here and fallen in love. Worked out who I was and what I wanted. If I'd stayed at the party, or called them straight after and demanded an explanation, would they have talked me into the role they wanted to fit me into? I'd run, and it was the best thing I'd ever done.

With any luck, it was over for me, just as it was for them.

Ben

A fire crackled in the wee stove in the bunkhouse's living area, a shiny chimney carrying the smoke out through the wall. Jackson had found a bookcase that stretched the height of the near wall, giving the place a homely feel.

At my side, my brother took it in, crossing to check out the bedrooms, his hair tied back and his kit bag over a shoulder.

"It's only meant to be temporary," I told him. "If ye like the work and want to stay, we'll find somewhere more permanent."

To my surprise, I had a buzz of nerves and apprehension over his opinion. I wanted him to stay. He'd arrived this morning with Ma, and I'd mentally rehearsed a few key conversations we needed to have. How gutted I felt over what had happened with Kelly. How I wanted back what we once had. All in good time, though.

Valentine slowly nodded. "Works for me. I bunked at the logging company with eleven other men, and it was a shite-hole in comparison. Who else will be living here?"

Jackson entered with Gordain.

I pointed at the younger man. "Perfect timing. Meet Jackson, my other permanent member of the team. Jackson, this is Valentine. It's just the two of ye staying here for now."

Valentine extended a long arm to shake Jackson's hand. "Grand to meet ye. Do ye snore?"

Jackson pursed his lips. "Not that I've ever been told. But if it's just the two of us here, we can take a room each."

My brother heaved a sigh, his expression tinged with regret. "This reminds me of boarding school. We had methods for handling noisy night-time sleepers."

To my complete surprise, Jackson rolled his eyes. "If that involved a bucket of water, I'll sleep out in the hangar."

"Might have done. Or worse."

Valentine didn't look my way, but I got a swift pang of how much I'd missed him. I hadn't seen this side of him, his casual amusement, in forever.

And I'd never once seen Jackson as anything other than serious.

"Here, let me show ye around. There's a trick to get the showers to work," Jackson said.

"We're going to need a code." Valentine followed him deeper into the bunkhouse. "Communal bathrooms have way too many opportunities for sights that can't be unseen, and if we're going to be buddies, let's not make things awkward. I don't want your envy hampering our friendship."

Jackson snorted a laugh. "What the fuck are ye talking about? Implying ye have an oversized—? Actually, don't answer that. How do we set up this code?"

The two of them continued, chatting together easily like

they'd known each other for years.

I released a breath of relief.

From the doorway, Gordain eyed me. "Looks like we've got the core of our team."

I tipped my head in acknowledgement. "I've got a good feeling about this."

"I do as well. Good job. While we're on the subject of the team, you've got your work cut out with a training programme. Keep it up with the deep research. Pairing that with close protection is a good fit for us. Leo has a couple of personal appearances coming up soon, one of them an evening performance. He agreed to it this morning."

My pulse crept up. This was exactly what we needed. To get the crew out on an event. As my brother familiarised himself with the living arrangements, I worked through with Gordain the finer details of what we had coming up.

Then I set out into the sunny, frosty day, a more important task on my radar.

I'd left my mother with Daisy at Castle Braithar and now returned to pick them up. Daisy needed a car. That was on my list to arrange. In the meantime, I was happy to chauffeur her around.

Even if she didn't need such close protection in future, I'd never ease up entirely on worrying about her, even though the revenge act she'd taken had been an outright success.

The newspapers had moved quickly, the authorities a little slower. The very next day, headlines had appeared of illegal shipments moving controlled goods through California, then arrests were announced. Paul and Sigrid were fighting for their lives, their office manager arrested, and others, too.

Accordingly, Jackson tracked their pet kidnapper, or

whatever the fuck Landon Larson was, back out of the UK.

Daisy had won.

I neared the castle, a grin curving my lips. With any luck, I'd be able to surprise her with something I'd put into play earlier. Things moved fast around here, despite our small-town vibe.

Daisy exited with Ma right as I parked. I leapt out to greet them, not over how easily they chatted and how much they had to say. Daisy had brought her cleaning kit, so I loaded it into the back and drove them out to Mr Campbell's place.

For the past couple of days, Daisy had worked with Isobel to clear the old boy's personal possessions. They'd taken their time over it, a respectful conclusion to the man's life.

Daisy had kept his wedding album with Isobel's blessing.

When she finally agreed to marry me, I'd give her whatever kind of wedding she wanted.

We pulled up at the house, today being the final clean before the place was relet. Daisy waved at Isobel, and the two went inside.

Ma paused me outside, her gaze tracking my lass. "You're happy."

I gave her a smirk in reply. Happy was an understatement.

My mother elbowed me. "When you have your own kids, you'll realise what I'm feeling right now. There is nothing better than seeing your children thrive. Even ones who grew taller than you twenty years ago."

Isobel appeared in the doorway, Jamie-Beth, her scamp of a daughter at her side. She linked her gaze to mine, then gave me a small nod, all the information I needed in that little gesture.

I resisted the urge to punch the air and instead turned to

Ma so Daisy couldn't see.

My mother squinted. "What was that?"

Setting my voice low, I let her in on my secret. "I asked Isobel if I could rent this place. She just confirmed it."

"You're going to live here? With Daisy?"

"Of course with Daisy, if she wants it. There's space for her in the garage to keep equipment. I'll set her up a desk to work from."

Ma clapped her hand to her mouth, her expression everything I felt inside. "You need to marry her in order for her to stay," she said in a rush.

I made the action of casting a rod then winding up the reel, teasing my mother that she was fishing for information.

She wiped her eyes then moved in on me with a hug.

Then I turned and hollered for Jamie-Beth. "JB, come here."

She trotted over.

"How about ye help this grumpy bear make this place his permanent cave?" I asked her.

The tiny lass widened her eyes. "Oh my god. Can I tell Daisy?"

I nodded, and she scrammed, back in the direction of the cottage that would soon be home.

And the woman who'd turned my life around from the very first touch.

EPILOGUE

Jackson

In convoy, I drove back to the McRae estate, bringing up the rear to Leo escorting his family home. It had taken a few days for baby Torran to be released from the hospital, but at last they were on their way.

There had been no problems. Leo hadn't been spotted. I hadn't needed to protect them from anyone trying to sneak a photo.

I peered in my rearview mirror. An elderly lady drove the vehicle behind. The streets otherwise quiet. No reason for worry.

Still, my skin crawled.

Attacks of paranoia were familiar territory for me. I'd had them for years, ever since suffering the worst loss my family could endure.

This was different.

Adrenaline rose and fell in me. Like my body was trying to warn me of something approaching. Some danger I couldn't see and no other signs warned of.

We sped on, the early dusk darkening the long and icy journey.

By the time we'd turned onto the road that followed the loch, it was four p.m. and night had fallen. The village appeared on the left. Little dots of warm light from cottages and the few still open businesses.

A familiar Mini sat by the roadside just beyond the village boundary. It belonged to Ariel.

My best friend's younger sister.

I squinted at it, not able to spot the woman herself. There were no streetlights here, nothing showing me anything was wrong, but the strange feeling in my gut intensified.

We cruised on, Leo not slowing, and I took a good look at Ariel's car as we passed though still not seeing her.

Then the Mini was in my rearview and I was sweating.

What was it? Why was I suddenly even more on edge?

Thoughts of Ariel typically stole my focus, and I had the bad habit of checking in on her via her brother. Now those thoughts came with a warning.

Since discovering that Daisy's aunt and uncle had sent a man after her, I couldn't shake the idea there was something more to it. Ariel had described Landon Larson as being overly interested in her to the point of assault.

Once, that arsehole had put his hands on her.

What if he'd found her for his own purposes?

My heart thumped, that spike of intuition getting stronger.

He'd gone. His passport had been flagged leaving Manchester a few hours after the news stories broke.

But I hadn't checked again since.

Behind, barely visible in the gloom, a pair of red tail-lights appeared where I'd seen Ariel's car. Definitely not the distinctive Union Jack ones of the Mini.

A second car had stopped near hers. The driver hadn't passed us so he had to have come out of the village, or one of the very few lanes.

My heart iced over.

She could be meeting someone. Going on a fucking date. Any number of things that were none of my business.

Even so, I hit my car's phone controls and dialled Leo.

He answered in a second. "Problem?"

"No. I'm going to leave ye at the gateposts and call G to see ye in. There's something I need to check on but it doesn't involve your family's safety."

Once they were on the estate, my job was done.

"No sweat. Gordain's already waiting. Go do your thing and we'll catch you later."

Viola and Finn both called out thanks then we disconnected, the happy sounds of the family diminishing to loaded silence.

My pulse thumping in my ears.

Without pause, I spun my car around.

A fast one-eighty then down the loch road. It wasn't any real distance, but I put my foot down.

Pushed up my speed.

Raced back to the spot I'd seen Ariel's car.

It was still there though alone now. I pulled over behind it, my headlights flooding the scene.

The driver's side front corner with her headlight had been smashed.

Her door was open.

I leapt out and jogged over, my engine still running. There were items on the ground beside the open door. Pieces of paper, fluttering on the packed snow. Her keys.

A single shoe.

Without a doubt, and with cresting panic, I knew what had happened.

Ariel had been taken.

Order Jackson and Ariel's romance.

https://mybook.to/SaveHerfromMe

The two of them agree to a sexy deal you won't want to miss.

Like the sound of tattooed Highlander Gordain, Ben's boss? Read a free bonus scene for his story and find out all about his piercing.

https://dl.bookfunnel.com/rmd3162v79

(Note: I write a lot of free bonus scenes. Downloading any signs you up to my newsletter reader list. You'll get a full list there, and can unsubscribe at any time.)

ACKNOWLEDGEMENTS

Dear reader,

Thank you for reading Ben and Daisy's story. The heat! The way Ben was living their love story without even realising! So much love to be found in Scotland.

I know you long term readers are going to be crazy about the character cameos. That'll be a theme with these books. I get so many messages asking for future glimpses including who had babies, how they're getting along. I am very happy to write these little easter eggs in here and there.

Email me at jolie@jolievines.com to tell me of any specific updates you'd love to see.

Want that series order now? Here you go:

-Marry the Scot (first generation, a family of brothers, the lasses who steal their hearts, and a crumbling Castle McRae. Start with Storm the Castle)

-Wild Scots (second generation, fast paced new adult. Jump in with Hard Nox)

-Wild Mountain Scots (the men of the mountain rescue. Think big and protective plus snow)

-Dark Island Scots (a spin off dark and gritty romance series about a group of kidnapped men. Must be read in order. Start with Ruin)

-McRae Bodyguards (comes after the final Wild Mountain Scots book with protective heroes and women with revenge missions)

Join my FB reader group and tell me your favourite hero (a minor obsession of mine)

And add yourself to my newsletter here

Big thanks go to my readers who make writing a joy. To Elle, Zoe, Emmy, Sara, Shellie, Liz, Cleo, Lori, Amanda, and Erika – you're the best. To my ARC and Street Team, I know you're going to go crazy for every one of these stories.

Lastly, as always, I thank N&M, the reason I need good headphones to get anything done.

Jolie x

ALSO BY JOLIE VINES

Marry the Scot series

1) Storm the Castle

2) Love Most, Say Least

3) Hero

4) Picture This

5) Oh Baby

Wild Scots series

1) Hard Nox

2) Perfect Storm

3) Lion Heart

4) Fallen Snow

5) Stubborn Spark

Wild Mountain Scots series

1) Obsessed

2) Hunted

3) Stolen

4) Betrayed

5) Tormented

Dark Island Scots series

1) Ruin

2) Sin

3) Scar

4) Burn

McRae Bodyguards

1) Touch Her and Die

Standalones

Cocky Kilt:

a Cocky Hero Club Novel

Race You:

An Office-Based Enemies-to-Lovers Romance

Fight For Us:

a Second-Chance Military Romantic Suspense

Visit and follow my Amazon page for all new releases

https://amazon.com/author/jolievines

Add yourself to my insider list to make sure you don't miss my publishing news

https://www.jolievines.com/newsletter

ABOUT THE AUTHOR

JOLIE VINES is a romance author who lives in the UK with her husband and son.

Jolie loves her heroes to be one-woman guys.

Whether they are a brooding pilot (Gordain in Hero), a wrongfully imprisoned rich boy (Sebastian in Lion Heart), or a tormented twin (Max in Betrayed), they will adore their heroine until the end of time.

Her favourite pastime is wrecking emotions, then making up for it by giving her imaginary friends deep and meaningful happily ever afters.

Have you found all of Jolie's Scots?

Visit her page on Amazon and join her ever active Fall Hard Facebook group.

Printed in Great Britain
by Amazon